SUMMER OF SECRETS

SUMMER OF SECRETS

A Stonecliff Mystery

ALICIA STANKAY

ISBN-13: 9781548166120
ISBN-10: 154816612X

This book is dedicated to my husband, Red, with eternal love and gratitude for his support in all my creative endeavors. Proofreader to picture-framer, he's the best!

CHAPTER 1

Kyra Martin stood in Aunt Mary's kitchen, expecting her aunt to come bustling through the doorway at any moment. When the memories of the funeral service this morning threatened to overwhelm her, she turned to look out the window. Purple and yellow irises danced in the breeze in one corner of her aunt's garden, and large pink blooms of rhododendron decorated the fence. How could those flowers be so alive and yet Aunt Mary was gone?

Sighing, she pushed her sadness to the background and rubbed her forehead, trying to remember where her aunt hid the wine stash. She shoved aside the pots and pans in the cupboard and found a bottle of merlot and one of chardonnay. After dusting the bottles off, she placed the chardonnay in the refrigerator for later and opened the merlot. She filled two glasses and then called for Brad.

Her husband appeared and gratefully reached for his glass. After a long sip, he murmured, "At last I'm feeling a little more normal. What a day!"

He slipped an arm around her shoulders and she relaxed against his comforting presence.

"Funerals are so exhausting, physically and emotionally," she agreed. "At least Aunt Mary had a good life without many health problems, and she slipped away in her sleep."

Aunt Mary had always been a big part of Kyra's life, especially after her mother had died when she was twelve. Her aunt was her father's older sister and had been the only living relative from either family. Kyra spent every summer with her because her father had worked so many hours, and she knew she would inherit this house. She looked around and sobs caught in her throat.

When Brad saw the tears in her eyes, he gathered her in his arms and kissed the top of her head. She finally allowed herself to cry after holding herself together all day. Afterwards, they kissed for several long moments before Kyra broke away.

"I was thinking of keeping this house for a while," she began, knowing she was opening a touchy subject.

"What?" Brad's sympathy had disappeared and he stared at her. "Why in the world would you want to do that?"

Kyra took another calming sip of wine before saying, "You know I've wanted to get away and finish the book I'm working on. Maybe now is the perfect opportunity."

"But Stonecliff is three hours from home. That's a little far to commute every day from Pittsburgh. What about your job?" When Kyra didn't immediately respond, he moved closer and reached for her. "And what about me?" he murmured in a seductive voice.

She forced herself to step back to avoid his arms. "Please, Brad. I think Aunt Mary's death made me realize I need to take a little time to focus on my writing. It's an opportunity for me to follow my dream."

"And what about me? I'm your husband, in case you've forgotten, and I have needs, too. I don't see why you can't write at home in the evenings or on the weekends."

She could feel her certainty slipping in the face of Brad's arguments. Then she thought of Aunt Mary and how she always told Kyra to go after the things she wanted in life and not give in to the less controversial solution. She suspected her aunt had done something she regretted in her younger days and didn't want her niece to suffer the same fate. Kyra avoided Brad's gaze and looked around her at the place she'd always called her second home. She loved this kitchen with its warm peach and cool blue colors and the Amish-built oak table. Despite the loss of her aunt, she felt a strong tug of belonging here that she couldn't resist.

"I promise it will only be for a month," Kyra said decisively. "If I can't whip my book into some kind of shape by then, I'll put the house on the market."

Brad huffed, swallowed down the wine left in his glass, and filled it to the brim again.

"I don't believe this. It sounds like you're trying to get away from me to relive your happy memories." He frowned before gulping more wine. "Despite what you've read, you really can't go home again. It's always a different place."

Kyra tilted her head and thought about what Brad said. "You're right, of course. But sometimes that's what you want, a different perspective, and that's exactly what I need to finish my book." Seeing the sadness and confusion on Brad's face, Kyra stepped forward, rested her head on his chest, and wrapped her arms around him. At first, he resisted and then he hesitantly returned the hug, releasing an annoyed sigh.

After a few moments, he said, "You didn't say what you'd do about your job." His voice sounded smug, as if he'd discovered the reason why she couldn't carry out her plan.

Muffled somewhat against his chest, she murmured, "I still have about ten days vacation left from last year. Remember, you got that new job and didn't have as much time off as I did. Then I'll take two weeks of vacation this year. The other two I'll keep for us to vacation together."

Brad pushed away from her and stared into her eyes. "You had this all planned since the time you heard about your aunt's death."

She shook her head. "No, I didn't. Everything just came to me a couple minutes ago. It was like Aunt Mary orchestrated everything the moment I entered this house again."

"Don't be ridiculous!" Brad let her go and polished off his wine. "Just say it's what you want to do and it doesn't include me. Don't blame your dead aunt!" When Kyra gasped at his callousness, he grumbled, "I know we've been having some problems, but I didn't think you were making plans to leave."

"You're overreacting." Kyra struggled to keep her voice calm. Was she looking forward to a month without Brad too much? Did she need this time alone to prove her own worth to herself? As she hesitated about what to say, Brad reached for her.

"Oh, Kyra, I'm sorry. I'm being a jerk, just when you need me the most."

Kyra allowed him to hold her, even as her mind raced. Was he pretending? Softening her up before pushing his own agenda? Then she hated herself for thinking about Brad that way.

"Maybe you're right," Brad continued, running his hands down her arms before stepping back. "Maybe that's a good idea. You won't mind if I visit for weekends, will you?"

What could she say? He was being conciliatory, and saying no would only create problems again. "Of course not," she said and managed a smile. "That sounds great."

Much later that night as they lay in her old bedroom, Kyra gazed up at the spot of light above the bed. She remembered staring at that reflection from the street lamp as a young girl until she fell asleep, but it wasn't working tonight. When Brad began snoring, she slid carefully out of bed, put on her slippers and a light robe, and crept down the hall, stepping over the squeaky boards on her way downstairs.

In the den, she clicked on the lamp and settled behind Aunt Mary's antique rolltop desk. She decided her laptop would fit nicely into the front of the desk with the rolltop opened. She'd loved this desk as a girl, especially all the pigeonholes along the back for separating mail or placing office supplies and other miscellaneous items of another era. She couldn't resist poking her fingers into the various openings now to see what Aunt Mary had deemed important enough to keep over the years. The first thing she found were several cards she had sent to her aunt for her birthday and Christmas. When she opened them and saw her immature writing, tears sprang to her eyes.

"Oh, Aunt Mary, I miss you so much," she whispered. She touched the red embossed Santa suit on the first card and sighed. She supposed she'd have to make a pile of all these keepsakes and eventually throw them away, even though it felt like severing all ties from her aunt. She simply wouldn't have anywhere to keep everything, especially if she did end up selling the house.

Kyra poked and pried, continuing to pile everything into a box beside the desk. As she slid her fingers into the last pigeonhole, she thought it was empty until she found a small envelope pushed into the back. Inside was a single piece of folded writing paper designed like a card. The outside held several flat dried wildflowers encased in clear paper, obviously handmade. Gently opening it, she saw a letter written in beautiful faded script from a time when handwriting mattered. Her hands trembled as she read the first words: *To my dearest daughter, Kyra.* She looked up in shock and her breath caught in her throat as she set the letter carefully on the desktop. When she glanced down at the signature, it said: *Your loving mother, Mary Wyndham.*

Kyra rocked back and forth, unable to take it all in. How could Mary be her mother? She was her dad's sister and she was years older than her father. For several minutes, she thought about tearing the letter up and pretending she'd never seen it so nothing in her life would change. Then she sighed in resignation, knowing that the change had already happened, and it was important for her to understand it. She flattened the letter with her hands and started over.

To my dearest daughter, Kyra,
I know I will never send this letter, but it gives me great joy to write it.
My daughter—such lovely words. I wish now I had made a different
decision, but it's too late. I bowed to convention and made the best choice
I could at the time. Circumstances contrived to solve my dilemma when I
heard Scott and Beth longed for a child, and she wasn't able to conceive.
It eased some of my grief to give you to my brother and his wife. At least I
know you're safe and loved, and that's more important than my feelings.

If ever I decide you need help, I will be there in a flash to offer my services. I'll make sure you never want for anything. Or maybe that's not quite right—everyone should have something to strive for and learn how to deal with mistakes and move on. But, if society gives you bad advice about doing the "right thing," then I would suggest other possibilities to offer you a different perspective.

Well, my love, I guess I haven't solved my problem here, but I hope I clarified things in my mind. Perhaps, one day, I'll have a chance to become better acquainted with you and share some of my belated knowledge.

Your loving mother,
Mary Wyndham

After reading over the letter twice, Kyra thought about all the months she'd stayed in this house over the years. Suddenly everything had changed, and now the anger of losing her past as she knew it conflicted with the happiness of knowing her beloved Aunt Mary was actually her mother. Why hadn't her aunt finally told her the truth? Tears slid down her face and she reached for the letter again. Part of her mind understood Mary's motivations: she didn't want to intrude on Kyra's love for her adopted parents. If society at the time had frowned on single mothers, Mary thought she'd do the next best thing by giving her daughter to her brother and his wife. At least then she'd still see Kyra as she grew up.

Kyra slid the sheet of writing paper back into the envelope and hugged it to her chest. Just for a little longer, she wanted to keep it a secret and ponder how she would adjust to this change in her life, and eventually, find ways to honor this woman who had given birth to her. She turned off the light and sat for a little while longer, remembering her early years with Mom and Dad, and then the summers spent with Mary in her teen years and early twenties.

Finally, she climbed the stairs and crawled back into bed with Brad, and much to her surprise, she fell into a deep sleep. In the morning, they drove back home and returned to their daily routines for the rest of the week. Kyra made the arrangements for her time off at work before devoting the weekend to Brad.

"Are you sure you'll be all right?" Brad asked for about the tenth time Sunday night. They were standing in the kitchen as Kyra filled the coffeemaker and clicked the timer for seven o'clock the next morning. When Brad headed to work, she'd be leaving for Aunt Mary's house.

"I'll be fine, honey. And I'll call every night like I promised. You'll hardly miss me."

Brad cleared his throat and looked skeptical. "You know, my friends will probably think we're separated or getting a divorce. It sends the wrong message." He shook his head. "I can't wait until this month is over."

Kyra wanted to scream because her month away was still all about Brad. Instead, she murmured, "Why don't you just tell them I'm working on my book? That's what I've told them at work, and no one seemed to think that was strange at all. Is it because you still don't take my writing seriously?"

Brad turned and strode away toward the stairs. He stopped as he put his foot onto the first step, turned and said, "I hate to break it to you, Kyra, but do you really believe you're going to become some best-selling author? Do you know how ridiculous that sounds? You know, and I know, that will never happen. It's a waste of time when you could be doing something more important."

Before she could reply, he took the steps two at a time until he was out of sight. She stood in the kitchen, shaking with anger and disbelief. Obviously, he'd been pretending all along to support her writing, figuring that she'd get bored with it eventually and move onto something worthwhile. Like maybe neatly ironing his shirts or polishing his shoes to a fine gloss? So angry she wanted to throw their coffee cups across the kitchen, she decided to sleep in the living room so she wouldn't be up all night fighting with Brad.

After a few calming breaths, she moved into the living room and piled a few throw pillows on one end of the sofa. She slipped out of her jeans and used the afghan from the chair as her blanket. Focusing on the excitement of a month's free time to work on her book, she fell into a troubled sleep.

She awoke to the feel of arms around her and Brad's head on her chest.

"God, Kyra, I am so sorry. I've been up half the night sitting in the chair watching you. I can't believe I was so rotten to you. Please, say you'll forgive me."

"Oh, Brad, you've got to stop acting this way. Supporting me one minute and then accusing me of wanting to leave you the next. I've told you again and again I love you and just want time to work on my novel. Please accept that my writing is important to me, but it doesn't make me love you less. If you can understand that, then yes, I forgive you."

He nodded, saying, "Maybe I found it so hard because I don't feel any desire to do something creative like you do. But I really need you so I'll try to understand. At least I know I'll have the weekends to look forward to this coming month, and you might even be ready to come home sooner. You never know what will happen." Before she could reply, he glanced at his watch and frowned. "I'd better hustle now; I didn't realize how late it was. Call me at work when you get to Mary's house."

After Brad hurried from the room, Kyra lay back down for a few minutes. She wished she could believe him, but she was afraid the weekend get-togethers would be a disaster. Every Sunday night he'd be upset again, asking if her novel was done yet, and suggesting she should come home to finish working. She would have to come up with a strategy to stave off the emotional leave-takings by showing the work she had planned for the next week and proving she needed to stay at Aunt Mary's house. Her head ached by the time Brad finally rushed out the door as she sipped her second cup of coffee.

After showering and dressing, she carried her suitcases downstairs. In the den, she packed up her laptop, all her written notes, and the flash drive with the outline and chapters of her book. As she opened the door to the garage, the phone rang. Sighing, she picked up the phone, expecting to hear Brad, but it was an unknown man's voice.

"Hello, is this Kyra Martin?"

"Who's calling, please?" she asked, suspecting a telemarketer.

The phone clicked in her ear and she heard the dial tone. Placing the phone back on the table, she frowned. Not a telemarketer then since he didn't go into his sales pitch, but who would ask for her by name and then hang up? Shrugging it off, she finished packing her things in the car and backed out of the driveway, closing the garage door after her. Just to be careful, she glanced around the street on her way out, but nothing looked out of place.

CHAPTER 2

The first thing Kyra did when she reached Stonecliff was stop for a supply of groceries and another bottle of chardonnay. After she put everything away in the kitchen, she hurried into the den and sat at the rolltop desk. The letter lay where she had dropped it the other night, so she could no longer convince herself it was all a dream. She read the letter again, trying to grasp the fact that she'd always thought of her aunt as an old lady, although old was certainly a relative term. She calculated ages now. Her aunt had just died at seventy eight, which meant she'd have been forty-eight years old when Kyra was born. That was rather old for giving birth, but she'd certainly heard of change-of-life babies. She smiled; she couldn't help it, thinking of the summer months she'd spent here, all unsuspecting that she was actually with her mother.

Then she wandered around the house, thinking about how empty it felt without Aunt Mary. Although she knew Mary wasn't her aunt, it was easier to think of her that way, at least for now. Everywhere she turned brought back another memory. Mary had hung a succession of Kyra's photos on one wall, as she grew from gangly girl to a shy teenager to a jubilant college graduate. The last few photos showed Kyra and Brad on their wedding day. She studied them for a long time, staring at Brad's face and trying to read into the smile he offered to the camera.

Sighing, she remembered her own mother, the woman who had raised her, who'd never gotten to see Kyra as she grew up, graduated high school and college, and married. Beth Wyndham had died of breast cancer when Kyra was only twelve, and her death had been overwhelming for her at the time. Thankfully, Mary had been there for her when her father eased his sorrows by immersing himself in his engineering work. Maybe Mary never told her about being her birth mother because she worried it would change the way she felt about Beth Wyndham. Of course, that would never happen because Kyra would always love and miss her mother.

Finally, Kyra turned away from the photos and her memories before she felt frozen in sadness. She made a cup of tea and then returned to the den where she set up her laptop on the rolltop desk. After surveying the results with satisfaction, she scrolled through some of her book, but her mind refused to shift into writer's mode. Distracted, she realized she'd never finished looking through the drawers in her aunt's desk the night she discovered Aunt Mary's letter.

The top drawer held pens, paper clips, address labels, and small notepads. The bottom drawer with hanging files only held one folder. When she opened it onto the desk, she discovered it was full of important papers. They were copies of the papers the lawyer, Mr. Berchtold, had already shown Kyra the day he explained that she was now Mary Wyndham's heir. After unfolding the last paper, she read the words saying Mary Wyndham had married Jasper Owens on November 1, 1964. This marriage license was not in the folder she'd been given at Mr. Berchtold's office.

How could that be? She wondered. As far as she knew, her aunt had never married. She'd lived in Stonecliff and worked as a secretary as long as she'd known her. Kyra had stayed with Aunt Mary every summer from the time she was twelve until she graduated from college ten years later. Because her father died during her freshman year in college, it made sense for Kyra to continue to stay with her aunt during holidays and summers. After she graduated, she returned to the house she'd inherited from her father and still lived there. Brad moved in with her after their marriage two years ago. But in all the time she'd lived with her aunt, no man had ever come around and her aunt never mentioned a husband. Kyra scratched her head in puzzlement.

She finally concluded that Jasper Owens had died early in their marriage, and her aunt found his death too upsetting to discuss. Just because she didn't find a death certificate didn't mean that it hadn't happened. Then she thought of another terrible possibility—maybe Jasper had left her or run off with another woman. Kyra could understand why Mary wouldn't want to talk about something like that. Still, she thought she could have comforted her aunt over the years had she known about the husband she lost, for whatever reason.

Sighing, she leaned back in her chair and closed her eyes. Her reflections were interrupted a moment later by the sound of a key in the lock. Startled, Kyra jumped up, thinking that Brad had followed her for some reason since he was the only other person she knew who had a key to the house. He wouldn't be able to get in, though, since she had placed the chain on the door. She hurried down the hallway just as the door banged open against the chain. Expecting Brad's shout to let him in, instead the door was immediately pulled shut again. Puzzled, she checked through the peephole and was surprised to see a middle-aged man she didn't know standing there. Why in the world would he have a key to Aunt Mary's house?

When he knocked, she opened the door, but left the chain in place. "May I help you?" she asked, studying the thin man with streaks of silver in his dark hair.

"Kyra Martin?" he asked, offering a phony smile.

Kyra couldn't be sure, but his voice sounded like the person who'd called at her house earlier in the day. If so, maybe he had assumed she wasn't in Stonecliff and it was safe to enter Aunt Mary's house. "Yes, I'm Kyra," she replied, holding up her cell phone. "I'd like to know who you are and why you have a key to this house. Otherwise, I'm calling the police right now."

Raising his hands, he said, "I don't think that will be necessary. I know about you and the fact that you've inherited this house, but I'm actually Mary Wyndham's son, Ethan Owens. I think I have a claim to her property, too."

Startled, Kyra couldn't believe his words, and she began to wonder if the marriage certificate she'd just found had been planted in the desk. She glanced up and down the street, but unfortunately, it was empty. "If that's true, I think you should get in touch with Mary's lawyer, Simon Berchtold. In the meantime, please give me that key you're holding."

The man frowned and quickly pocketed the key. "I don't think I can do that. My mother gave me this key, saying I was welcome anytime I wanted to visit. I'll be glad to talk to Mr. Berchtold, but in the meantime I'd like to look around this house and find my mother's recent will. She promised this house to me." His eyes narrowed and he pointed to the chain.

She shook her head, saying, "No, I don't think so. Until I hear differently, this is my house, and you're not welcome here. Please make an appointment with the lawyer." Showing him the phone again, she began punching in 911. "I'm going to call the police if you don't leave immediately."

He tried to stare her down but Kyra slammed the door in his face, and then she ran to the back door to make sure the chain was on. Hearing the pounding on the front door, she used her cell phone to call Mr. Berchtold.

"Please, please pick up," she begged as she finally heard the phone being answered.

"Berchtold and Berchtold," the secretary said in a bored voice.

"Hello, this is Kyra Martin. I need to speak to Mr. Simon Berchtold. It's an emergency."

"Hold please."

By the time Kyra managed to contact her lawyer, the pounding had stopped. As she moved to look out the front window, she saw the supposed Mr. Owens getting into a small blue sedan. As she relaxed, she relayed the events of the past fifteen minutes.

Mr. Berchtold sighed. "I'm so sorry, Ms. Martin. It's strange how claimants show up from everywhere once property and money from a will become available."

"But why did this man have a key to the house? It's frightening."

The lawyer hesitated before finally suggesting that the man may have worked for her aunt at one time, and somehow had a duplicate key made. "I'll send over a locksmith this afternoon to change all the locks on your house," he offered.

"Thank you. That will help my peace of mind." Kyra still wasn't able to let the incident go. "You don't have any information about my aunt ever marrying, do you?"

Mr. Berchtold quickly demanded, "Do you have a reason for asking that?"

Not liking his tone of voice, she decided to keep the information about the marriage certificate she had found from the lawyer. "I just wondered since this man seemed so insistent that he was the legitimate heir to Mary Wyndham."

He laughed. "As I said, let me look into the matter, dear, but I'm sure I can take care of Mr. Ethan Owens. I doubt you'll be hearing from him again."

"Thank you again, Mr. Berchtold. I'll be on the lookout for that locksmith this afternoon. I really appreciate your help."

After a few more assurances, the lawyer hung up. Kyra stood for a few minutes before slowly returning the desk and studying the marriage license still sitting where she had left it. It looked official, and she thought of asking Brad to bring theirs from home this weekend to make a comparison. But that would mean letting him know about Ethan Owens and she wasn't sure she wanted to do that, at least not yet. Sighing, she shoved the license into the folder and put it back where she'd found it. She worried again about why she didn't want to share her knowledge with Brad, afraid that he was correct and she wanted out of the marriage. Somewhere during the past year, they'd lost the loving intimacy of their first year together.

Even though Kyra worked full-time as a medical secretary, Brad never acted like she was pulling her weight in paying the household expenses. She was still the little woman who cleaned and prepared the meals. At first, she had enjoyed fulfilling those roles, but lately she'd become thoroughly sick of it. And when Brad started talking about children, Kyra balked.

"Not yet," she'd said, and that immediately started his tirade.

"That's what married people do, you know. Have kids. I thought maybe that would fill your creative need you're always talking about."

Kyra remembered how she'd exploded. "You mean I should concentrate on having kids and not doing something stupid, like writing a book."

That's when Brad would become loving again and try to calm her down. "Of course not, honey. I was just saying we're not getting any younger. At least say you'll think about it."

Kyra hesitated, but finally had agreed, just to keep him calm. But she was afraid Brad saw children as a way to keep control over her, and she wasn't sure he was the kind of man she wanted for the father of her children. If she ever intended to have any children. And didn't that alone indicate some kind of inherent problem with their marriage?

A knock on the door startled Kyra and she jumped up, bumping the folder, and the papers slid out across the desk. Grabbing her cell phone again, she walked to the front door and peered through the peephole. A young man stood there, looking around the front yard. When he turned back, Kyra saw the logo on his jacket: Bryant Locksmith Services. Sighing in relief, she unhooked the chain and opened the door, asking to see his work ID. Smiling, he held out his wallet with his employee number and name, Josh Parkins. He added that Mr. Berchtold had called his boss and asked for new locks to be installed at this address.

Several hours later, Kyra held the keys to her new locks and finally felt calm enough to begin working on her novel. She reread her novel so far and knew that the plot bogged down in the middle of the story. She needed some action to keep the reader's interest. She ended up putting the frightening episode with a false claimant to a will into her story, and then worked out how the man would be found dead two chapters later. Much better, she thought, and finally closed down her laptop because she was starving.

As the week went by, though, Kyra still struggled to adjust to the emptiness of the house. Aunt Mary's death left an ache in her heart, and she remembered how her aunt had helped her through early womanhood after her mother's death. She had frankly answered her questions and listened to her problems, suggesting solutions, but never seeming critical. On the days Kyra found it harder to concentrate on writing, she would hear her aunt saying, "If you believe in what you're doing, you'll find the time and energy to get it done." So she buckled down and managed to write three more chapters and work out a rough outline to the end of the book.

Mr. Berchtold called on Thursday to say that, although he'd located several Ethan Owens, none of them admitted to knowing Mary Wyndham or having a key to her house. Kyra hoped the whole incident was over. After much thought, she also decided she would discuss the strange episode with Brad. After all, if the man had proved to be dangerous, Brad should know about him. Now that the man had disappeared, Brad wouldn't have any reason to get all worked up.

Kyra's reasoning turned out all wrong. Brad was furious, complaining that he should have known immediately about Ethan Owens.

"He sounds to me like one of your old boyfriends!" Brad shouted before Kyra even finished telling him about the key in the door. "Who else would have keys to this house?"

"I just told you, Brad. He said he was Aunt Mary's son!"

"The son you conveniently never mentioned before!"

"That's because I'd never heard of him, either. I called Mr. Berchtold immediately, and he looked into it. So far he can't find anything to substantiate the man's claim. The locks have been changed, and I haven't heard from the man again. With any luck, it's all over." She dug in her purse and pulled out the extra key. "Take this before I forget to give it to you."

Brad took the key and sighed. "I still don't like it, Kyra. I wish you'd just come home with me now."

"Oh, Brad, not this same old argument again. My writing's going well, and I feel totally safe now. Let's enjoy the weekend together and forget about some guy named Ethan Owens."

After a little more persuasion, Kyra convinced Brad to calm down and suggested going out to dinner. She chose one of her favorite Italian restaurants where she used to go with Aunt Mary, a place called Dimeo's. The hostess recognized Kyra and took them to one of the back booths where they could absorb the cozy atmosphere of the candlelit tables. Brad finally relaxed as he sipped his Chianti wine and enjoyed the salad of baby lettuce leaves and tomatoes.

Over an hour later, Kyra led Brad back across the restaurant toward the door. Glancing into the dim bar filled with the sound of convivial drinkers, she sucked in her breath. Ethan Owens sat on the end of the bar staring right at her.

"Brad! He's here," she hissed, grabbing onto Brad's hand.

At the same moment, a large group from the table nearby moved toward the door, and blocked her vision to the bar entrance. She pushed past them, but it was too late. Ethan Owens was gone.

"Quick! He must have gone out the back door." She dragged Brad through the bar toward the dark hallway beyond the end of the barstools.

"Kyra, stop it! You're making a spectacle!" Brad pulled her to a standstill. "People are looking at us."

When she tried to disengage their hands, he hung on tighter. "He's getting away! I want you to speak to him."

"Who? Who the heck are you talking about?"

"Ethan Owens! I told you he was sitting at the bar. He followed us!" Frustrated, Kyra knew it was already too late. "Why didn't you pay attention to me?"

Brad placed his arm around her shoulders and guided her toward the exit. "Let's get out of here," he murmured. "We'll talk more in private."

Accepting defeat, she walked with him out of the restaurant and toward the car. Then she shrugged out of his arm and stopped to search the cars around them, looking for a small blue one. When she didn't see any sign of Ethan Owens, she sighed and opened her car door.

"What is wrong with you?" Brad demanded. "You acted like a crazy woman in there. I was so embarrassed."

"Brad, I told you how frightened I was this week when that Owens guy tried to get in the house, and now he was sitting in the bar watching us. Don't you think that's a reason to be upset?"

"If he was there," Brad said, emphasizing the "if." "However, I didn't see anybody. I'm beginning to think you shouldn't be living on your own in your aunt's house. It's probably a little scary thinking of your aunt who just passed away." He reached for her chin and tilted her face upward. "You're so beautiful, Kyra, and it's driving me crazy worrying about you living in that house alone. Please come home. I'll give you all the time you want to write."

Kyra stared up at him, seeing the crease of worry between his eyes and the softening of his features. If only he had believed her words, she might have let him convince her of his compassion.

"I'm sorry you don't believe me," she said, climbing into the passenger seat. "I'm going to stay so let's drop the subject."

The weekend passed in superficial talk and awkward silences. They slept together, but Kyra came to bed after Brad and got up earlier, and in between she clung to the edge of her side of the mattress. When Brad left on Sunday night, it was a relief for both of them.

CHAPTER 3

Monday morning Kyra had an appointment with Mr. Berchtold to hear the official reading of the will and sign forms. When she reached the office a little before ten, the secretary nodded and motioned to one of the comfortable chairs in front of a coffee table filled with glossy magazines. Kyra idly wondered if there had ever been another Berchtold at Berchtold & Berchtold, but was afraid to ask the woman with the forbidding expression sitting behind the desk. Mr. Berchtold's nephew worked at the office, but his last name was Craig.

The inner office door opened, and stern-faced Mr. Berchtold stood there.

"So good to see you, Mrs. Martin. Please, come in."

Once she was settled in her chair, Kyra asked if Mr. Berchtold had found out anything else about an Ethan Owens. She explained about seeing him at Dimeo's on Friday night and how he'd disappeared when she tried to point him out to her husband.

"I'm sorry, but I haven't come up with any information on him, but I have a few other facts that may be disturbing to you."

Kyra frowned and asked, "What are you talking about?"

Mr. Berchtold shuffled some papers and then handed one across the desk to her. It was a copy of her birth certificate, naming Mary Wyndham as her mother and Leonardo Napoli as her father. Kyra looked up and nodded. "Yes, I found a letter from my aunt in her desk the night of the funeral. Although it was addressed to me, she had never sent it. She explained that she was actually my mother, and the reasons why she gave me up for adoption to her brother and his wife." For a moment, calmness deserted her, and Kyra closed her eyes and placed a hand on her trembling lips. Saying it out loud made her shock and love and confusion so real.

When she opened her eyes, Mr. Berchtold looked up and murmured, "If you'd like to finish this some other time . . ."

Kyra shook her head. "No, I'm okay now." She glanced at the birth certificate again. "My aunt didn't mention anything about my father in the letter, and I know nothing about Mr. Napoli."

"I see," Mr. Berchtold murmured as he handed over more papers showing a formal adoption of Kyra Wyndham to Scott and Elizabeth Wyndham on April 3, 1985, two days after she was born.

Kyra studied the papers, thinking of Mary's words about how she shouldn't have given into pressure and instead kept her daughter. Sighing, she looked up at Mr. Berchtold and he cleared his throat.

"If you're ready to proceed, I'll give you the pertinent points of Mary's will and you can read over everything later."

"First, one more thing. Do you know if Mary ever gave birth before having me? In her letter, it sounded like I was her only child."

Mr. Berchtold cleared his throat, obviously uncomfortable discussing Mary's possible indiscretions. "No, I don't believe so, and I definitely don't have any other birth certificates."

Kyra nodded, even as she thought of the marriage license sitting in Mary's desk. She hesitated to mention it because she didn't want to complicate matters, especially if it had been planted there by the man claiming to be the son of Aunt Mary and Jasper Owens. By the time she left the office, Kyra was the official owner of Mary's house and property and the tidy sum of money in her bank account. Since it was almost noon, she decided to stop for a celebratory lunch.

The Victorian Café was located inside The Cartwright Hotel, the largest hotel in Stonecliff. Kyra settled into a booth near a small fountain surrounded by red and yellow tea roses. After ordering a glass of champagne with the main entrée of salmon, broccoli, and rice pilaf, she relaxed and surveyed the room. She recognized two of her aunt's friends from her pinochle club who were sitting in the far corner. They had visited the funeral home to offer their condolences to Kyra and Brad. When the women looked up, Kyra waved and received friendly waves in return. Her salad came then and she concentrated on enjoying the moment before she returned to work on her novel.

Before Kyra finished her meal, the ladies stopped at her table.

"Our condolences again, my dear," said Mrs. Dawson, a white-haired lady. "It was a lovely funeral service. And how are you doing now? It must be difficult living in your aunt's house without her being there."

Tears stung Kyra's eyes, but she managed a smile. "It's hard, but soothing at the same time. I have so many happy memories of living with Aunt Mary, along with the sadness of knowing I'll never see her again."

"Are you thinking of moving into your aunt's house now?" Mrs. Wright asked, her silver bracelets jangling as she patted Kyra on the shoulder.

"No, I don't think so. I'm staying there temporarily while I work on my writing, but I'll probably have to sell the house. My husband and I still live in Pittsburgh."

"Maybe you can just rent it out for now in case you decide to move in the future," Mrs. Dawson suggested. "I know how much Mary enjoyed your visits."

Kyra smiled up at them, thinking that they wanted to see her around to remind them of their good friend. "I always loved visiting Aunt Mary, too, but I really don't think we'll be able to keep up with two houses. But don't worry; I won't be making any definite decisions about the house for another month or two. In the meantime, why don't you stop over for lunch one day this week? Maybe Wednesday?"

Checking their schedules for other appointments, they both discovered they were available.

"Twelve-thirty?" Kyra asked and they agreed on the time. After they walked away, Kyra finished up her coffee and asked for her check. The waiter smiled and said, "You're very fortunate. That man over there has already taken care of the bill."

"What? What do you mean?" Kyra looked in the direction the waiter pointed. Ethan Owens sat at a table in the corner and he nodded and stood up.

"No," Kyra said, surprising the waiter. "Tell that man I do not accept and write up a new check for me."

"But, miss, I can't do that. The man has already paid."

Tight-lipped, Kyra demanded, "Then get the manager for me. And stop that man from leaving!"

Ethan Owens had reached the door. He turned one more time, gave a semi-bow, and stepped into the lobby. Kyra jumped up and rushed across the restaurant, but by the time she got out the door, the man was nowhere in sight.

"Damn!" she muttered under her breath. The waiter followed her, babbling about how sorry he was. "If I had known there was a problem . . . I mean, I thought it was your birthday or something . . . I'm so sorry." The young man's face was flushed and he looked truly upset. "Miss, please, I don't want to lose my job."

The door opened again and an older woman appeared. She was dressed in a gray pant suit with her hair in a bun and carried a pile of menus. "Is there a problem, Gregory?" she demanded, and the boy turned his beseeching face toward Kyra.

Kyra took a deep breath, summoned up a smile and said, "Nothing's wrong. I just wanted to thank my colleague for a free meal, but he rushed away too quickly. I'm sorry if I startled everyone in the restaurant."

"I'm Mrs. Johnson, the manager here. If Gregory did something wrong, I'd like to know." Her words were frosty and Kyra took an instant disliking to her. She replied, "Don't worry, if there had been a problem with my service, I'd let you know. However, I simply got too excited and acted without thinking. The fault was mine so please accept my apologies."

"Of course," Mrs. Johnson said, and ushered Gregory back into the restaurant.

By the time Kyra walked through the lobby and out into the street, Ethan Owens was long gone. Frustrated, she got into her car and drove back to Aunt Mary's house.

Once safely inside Mary's house, Kyra debated about calling the police to report Ethan Owens as a stalker. She wasn't sure of the criteria for stalking, but certainly fear played into it. But what could she say? He had a key to her house, claiming he was Mary's legitimate son, although Mary had never mentioned him and Kyra had never seen him before. Even Mr. Berchtold didn't know who he was. Then he evidently followed her and Brad to the restaurant where they had dinner on Friday, and now he paid for her lunch today. Whether it was stalking or not, it was creepy.

After picking up the phone, she hesitated, thinking about Brad's response. He'd want her out of Mary's house immediately, and she'd lose her freedom to work on her novel. She put down the phone and wondered about why she'd chosen the word "freedom" to explain what she'd lose if Brad got involved. He'd say it was to protect her, but she'd just feel suffocated. Walking around downstairs, she checked to make sure all the windows and doors were locked. She thanked Aunt Mary for adding air conditioning to the house about twelve years ago because now she wouldn't have to worry about leaving windows open.

When she was certain the house was secure, she went back into the den to review what she'd written last night. Determined to finish her book before the month was up, she knew she had to work faster. After she completed the first draft, she'd need time to edit and proofread, but at least she'd have a completed story. Thoughts of Ethan Owens kept drifting into her mind as she wrote, and she decided a stalker might fit nicely into her plot. She'd have to add a few hints earlier in the story to make it seem realistic, but that wouldn't be too complicated.

By late that afternoon, the heroine had turned the tables on the stalker. As he crept up the fire escape to her New York apartment one wintry evening, she doused him with a bucket of cold water filled with ice cubes. As he slipped and slid on the icy iron walkway, he fell two stories down onto the ground and broke a leg. The police didn't believe his story about rescuing a stranded kitten.

As Kyra opened a can of hearty chicken soup for her dinner, she realized that the stalker would come back to attack her heroine to revenge himself. In his eyes, she had caused all his problems, despite the fact that he had been wrong in the first place. She decided to work out that scenario later, and eat her soup and crackers while she read one of the writer magazines she had picked up earlier in the day.

The tinkling sound of broken glass jerked her out of her absorption in an article about using the right setting for the plot of a novel. Jumping up in alarm, she grabbed her cell phone off the counter. She ran toward the front of the house to see what had happened. Shattered glass lay under the front window, and the brilliant orange of the setting sun blinded her from seeing what lay outside the window.

"Who's there?" she screamed, trying to hit 911 on her cell phone.

A dog barked and slammed against the house, snarling. He barked again and again, and then she heard footsteps pound away on the sidewalk.

"Miss, miss, are you all right?" a man shouted.

When a cloud covered the sun, Kyra was able to make out her next-door neighbor Sam standing outside the window with his collie, Tex.

"I'm fine, Sam," she replied, going to the front door and opening it. "Just a little shaken up." Tex barked a greeting and stood there wagging his tail.

Sam frowned and pointed to the window. "I saw some jerk throw a rock at this window from my kitchen. I opened the door and let Tex out. That guy didn't stick around long after that!"

"But why?" Kyra wondered. "Why throw a rock at this house for no reason?"

"Aw, you know kids today. They don't need reasons to get into trouble. I'm real sorry about the window, but I can patch it up until you can get a repairman to come tomorrow."

She managed to smile shakily at Sam and thank him despite her fright. About a decade younger than her aunt, he had lived next door for many years, and Mary often asked him to help on little jobs around the house. Before Kyra let Sam do his repair job, she called the police to report the incident. A patrolman stopped by and surveyed the damage, but said there was little he could do. Sam offered a vague description of a man wearing jeans and a dark hooded sweatshirt, probably young by the way he moved, which the patrolman dutifully wrote in his notebook.

"In case we have a rash of such incidents, we'll have information to coordinate," he explained. "However, if this is just one episode, there won't be anything we can do. It's good to report this type of crime for insurance reasons, of course."

Once Kyra stopped shaking and the window was protected by a large square of heavy cardboard, she closed the drapes and turned on all the lights in the downstairs rooms. Sitting on the living room sofa with her feet tucked under her, she reviewed what Sam had said about the man. If he was right about the guy being younger, then it definitely wasn't Ethan Owens, who had to be around fifty. But Owens could have hired the boy to throw a rock into the window to scare her so she'd leave. For some reason, Owens wanted her out of the house so he could look around. But what was he looking for?

Sighing, Kyra picked up the phone to call Mr. Berchtold's private line. She hated to bother him at home, but she thought he should know about any incidents relating to Mary's house.

"You think someone wanted to break into the house?" he asked, surprise in his voice. "Whatever for?"

"I don't know," Kyra replied. "I don't even know if the guy wanted in the house. I think it was a scare tactic, but it still makes no sense. Did Mary ever report any of problems like this?"

"No, definitely not. In all the years I dealt with Mary Wyndham, she never said she had anything unusual happen."

Kyra sensed disapproval in his tone, and realized he inferred she was bringing these incidents down on herself.

Hesitating, he continued, "Maybe that man had some reason to believe he could find drugs or something else illegal in your home?"

"Of course not! Mr. Berchtold, you've known me all my life. How could you say that?"

"I'm sorry, my dear. But it does seem rather strange that these things are happening since you're staying there alone in the house. Perhaps you should think about selling."

"Now you sound like my husband!" Realizing her voice shook with anger, she forced herself to speak reasonably. "Mr. Berchtold, I've already reported this incident to the police, but I thought that since I was a client of yours, you might want to know. From now on, I'll no longer bother you. And after the will is probated, I'll be looking for another lawyer to take care of my legal business."

"Please, Mrs. Martin, I'm sorry if I offended you. It just seems so strange that Mary never had any incidents such as those happening to you now, but I shouldn't have made a judgment like that. Please, accept my apology."

Kyra sighed as she stared at the drapes hiding the broken window. "I'll accept your apology, but I would appreciate it if you would give me any information you have about Mary's early life before I was born."

"Why? What are you looking for?" he asked sharply.

The way he said it made Kyra wonder if he did possess some knowledge about Mary's life that he purposely had kept concealed from her.

"I'm not sure what I'm looking for," she replied. "I know about Mary when she was a child and young woman from my father and some pictures at home. Then there's a big gap before I came to live with her every summer when I was twelve." When he didn't respond immediately, she added, "I'm thinking of writing a family memoir, and I'd like to have more information."

"I see. To be honest, I didn't become your aunt's lawyer until right before you were born, so I don't know much of her previous history." He chuckled. "But if that will keep you busy and away from all these imaginings, I'll have my nephew delve into her background for you. He'll report to you by the end of the week."

Kyra gritted her teeth and bit back a rude comment at his patronizing attitude. She managed to say goodbye without swearing at him. From now on, no matter what happened, she decided she wouldn't ask for help. She was thoroughly sick of being treated like the swooning lady on the sofa who needed to rely on the men folk of the family to save her.

Kyra hurried to the large hall closet and searched though the sports equipment packed into the back corner. Although she hadn't played any organized sports, Kyra did enjoy games of pick-up baseball, tennis, and badminton in the summers while visiting her aunt.

"Aha!" she exclaimed, dragging out her softball bat. Hefting it, she muttered, "Perfect!"

Two hours later as she dozed on the sofa, the loud crash of a broken window jerked her upright. As glass sprayed across the living room floor again, she grabbed her bat and rushed across the room. She flicked off the switch so she wouldn't be silhouetted against the light. Then she opened the door and stomped out onto the front porch.

CHAPTER 4

The front yard lay in deep shadows from the street lamp on the corner. Kyra caught the sight of movement from the corner of her eye and she ran toward the maple tree in Sam's yard. Hearing a low growl, she stopped. Tex bounded away from the tree and his form melded against another form at the end of the driveway. A man grunted and the shapes rolled in the grass as Kyra ran across the yard. Sam burst from his house and rushed toward Kyra, calling, "Let Tex do his job. I don't want you hurt."

Tex suddenly yelped, and the man separated himself from the dog and limped away into the trees. Tex struggled to his feet and took off after him, but returned several minutes later as a car started up in the street behind Kyra's house.

"Damn! He got away." Sam knelt down to pet Tex and carefully checked him over. Kyra watched as he pulled his hand away. "What the hell. . ." Shifting toward the street lamp, he examined the dark moisture on his hand, exclaiming, "That guy used a knife on my dog."

"Oh, no!" Kyra's arm trembled and she let the bat fall to the ground. If she had accosted the lawbreaker, would he have knifed her, too? "What is going on here? I'm so sorry."

"Not your fault." Sam guided her back to her house with Tex following. "I want you to call the police again, and afterwards I think you should go to a motel for the night. Maybe even call your husband, too."

At the mention of Brad, Kyra straightened her spine and cleared her throat.

"I don't think I should worry him right now, but I will call the police." Stepping onto the porch, she pulled her cell phone from her pocket and made the second such call of the evening. "Now I want you to take Tex to the vet's and I'll pay for the visit. No argument, Sam!"

"Sure, no problem." Sam plunked down on the top step with Tex beside him. He rubbed his hand down Tex's side and then nodded. "He's already stopped bleeding, so we're not leaving until after we've told our story to the police."

Knowing how cantankerous Sam could be, Kyra agreed and sat down beside him. A different policeman showed up this time, but he scribbled all the information as they recounted the story.

"And you're saying someone also threw a rock through another window a couple hours ago?" The thin middle-aged cop studied Kyra's face in the glare of the overheard porch light. "Pretty peculiar, wouldn't you say? Sounds like you're on someone's shit list. Excuse the language."

"The language I can excuse, but not the inference." Kyra drew herself up to her full five foot eight height and stared into the policeman's eyes. "Will this be written off as another case of 'blame the victim,' Officer McCann?"

"No, of course not, ma'am. I'll write up the report just like I always do." The policeman's tone matched Kyra's in frostiness, but she believed he meant what he said. He surveyed the damage to the other front window and scribbled in his notebook.

"Thank you," she said.

He nodded and turned to Sam, asking about the collie's injuries. "We'll make sure that a patrol car drives by regularly all night in case this prankster decides to show up again. And don't hesitate to call 911 if anything else happens."

After the policeman left, Kyra sent Sam off with Tex to the emergency veterinarian. He insisted on coming back and sitting on her porch for the rest of the night after Tex was cleaned up and his minor wound stitched. Kyra dozed on and off as she rested on the sofa, but was thankful when the first rays of light peeked through the drapery. She fed Sam a breakfast of bacon, eggs, and coffee before he went off to pick up Tex at the vet's office.

Sipping her own coffee, Kyra called to have her windows replaced. First the locks needed changed and now the windows, she thought. She believed that Ethan Owens was responsible for all these scares, but for some reason, Simon Berchtold didn't seem capable of identifying him. Or wasn't interested enough in pursuing that line of inquiry. If so, why not? Kyra felt as if her whole world had shifted on its axis ever since Aunt Mary had died, and she couldn't figure out why.

Although she had inherited Mary's house, everyone wanted her out of it. Brad wanted her to sell it, Ethan Owens claimed it was his inheritance, and Simon Berchtold suggested she'd be safer if she sold the house. As far as she knew, those three people weren't related in any way, so what were their motives for wanting her out? Or could they be united in some way that Kyra didn't understand? She rubbed her forehead and sighed in frustration.

Deciding she needed to speak to someone else who knew Mary and her past history, Kyra remembered that she had two of Mary's friends coming for lunch this week. She decided they might be the best source of background material, probably better than Mr. Berchtold's nephew, who might reveal only limited information. She could also pump Sam for whatever knowledge he might have from the years of being Mary's neighbor and helpful handyman.

She poured another cup of coffee and hoped the company she'd called to do the window repair would send the glazier soon. She wanted to shower and get into fresh clothes, but not while she had two broken front windows. In the meantime, she'd work on her book and try to ignore all her worries. The novel was her prime objective right now, and she had every intention of holding a completed manuscript in her hands at the end of the month. Every time she faced a new problem in real life, she tried to add a corollary complication into the story. At the rate her life was going, the story would hold a thrill every minute. Thinking that might be good for plotting, but was a little worrisome for real life, Kyra tried to settle down to rereading the most recent chapter before continuing her writing.

She shuddered a bit when her main character stumbled over a body in her basement one night, and just typing the scene caused her to pull her hands away from the keyboard. Did she really want Jennie to find a body like that? The tone of her story had suddenly turned dark, much darker than she'd originally planned. Maybe she should go back and rewrite the chapter. She had made her character's fear so real that Kyra could feel it, too, and that's when she realized the sun had disappeared and storm clouds crowded the horizon.

She shivered in the chill of the air-conditioned house and hurried to raise the temperature. Passing the door to the basement, she stared at it with dread. What if a body lay at the bottom of the stairs? *Stop it, silly! That's your story, not reality. If you keep up like this, you'll be running home to Brad and he'll say that he told you so.* Gritting her teeth, Kyra walked around the first floor and then peered out the front window, hoping to see a home improvement truck pulling into her driveway. The usually busy street lay empty and deserted, as if a sinister episode of *Twilight Zone* was being filmed.

Since she hated how easily she was frightening herself, she pulled open the basement door and flicked on the light. She walked down the stairs to where they curved at the halfway point. From there, she could see the smaller room on the left where the furnace and hot water heater resided, and the large main room directly ahead that was used for storage. Aunt Mary had shelves of old canning bottles, along with half-used paint cans and brushes, and broken appliances. A work area held tools, boxes of screws and nails, and other miscellaneous items. Double laundry tubs with an antique washer and dryer filled the left side of the room, but they hadn't been used for years. As she aged, Aunt Mary had bought a modern washer and dryer and moved them to a small room beside the kitchen, so she no longer had to traipse up and down the stairs to do her laundry. Kyra thanked her aunt every day for this convenience.

From her vantage point, she could see the door to the back room of the basement. She knew that room was never used because the floor was packed dirt covered with fine gravel, unlike the concrete of the front section. Shrugging off any need for further exploration, she could see that that no bodies lay at the bottom of the steps or anywhere else on the basement floor. Sighing in relief, she turned around on the stairs and hurried back to the den.

Sitting down in front of her laptop again, she ignored that little twinge of unease that reminded her she didn't actually search the entire basement. She forced herself to concentrate on her story and go back to discussing murder and mayhem. She wasn't sure why that body had shown up, but it fit into the plot, and that was all that mattered. Her heroine was much braver than Kyra, and she studied the dead man's body before calling the police. He hadn't been dead long, and Jennie recognized him as the man who'd been coming out of her lawyer's office while she sat in the waiting room.

Kyra's hands moved away from the keyboard again, and she wondered why she'd written that. She stopped to think about the people she'd seen at Mr. Berchtold's office recently, but no particular man came to mind. She remembered a well dressed woman wearing an apricot suit, but definitely no man at all. Then she realized that the person she pictured was the man who had come to her door the other day, identifying himself as Ethan Owens. That's the body of the man she'd written about—thin with dark brown hair and a crooked nose, wearing a gray sport coat with blue jeans. Now why had she written about Ethan Owens? She didn't like the guy's attitude, but she certainly didn't want to kill him off. What was the matter with her?

The doorbell rang and Kyra jumped up. *Hooray! The window guy was here.* Hurrying to the front door, she checked through the side window to be sure it was safe. Not a man at all, but a woman dressed in a pink suit wearing high heels and looking every inch the professional. Definitely not the window repairman or repairwoman. And she looked similar to the lady she'd seen recently in Mr. Berchtold's office, but of course that was silly. It had to be purely coincidence. Didn't it?

Inching open the door, Kyra said, "May I help you?"

"Yes, I'm Mrs. Taylor. Am I speaking to Kyra Martin?"

"That's correct."

"Do you mind if I come in?" she asked. "I'm a real estate agent and I'd like to talk to you about your house."

CHAPTER 5

Kyra stared at the woman and wondered who had sent her. "You must be mistaken. I don't need a real estate agent since I'm not selling this house."

The woman smiled and said, "If I could just come in for a minute. I understand you haven't put the house on the market, but you might like to hear what I have to say."

Kyra shook her head. "I can't imagine what you'd say that I'd be interested in." Before she could continue her refusal, a beige van pulled into the driveway. The sign on the side read Stanley's Home Improvement—Windows Our Specialty. "Sorry, but I've been waiting for this company. Now isn't the right time for me to see you."

Mrs. Taylor stepped back and studied the two cardboard-covered windows. "Look, I hate to say this, but it looks like someone wants you out of this house. Why would you want to live here when it seems someone is determined to scare you away?"

Anger made Kyra's hands shake as she replied, "That's exactly why I intend to stay here! And what business is it of yours to know what's happening at my house?"

"Excuse me, ma'am, I'm Jim Knox," said a man dressed in a beige work shirt matching the color of the van. He pushed past Mrs. Taylor and smiled at Kyra. "I'm here to fix your broken windows. I can see the problem from out here and I'd like to come in and take measurements."

"I'm so glad to see you." Kyra stepped back and he entered carrying a tool box, waving his partner to join him. Just then the storm that had threatened broke, and Mrs. Taylor edged closer to the door to avoid being soaked by the rain.

"Please," she said again. "Just give me five minutes of your time."

The window guy glanced back at Kyra, as if to see if she needed his assistance. She rolled her eyes before saying, "Fine. Five minutes and that's all."

She led the woman into the den, leaving the door open. She pointed to one of the wing chairs by the reading table and sat in the other one.

"I have an offer here from an anonymous buyer who's had his eye on this property for many years. He understood your aunt wouldn't be interested in a sale, but he felt fairly certain when you inherited that you wouldn't be living here."

Kyra held up her hand. "Why would this person think that? Who is this person?"

"I'm sorry, but I can't divulge his name right now. However, he lived here in Stonecliff for many years and knew about you and your aunt. Since you live hours away and work there, why would you keep this house?"

"I don't have to give you any reason for what I do. I have no intention of selling, so we're back to square one."

"He's offering you half a million dollars." Mrs. Taylor touched her perfectly coiffed hair, allowing a supercilious smile to touch her lips. She figured she'd delivered the coup de grâce.

Kyra stared at her for a moment, speechless. Finally she demanded, "Why in the world would he pay so much for this small two-story two-bedroom house? Is there gold buried here or something else, gas or oil deposits?"

Mrs. Taylor laughed and shook her head. "Hardly. It's simply a dream of his to live here and because he has the money, he sees no reason why this can't be a win-win situation."

"Oh, I get it now. He believes money can buy anything." Kyra looked toward the rolltop desk and thought about the many secrets she was discovering about her aunt. No way would she sell until she understood more about her aunt's past life and felt comfortable selling her legacy. "I'm sorry, but I'm not interested in selling now. You'll have to tell your buyer 'no' and lose that large commission you expected to receive."

The real estate agent stared at her in disbelief. "You do understand I'm talking about $500,000? That's a huge sum of money for you, and all you have to pay are the taxes. Would you like to check with your husband first before you turn me down?"

Anger shot through Kyra and she jumped out of her seat. Pointing toward the door, she said, "Please leave, and tell your buyer I turned down his or her offer."

"You're making a mistake." Mrs. Taylor gathered her purse and a sheaf of papers and stood up, smoothing down her skirt. She pulled out her card and set it on the desk. "I'll leave my card here, just in case. You understand you won't get another offer like this, ever. You'll be lucky if you manage to sell this house for a quarter of that later on."

"I'll worry about that, when and if I ever decide to sell." Misgivings about her decision already assailed her, especially if Brad ever heard about the agent's visit and the deal she'd been offered. Having the agent ask if Brad should be consulted had sent her over the edge, and she resented the supposition that she couldn't make a decision without her husband.

Kyra followed Mrs. Taylor through the house and noticed the curious looks of the window guys. The rain had slowed to a drizzle and the agent hurried to her car as quickly as she could in her fancy pink high heels. She backed her car out of the driveway and drove away. Only then did Kyra heave a great sigh of relief.

"Pushy bitch," Jim Knox muttered, glancing up at her. "I'm glad you showed her the door. She tried to buy my mother's house after my dad passed away. Told her the house wasn't worth much in today's market, and offered some measly sum. Turned out some developer wanted to buy all the houses on her side of the street and build fancy condos."

"I didn't like her attitude," Kyra said. "And she definitely doesn't like being told 'no.'"

"Do her good; she needs knocked down a peg." Jim pointed to the window. "Now, these here windows are standard size, and we can pick up replacements at the warehouse right after lunch. In the meantime, I taped this temporary cardboard nice and tight so the rain shouldn't get in. We'll have it all done by early evening. That okay with you?"

"That's wonderful! I just hope no one takes a rock to the windows again tonight. It was pretty scary."

"You need someone to keep an eye on your house," the other young man said.

"Why, Doug, you offering your services?" Jim grinned at his partner.

Doug shook his head. "You know Tina'd kill me if I didn't come home and help with the twins. She about goes crazy all day with the diapers and feedings and rocking."

"That's okay, guys," Kyra interrupted their banter. "I have a neighbor and his dog that will probably take over that job tonight. The dog nearly caught the rock-thrower last night so I don't think he'll show up again."

"What's really weird is I remember this house now." Jim studied the room and then stared outside. "Yep, I was here about seven, eight years ago. Same thing—someone threw a rock through the window. Old lady was pretty upset when she came home from a vacation and found the broken window, and I felt real bad for her. It never did happen again to my knowledge. Well, until now."

"You're sure about that?" Kyra remembered Simon Berchtold saying nothing like that ever happened when Mary lived here. Was it possible he didn't know? Or did the lawyer lie to her?

Jim nodded, saying, "Yep, I'm sure. Now sit tight and we'll be back in a couple hours."

Trying to shake off her unsettled feelings, Kyra made herself a cup of tea and sipped it slowly. When she felt more relaxed, she returned to the den and opened up her laptop. She read over the pages of the most recent chapter and began typing. She couldn't let outside events deter her from writing because she wanted to prove to Brad that this month away was a success. Now that her character Jennie had discovered a dead body at the bottom of her basement stairs, she had to explain how it got there. If Jennie didn't push him, then someone else did, and maybe that person was still in the house with her. That thought made Kyra glance quickly around the room before continuing her story.

Jennie had come to visit her great-aunt after an unexpected call from a neighbor saying the aunt hadn't been seen in days. The neighbor had knocked on the door and called on the phone, but there wasn't any answer. Jennie had found the house neat and orderly and had no reason to believe anything bad had happened, until she discovered the body of the man. As Kyra wrote about Jennie hearing a metallic noise, she realized the storm had returned. Rain sluiced down the windows of the den and thunder drowned out any sounds in the house.

Uneasy again, Kyra stood up and flicked on the lights in the den before moving to the lights in the living room. The air conditioning clicked on, making her jump. She laughed and headed into the kitchen to make some lunch since she was distracted from her story anyway. Busy with her sandwich preparations, she didn't realize at first that she could feel a slight breeze touching her arms. How odd. The air conditioning had already gone off and the ceiling fan wasn't on. Scanning the room, she saw the window above the sink was open about an inch.

Slowly setting her sandwich down on the table, Kyra walked toward the sink and with a shaking hand reached over to close the window. She was almost positive she had made sure this window was closed and locked the night before. Frightened, she whipped around, observing the hallway and the section of the living room she could see. Like her character Jennie, she was afraid someone was in the house with her. She slipped across the room to the kitchen door and checked the latch. It was locked.

The heavy rain hitting the house and the intermittent thunder fed her fear, and Kyra tried to convince herself that she was overreacting. The window contractors would be back shortly, and she should just sit down and eat her sandwich. She compromised by picking up the phone and calling Sam, only to discover Sam wasn't home.

"Okay, what's Plan B?" Kyra muttered to herself. Before she could make a decision, the doorbell rang. Hurray! It had to be the window guys. She'd even welcome Mrs. Taylor. In a moment of caution, she grabbed a knife from the cutlery block and headed toward the front door. At first she couldn't see anything through the curtain of rain and then she realized she was looking at brown packing label on a new window. Sliding the knife behind her, she opened the door.

"Hey," said Jim Knox. "Here's window number one. Doug's got the other one, so could you hold the door, please?"

Relief surged through her and she waved toward the living room, forgetting about the knife in her hand. "I'm so glad to see you," she said.

Jim reared back and looked at her in surprise. "You were expecting Jack the Ripper?"

"Oh, sorry, no, I was just making a sandwich."

"Yeah, right," he said, still looking uncertain.

After Doug entered the house, Kyra asked, "Did either of you go into the kitchen for a drink of water or anything else earlier?"

"Ms. Martin, is there a problem?" Jim frowned as he began stripping off the cardboard from the window he'd brought.

Kyra explained about the open window, but both men shook their heads. The storm had drifted away and the sky had lightened, and with the change in atmosphere, she was beginning to feel silly.

"Do you want us to check over the house?" Jim asked. "It's a little creepy to be surprised like that."

"No, no, I'm sure it's my imagination. You probably want to get those windows installed before it starts storming again."

Kyra ate her sandwich quickly and then walked around the house while the men were within screaming distance. She even got up the nerve to check out the basement again, but she didn't see anything out of the ordinary. When she was assured no one was hiding away, she cursed herself for being a fool. After getting a large glass of iced tea, she returned to the den and sat down at Aunt Mary's desk. She couldn't wait to get back into writing about Jennie's adventures. She sniffed and noticed the odor of cigarette smoke.

Frowning, she hurried out to the living room where the men were hard at work.

"Did one of you light a cigarette?" she asked. "I don't allow smoking in the house."

Both men turned blank looks toward her.

"Nope," said Jim. "I quit about five years ago, and Doug here never smoked. Besides his old lady would smack him upside the head if he ever tried it around the babies."

Doug grinned at her. "That she would."

"Oh, sorry. I thought I smelled . . . well, never mind."

Puzzled, Kyra slowly walked back to the den. Sitting down, she reached for her notebook to review her notes and cigarette ash fell into her lap. More ash lay strewn across her laptop keyboard. Someone had launched a scare campaign against her. And it was working.

CHAPTER 6

Sam came by as the contractors were finishing up to check out the new windows. Kyra told him about her possible intruder and asked if he wouldn't mind keeping an eye on the house for a night or two. She offered to pay him, but he refused to accept any money, so she said she'd make him breakfast as payment.

"I think you should call the police again," Sam said after sniffing the den. "Maybe you shouldn't have cleaned up already."

"And what would they do?" Kyra shook her head. "They couldn't identify what brand of cigarette the ash came from, and they'd insist that one of those workers simply lied to me about smoking in here."

Rubbing his hand over his face in thought, Sam agreed. He walked over to the desk and slid the rolltop up and down a few times, careful not to bump the laptop. "Still works great. Mary asked me to take a look at it a few years ago because it was sticking, and I lubricated it real good."

Kyra thought of all the years Aunt Mary had called Sam over to check a leaky faucet or help her move a heavy piece of furniture to clean. Looking at him now, she wondered if he had hoped for more from their relationship, even if he was ten years younger than her. She felt odd thinking that way, especially since she'd discovered the possibility of her aunt being married. Maybe that was why Kyra never saw any indication that Mary was interested in getting married or having a man around the house.

Sam sighed and turned to Kyra. "I'll head over to my house and take care of Tex. After dark, I'll set up in the shadows of your porch and we'll see if we can catch a rock thrower!"

"I feel bad about ruining your night's sleep," Kyra began but Sam cut her off.

"Don't worry. I don't sleep much anymore anyway. I'm up half the night tossing and turning. Then I go play some solitaire in the kitchen and sip a little whiskey 'til I'm ready to sleep again."

At dusk Kyra dug out a plastic lounge chair from the garage and set it in a corner of the porch away from the street light. She added a light blanket and small pillow to make Sam comfortable and then tried to review her day's writing in the den. When she heard Sam and Tex settle themselves on the porch, she tried to relax. Finally giving up, she moved to the living room and began reading a detective story. With the curtains closed and low music playing, she felt antsy because she had no idea what was happening outside.

Worried that whoever was trying to frighten her was even now creeping up to her back door, she hurried to the kitchen. She peeked through the curtains into her backyard. A slight breeze rustled the leaves on the maple trees and the rhododendron bushes squatted like menacing trolls along the edge of the property. Odd shadows lay here and there in the middle of the yard, but Kyra assumed they belonged to clusters of perennial plants Aunt Mary had planted years ago. None of the shadows was big enough to hide a man.

Taking a deep breath, she forced herself away from the window and decided it was time for a shower and then bed. She hadn't slept well last night, and she'd been on a roller coaster ride all day with one strange incident after another. She lay for a long time waiting to hear the crash of glass, but eventually exhaustion claimed her. Kyra didn't awake until light peeked through her blinds the next morning. She rested drowsily against her pillows, relaxing in the knowledge that the house had been safe for the night. Could her reign of terror be over?

Although Kyra knew it was still early, she wanted to start the coffee and ask Sam in for bacon and eggs. It was the least she could do. After she cleaned up breakfast, she'd move on to planning her luncheon for Mrs. Wright and Mrs. Dawson. Sam reported a quiet night, and gladly polished off his breakfast with several cups of coffee.

"I'm off to catch a couple hours of sleep now," he said, patting Tex who lay by his side.

"I don't think you should come over tonight." Kyra sipped her own coffee before smiling at Sam. "Maybe it's no longer necessary for you to go out of your way."

Sam grinned back at her. "I appreciate your concern for me, but I'm fine. Me and Tex walked around the yard several times last night and didn't notice a thing. But it was probably because we were around that nothing happened. Let me help for a few more days."

"Then I insist on paying you," Kyra said.

Again, Sam shook his head. "Mary would want me to do this for you. Breakfast is payment enough. Now if you need me for anything this afternoon, just give me a holler."

Kyra leaned over to hug Sam before reaching down to pat Tex. "Thanks, guys, you've been real life savers."

For an hour after Sam left, Kyra sat in the den reviewing her last chapter and trying to write, but her brain wouldn't cooperate. She finally closed the laptop and decided to run the sweeper and dust the downstairs rooms. When she finished her cleaning, it was almost eleven o'clock, so she headed out to the kitchen to prepare her salad and make some fresh balsamic vinaigrette dressing. She trimmed a half dozen chicken tenderloins, dredged them in an egg wash and then through a parmesan coating. She placed them on a tray coated with olive oil and popped them into the oven. When her company arrived, she'd cut up the chicken and serve it on top of her salads along with slices of garlic bread. For dessert, she had defrosted a loaf of apple bread she made several days ago, and she'd slice that down to serve with fresh coffee or tea.

Kyra ran upstairs to freshen up, and the doorbell was ringing on her way back down.

"Mrs. Wright, Mrs. Dawson, I'm so glad to see you."

As the women entered, Mrs. Dawson patted her on the arm and said, "That sounds much too formal, my dear. Why don't we get on more comfortable terms? I'm Trudy."

"And I'm Nora," piped up Mrs. Wright, jangling the bright-colored bracelets on her arm. "I picked these up at the flea market last week. Don't you think they're delightful?"

"They're gaudy and annoying," Trudy said, rolling her eyes. "But I'll put up with them because you enjoy them."

"We've been friends too long," Nora whispered to Kyra. "You have to watch out because sometimes . . ."

"We finish each other's sentences."

Kyra laughed and ushered them into the kitchen. "I don't mind. I have a friend like that, too, but I haven't seen her in the last year or two."

"Oh, my dear, that shouldn't matter. You must take time to get in touch again."

Kyra nodded and smiled, suddenly feeling the loss of her friendship with Sandy. Ever since her marriage to Brad, the gulf had widened between herself and her friend. Going to work and spending time with Brad had taken up most of her time and energy. And Brad had made it clear that he didn't care for Sandy's loud laugh and ironic sense of humor, traits Kyra had enjoyed.

Trudy glanced around the kitchen and sighed. "Goodness, I didn't realize how much I missed Mary until I'm standing here looking at her favorite dishes on the shelf and that Amish oak table she loved."

Kyra hesitated, hating to interrupt their memories, when Trudy turned and gave her a quick hug. "But we're so glad you're here, my dear. Aren't we, Nora?"

"We certainly are. And it smells delicious in here. Is that some kind of chicken?"

Trudy laughed and poked her friend. "Nora's thoughts never stray far from food. You'd better serve lunch or she'll drive you crazy guessing what you made."

Kyra had always liked Aunt Mary's friends, but it felt strange at first to sit with them around the table without her aunt's presence. Halfway through the meal, she decided she was comfortable enough with them to talk frankly about Mary's past. She was dying to know if they knew her "aunt" was really her mother.

"I'm curious to know how long you were friends with my aunt. I remember your visits from the first summer I stayed here." Kyra looked around at their smiling faces.

Nora waved her arms and the bracelets jangled. "We were friends for ages," she said. "Even before you were born."

"Really? No wonder you miss her so much then." Kyra hesitated, trying to think about how to discuss her birth. "You must have been surprised when I was born."

Trudy narrowed her eyes and studied Kyra. "Why would you say that? Your parents had wanted a child for ages, so it was a happy occasion."

"Of course, you're right. They did want a child for a long time, but I believe Aunt Mary helped them out. Isn't that correct?"

"Why would you think that?" Nora frowned and looked quickly toward Trudy. "I can't imagine what you thought Mary had to do with it."

"Oh, give it up, Nora," Trudy murmured. "She obviously knows about what happened."

I nodded. "I've already discovered that Mary was actually my mother, not my aunt. I just wanted to be sure you both knew before I said something I shouldn't."

"Oh, dear, I hope you're not upset." Nora looked upset herself. "Mary loved you very much. But it was much harder then to raise a child without a father, even though Mary was middle-aged at the time. People would talk, and then your poor mama had several miscarriages and the doctor said—"

Trudy held up her hand. "Enough! I think Kyra understands all that, Nora." She turned to Kyra. "I sense there's something else you want to discuss."

Kyra bit her lip and debated about asking her next question. "Um, did either of you know if Mary was ever married?"

"Married? I don't think so," Nora said, her forehead crinkled in thought. "But then I didn't know Mary until a couple years before you were born. Trudy, how about you? You've lived here in town longer than I have."

Trudy hesitated, causing Kyra to stare at her in surprise. Then she shook her head and smiled. "Not to my knowledge. Why did you ask?"

"It's because a middle-aged man showed up at my door last week claiming to be Ethan Owens, Mary's son by a man called Jasper Owens. He was rather insistent and wanted to take a look inside the house. Said he was the rightful heir."

"What? That's ridiculous!" Nora's bracelets rattled as her arms shook. "He was probably some thief trying to get inside and case the joint."

Kyra couldn't help it—she laughed.

"The joint?" Trudy remarked. "I hardly think . . ."

"Oh, you know what I mean." Then her face whitened. "What if he had more nefarious thoughts?"

Kyra stood up and put her arm around Nora's shoulders. "No, no, don't worry. I'm sure he has no interest in me. It's the house he wants for some reason."

"Did you talk to your lawyer?" Trudy asked, looking at the problem with a practical view. Kyra smiled, thinking that these two friends were exact opposites, but sometimes that made the best friendships.

"Yes, of course, and he knew nothing about an Ethan Owens. He checked around but couldn't find anyone by that name who had anything to do with Aunt Mary."

"Then you should forget about him." Trudy said those words in such a way that Kyra could see her mentally dusting her hands to show the end of the problem.

"Well, see, it's a little more complicated than that." By the time Kyra finished explaining the strange events of the past week, Trudy looked fiercely angry and Nora's face was pale and frightened. "Maybe I shouldn't have said anything about this to you. I'm sorry if I've upset you."

"Hah! It will take more than some obnoxious guy to give me bad dreams. I don't think your lawyer is doing his job very well. Or the police!" Trudy exclaimed.

"I'd ask you to move in with me, but I'm going to Florida for several weeks to stay with my daughter's family," Nora said. "I don't like you living here alone; it could be dangerous."

The thought of living with a nervous Nellie like Nora made Kyra cringe. Besides, she had no intention of moving anywhere since she refused to be frightened out of Mary's home.

"I didn't tell you to scare you, but to see if you knew something I didn't. Sam lives right next door and my husband will be here Friday night. I'm sure I'll be fine."

Nora patted her arm and murmured about Kyra being welcome to stay with her later in the summer, but Trudy seemed uncharacteristically quiet. Kyra glanced up to see her staring at the table deep in thought.

"Trudy?" Kyra said and she jumped.

"Oh, sorry, I must have been daydreaming a little."

"How could you daydream at a time like this?" Nora demanded, but Trudy shook her head and smiled.

Desperate to change the subject, Kyra said, "Who's ready for apple bread and coffee?"

When she saw her company to the door an hour later, Nora hugged her and made her promise to call the police if she was frightened for any reason. Trudy studied her face before saying, "We'll talk again soon."

"Sure, that sounds great." Kyra suspected Trudy was trying to tell her something that she didn't want Nora to know. Puzzled, she walked back to the kitchen to clean up before returning to the den to work on her story. Was Trudy a closer confidante to her aunt than Nora? Did Trudy know secrets that might help explain the marriage license Kyra found in the desk? To take her mind off her own confusion, Kyra worked on deepening the mystery in her novel to keep the reader guessing. She spent the rest of the day spinning out the suspense in her story.

Just as she drifted off to sleep that night, the phone on her night-stand rang. Jerking awake, her heart pounding, she grabbed for it and gasped, "Hello?" Brad only called her cell phone, so she feared it was Ethan Owens trying to annoy her.

"Kyra, it's Trudy."

"Oh, hi." She pushed one hand against her chest to ease the thump-ing within.

"I'm sorry if I frightened you. I usually can't sleep before midnight. Since you were a writer, I assumed you were one of those people who burned the midnight oil. It sounds like I was wrong."

"No, it's all right. I'm glad you called." Kyra pushed herself up to a sitting position and clicked on her bedside lamp. "Sometimes I do stay up quite late writing."

"But not tonight," Trudy murmured with a quiet laugh.

"I'm happy to talk to you because I think you have things to tell me. The wariness in my voice was because I feared Ethan Owens was contacting me."

"Oh, I never thought of that. I'm so sorry."

Kyra reached for the notebook and pencil she kept by her bedside because she never knew when inspiration would strike. "Please, let's talk about why you called. Was Mary married at one time?"

"Yes, and not happily, either, which was one reason she wasn't inter-ested in marriage when she got pregnant with you."

"Wait! Are you saying that earlier she did have a son with that hus-band?" Maybe Mr. Owens was telling the truth, Kyra thought.

"No, definitely not. When you mentioned that man today, I was quite surprised. Especially because her husband's name was Owens, Jasper Owens."

Kyra sucked in her breath, thinking of the marriage license in the folder she found in the desk. So it was true, at least the marriage. She told Trudy about her discovery, and her suspicion that Ethan had hidden it in the house deliberately to back up his story. "At the time, I thought maybe it was a forgery. However, I never found anything about a birth certificate for any child."

"I believe Ethan was Jasper's illegitimate child. If so, I wouldn't worry about any claim he's making on Mary's house." She hesitated before saying, "You said you didn't find any birth certificate?"

After Kyra had assured her that Mr. Berchtold had given her a copy of hers, Trudy added, "Despite all the mystery, I'm glad you're not upset about Mary being your mother. She worried about you so much sometimes, but she felt comfortable giving you to her brother and his wife."

"I had a happy childhood, Trudy, at least until my mother died. It was devastating at twelve to lose my mother, but Aunt Mary filled the gap so well, and she was always there for me. She helped me grow up in so many ways." Kyra felt the tears pricking and forced herself to take a deep breath and remain calm. "And at least you've cleared up some of that mystery you were talking about."

"There is one thing we haven't discussed, besides the identity of Ethan Owens." Trudy sounded worried now and rather hesitant. "I'm surprised Mr. Berchtold hasn't said anything to you about it."

Kyra glanced at the several notes she had made and wondered what Trudy was hinting at. Then she realized the one fact they hadn't discussed completely. "Jasper Owens. What happened to him? Did he die long ago since I'd never even heard of him?"

"Yes, he died." Trudy's voice was flat and Kyra detected a note of worry. "Maybe we should discuss this tomorrow. I wasn't thinking clearly and I shouldn't have brought this up now."

"What? Why shouldn't we discuss it? You can't leave me hanging like this—I'll never be able to sleep all night."

Trudy sighed, saying, "That's exactly what I'm afraid of. Please, I'm tired and the story won't seem as bad in the light of day."

"What story? Trudy, don't do this to me. I can't imagine how it could bother me since I never knew Jasper and I certainly don't care about him."

"I know, but you did care about Mary, and you're living in her house."

"If you try to hang up now, I'll drive over to your house and bang on the door until you answer!"

"Okay, fine; I understand your point of view." She hesitated and then said quickly, "He died after falling down the basement steps."

"Oh." Kyra thought of her story and how she'd written about a man falling down the basement stairs. She shivered at the coincidence before forcing herself to say, "That's sad, and no wonder I never liked going down to the basement. But accidents like that do happen all the time."

"That's not the worst of it. Everyone knew Jasper and Mary didn't get along well in the two years they were married. She was accused of pushing him down the stairs when he was drunk the day he died."

CHAPTER 7

Kyra's hand shook and she dropped the pencil onto the sheets. "What? How awful. But I don't believe Mary would ever do that!"

"No, of course not. No one's talked about it for years, and Nora doesn't even know. There was never any proof that Mary had done such a terrible thing. Since it was common knowledge that Jasper drank too much, the coroner at the time ruled it an accidental death. Mary had so many good friends, including some influential people, that the story eventually faded away. Her work as a judge's secretary helped."

"That's odd because Mr. Berchtold never mentioned Mary's marriage or Jasper's death to me." Kyra's mind buzzed around in confusion as she tried to imagine her "aunt" being accused of murder. Or would it have been manslaughter? She was rather hazy on the various terms used for killing people.

"Maybe he didn't want to worry you about something that was never proven," Trudy said in a muffled voice. Kyra realized she was trying to stifle a yawn. "And I think we should continue this conversation in the morning. Will you be all right?"

"I guess I'll manage." The yawn was infectious because Kyra caught herself doing the same thing. Looking at her watch, she saw it was now 12:20 in the morning. "It was my decision to insist you tell me everything, so it's my own fault if I can't sleep. I'm going downstairs and check on Sam first. I'll call you in the morning."

"Don't worry, Kyra. Everything will work out; I'm sure of it. Good night, dear."

When Kyra opened the front door to ask Sam if he needed anything, he waved her off. "Got a thermos of coffee here and some protein bars. The night's real quiet. Go get some sleep."

What she really wanted to do was grill Sam about Mary's husband falling down the stairs, but then she remembered he'd only lived next door for about ten years. He might not know anything, either. Sighing, she grabbed a water bottle from the fridge and plodded back up to bed. Writing in her notebook, she added a few lines to the information Trudy had shared with her. From now on, she planned on researching Mary's life just like she did for the characters and incidents in her stories.

Yawning in earnest, she turned off the light and slid back under the sheets. Afraid she wouldn't sleep, she used her old trick. She forced her eyes to stay open and stare at a spot of light created by the street lamp. The longer she stared, the more tired she felt until finally her eyes closed.

The patter of rain woke her early the next morning. The grayness outside her windows foretold a damp and dreary day. Seeing it was only a little after six, Kyra curled up and fell back to sleep. The sound of Tex barking jerked her awake again, and she suddenly remembered Sam sitting outside watching her house. She pulled on yesterday's jean shorts and a clean t-shirt and detangled her hair with her fingers before flying down the stairs. The thought of Jasper Owens rushing to his death on the basement steps flickered through her mind, but she quickly suppressed it.

Peering out the front windows, Kyra saw Sam on the porch throwing a stick to Tex. The dog slid through the wet grass to grab it out of the air. Relief flooded through her, and she opened the door to call out, "I'm starting breakfast now, Sam."

"Sounds great. I'll take Tex over home so he won't mess up your kitchen. Be back in a minute."

By the time Sam returned, the coffee was gurgling and the ham was browning nicely.

"No problems at all last night. I don't think whoever was behind the window smashing liked having the police involved."

Kyra paused in checking the French toast to say, "But how would he even know the police were here? Oh, you mean he was watching the house?"

"Aw, now, don't worry. I think maybe he's given up and will leave you alone."

"Maybe." She turned off the heat and slid the French toast and ham onto their plates. "But I don't think that real estate lady is finished with me. I'm sure Ethan Owens is behind that offer and it's his other prong of attack."

"Yeah. Can't scare 'em out, then buy 'em out."

Kyra smiled at Sam as she brought over his breakfast. "That sounds about right. Now let's forget about this problem and enjoy our meal."

Before Sam left, Kyra asked if he'd ever heard about Mary being married years ago. He shook his head, but said he wondered sometimes if she'd had a bad experience with love in her past.

"She always changed the subject when I said I was sorry I'd never found the right gal and gotten married when I was younger. Always felt like I'd missed out on something." Sam stared out the window as if remembering her exact words. "She'd say not everyone was cut out for marriage, and I was better off single than marrying the wrong person."

Kyra took a sip of coffee so she wouldn't have to respond. Without meaning to, she applied those words to her marriage to Brad, and it shook her up. Was she repeating the mistake Mary had made with Jasper? That wasn't fair to Brad because he certainly wasn't a drunkard, and if anything, he was over-protective. *But he does want you to be a dutiful wife and not insist on doing things your way,* her mind whispered.

Glancing across the table, she saw Sam frowning at her.

"You okay?" he asked.

Laughing, she said she was fine, and thanked him again for providing his security services for the last couple nights. After assuring him she'd call if any problem arose, she saw him to the door.

Before settling down to her writing, she called Trudy. After discussing how they had both managed a good night's sleep, Kyra said, "I checked with my neighbor Sam about Mary's earlier life, but he had no clue. He seemed to think she'd never married. I'll have to visit the local newspaper office and see if their papers are archived on the computer. I can always say I'm doing research for my book."

"Good idea," Trudy agreed. "I'll see what I can come up with by talking to some of the old-timers around here."

Kyra hesitated before saying, "Maybe that's not such a great idea. We don't want anyone to spread the news about how we're digging into Mary's life. I'd hate myself if you came to some harm because of me."

"Nonsense! If I've lived to the ripe old age of seventy-five, I'm not afraid of some stupid threats. Don't worry about me. Besides, I'm enjoying a little excitement in my life for a change."

Before Kyra could reply, Trudy continued, "Oh, dear, that didn't come out right. I didn't mean that this situation is anything but worrisome. I really don't want anything to happen to you, either."

Kyra laughed and soothed away Trudy's upset. "I'm sure we have nothing to worry about, but I'd like to know why Ethan Owens wants his hands on Mary's property so desperately."

"I've been thinking that over, and I believe it has something to do with the basement in that house."

Surprised, Kyra asked, "Why in the world . . .?"

"Jasper died going down to the basement, and I think he hid something worthwhile down there. Mary said he yelled at her if she questioned his frequent trips to the basement. Except for the police looking into Jasper's death, I don't think anyone has ever really searched that area in decades."

Kyra shuddered, thinking about undertaking a comprehensive search of that dank, barely lighted cellar.

"And I know for a fact that the back room still has dirt floors—they were never cemented over like the rest of the basement. Anything could be buried in there!"

"Oh, Trudy. You sound like you're thinking of buried treasure."

"I know it sounds silly, but who knows what shady deals he was involved in? Especially because Jasper had a terrible reputation for intimidating people. He could have even buried people down there!" At Kyra's sharp intake of breath, Trudy hurried on, "Sorry, dear. I've done it again and frightened you. Perhaps I should begin writing books."

Kyra found herself amazed at this white-haired, slightly overweight old lady's ability to come up with such fantastic scenarios. Trying to stick to logic, she said, "I think it's more likely he hid the record of all his blackmail victims in the basement, but I'm sure Mary would have found it and destroyed it after his death." When Trudy agreed, Kyra added, "Maybe you should collaborate with me on the murder mystery I'm writing. You could give me some plot suggestions."

Trudy laughed, before saying, "Now I know you're being kind, but I would like to get together with you again. Could we meet for lunch one day soon?"

"Of course, I'd like that, too."

After settling on the next Monday at a small restaurant Trudy suggested, Kyra hung up. Shaking her head, she walked down the hall toward the den. She tried to ignore the basement door on her right, but her steps slowed. She vaguely remembered that back room Trudy had mentioned because one summer a friend had dared her to walk all around the basement with only a small flashlight. She'd done it, but her heart was pounding in her chest by the time she'd made it back upstairs. With a laugh, she'd convinced the girl it was no big deal, but she never went back down there again unless she was with Aunt Mary.

Opening the door, she stood at the top of the stairs and flicked on the light. She carefully stepped down, and as she rounded the curve, the basement stretched out before her in all its cluttered disarray. Boxes, old furniture, shelves full of broken household items and old canning jars still filled the large open area. The door to the furnace and hot water heater stood open on the left side, just as it had when she checked out the area a few days ago.

Kyra tried to ignore the musty smell as she marched past all the miscellaneous items until she stood before that ominous door. Taking a deep breath, she whipped it open and reached along the wall for a light switch. She snatched her hand away when she encountered gritty cement block covered with a spider's web. The weak bulb hanging from the center of the main room did nothing more than highlight the shadows within. She cursed herself for not bringing the flashlight from the kitchen drawer.

Gathering her courage, she stepped into the room to rub her shoe across the floor. A poof of dust and dirt settled onto her foot as she heard alarmed squeaks and scrambling sounds echo across the room. Pulling her foot back, she shifted to allow in a little more light and stared around. Beady red eyes glittered back at her. Rats! She slammed the door shut and searched the floor of the main room. Trying to see everywhere all at once, she crept toward the stairway.

The doorbell pealed and she jumped at the unexpected sound. Glad of an excuse to run, she hurried up the stairs, taking them two at a time. By the time she reached the living room, an assault of knocking battered the door.

With the thought of Ethan Owens standing on her porch, she whipped open the door, ready to give him a piece of her mind.

"If you think I'm going to sell this house to you . . . oh!"

Simon Berchtold stood there, worry lines creasing his forehead. "Are you all right? I was worried when you didn't answer."

Kyra pushed her hair back from her face and managed to say, "Yes, I'm fine. I thought you were someone else. Sorry!"

"I assumed that." The frown changed to a small smile. "Do you mind if I come in?"

"Oh, sorry again. Please come in." Still feeling rattled after the rat encounter and the adrenalin rush from expecting an argument with her nemesis, Kyra led the way down the hall to the living room.

"Have a seat, Mr. Berchtold." He settled on the sofa and she sat opposite on one of the wing chairs. Glancing down, she saw her shoe encrusted with dirt and slid it behind the other one. Nervously running her hand through her hair again, it came back sticky with spider web.

"Oh, darn!" She jumped up. "Sorry, I'll be right back."

Hurrying to the powder room down the hall, she rubbed a towel through her hair, making sure no spiders fell out. She swiped it over her face and brushed off her shoe. Dumping the towel in the wastebasket until later, she returned to the living room.

Mr. Berchtold looked up from some papers he'd spread out on the coffee table and smiled. "All better?"

"Yes, thank you. Have you brought some more papers for me to sign?"

He shook his head. "I've come because my nephew finally found some information about your aunt's marriage."

"Oh, I see." The adrenaline flow had ebbed away and it was replaced by nerves. Ignoring the urge to bite her nails, Kyra asked, "So she was married at one time?"

"Yes, many years ago for a short period of time. I vaguely remember something about her early marriage now that Peter talked to me, but I was away at college at the time. Her husband's name was Jasper Owens, and Ethan Owens, the man you said accosted you the other day, was his son."

Since the news wasn't exactly unexpected, Kyra focused on the lawyer's specific words. "What do you mean '*I said* he accosted me'? Are you inferring he didn't really try to push his way into this house?"

Putting his hands up to calm her down, he said, "No, of course not. But we have to be careful with terminology. If Ethan is her husband's son, he may have some property rights."

"Wait a minute! You've already said I'm Mary's heir and the will's being probated now. How in the world could he have any rights?"

"We need to be sure this is the most recent will; that's all. I thought that maybe you'd let me look around and make sure that we're not missing any important papers."

Kyra stood up, saying, "Since you're her lawyer and she filed all her paperwork with you, I don't think there's anything more that needs done. Unless Ethan or his lawyer has something to show you about another will, then I don't believe we need to follow up."

"Yes, of course you're right. I just didn't want any kind of surprise to surface and cause any problems."

"Fine." Kyra sat back down. "Please make sure Ethan Owens is told that he has no claim on this property and make it clear he must stop bothering me. If I have to, I'll file a harassment suit against him."

"The problem is that we haven't been able to get in touch with him. Did he give you an address?"

When Kyra shook her head, the lawyer cleared his throat and hesitated before saying, "There's one other thing you should know. Mary's husband died in a fall down the basement stairs less than two years into their marriage." Glancing up at her, he stopped talking. "But you already knew that, I see."

"Yes, one of her good friends felt she should tell me before I heard any rumors."

He nodded. "I also have some updated information about your biological father, Leonardo Napoli. He was originally from Stonecliff, but as far as we know, he hasn't left Italy for many years." He hesitated before adding, "When Mary signed the adoption papers, she made it clear that Mr. Napoli wouldn't be claiming any rights to the child. Er, I mean you."

CHAPTER 8

When Kyra finally sat down in front of her laptop later that afternoon, she struggled to focus on her story. Thoughts about her unknown father kept intruding, especially because she'd never wondered about him before. Knowing she was Mary's daughter had been enough to absorb at first. Since Mary hadn't mentioned his name in her letter, Kyra assumed it hadn't been a long relationship. Even after she discovered Leonardo Napoli's name on her birth certificate, Kyra figured Mary had her reasons not to talk about him. Because she wanted to honor Mary's wishes, there wasn't any reason to pursue a relationship with him.

In the back of her mind, though, Kyra knew she'd heard of an author named Leonardo Napoli and had even read a couple of his books. His main character was an Italian detective known for his forceful ways of getting the truth out of criminals he brought in for questioning. Several of his plots used real-life crimes as the basis for his stories, although he always added a special note saying the characters, settings, and incidents in his novels were pure fiction.

She connected to the internet and typed in Leonardo's name, and immediately she saw that the author was originally from a small town in Pennsylvania, and he had spent most of his adult life in Italy. No mention of a child, of course, but she didn't doubt it was the Leonardo on her birth certificate. Although curious to put a face to his name, she searched in vain for a photo. In a way, it saddened her to think she'd never know her biological father, even as an adult, but she wouldn't let it touch her that much. Instead, she focused on the possibility of inheriting some of his talent, although his writing style was quite different than hers. Running her hands through her hair, she shrugged. She could speculate all she wanted, but it wouldn't get her novel finished.

Sighing, she read over yesterday's pages and forced herself to put her fingers on the keyboard and type. Eventually settling into a rhythm, she found herself thinking and acting like her main character and the afternoon passed. The murder victim was a man who tried to force himself inside the heroine's house, and Kyra realized he looked a little too much like Ethan Owens. She probably should change his description if she ever managed to publish this book, but for now it made it easier to kill him off. His motive involved intimidation of the heroine and not making claims on her property. Remembering how she felt when Ethan stood at her door helped Kyra give her character the same fear and confusion.

Later, after an early dinner of salad and a grilled cheese sandwich, Kyra took a glass of iced tea out to the patio to relax and read a magazine. The backyard encompassed about an eighth of an acre where Mary had planted mostly perennials such as daisies, carnations, and butterfly bushes. Two maple trees provided shade in the middle of the garden and the rhododendron bushes lined up against the fence at the end of the property. Kyra had hidden within those bushes sometimes when she first came to stay with Aunt Mary. Still grieving from the loss of her mother, she had felt deserted by her father when he left her here for the summer. Slowly, Mary had drawn her out and asked her little things about her mother until she began to trust again. Mary said she was free to cry anytime or talk about her mother until some of the grief had eased.

Tears leaked from the corners of her eyes as Kyra felt the loss of her mother and Mary all over again. That's when Tex bounded around the corner of the house and jumped onto her legs for a big hug. Laughing, she leaned over and rubbed his back and petted his head.

"Tex, down," shouted Sam as he puffed into Kyra's backyard. "Sorry about that!"

Kyra knuckled the tears away and said, "No problem, Sam. I was feeling out of sorts and Tex perked me up. He's just what I needed!"

"Well, if you're sure . . ."

"Don't worry, I'm sure." She smiled at Sam and pointed to the chair opposite her at the glass table. "Have a seat, if you're not busy."

"Just for a minute. I should get back to the bushes I was trimming. Wanted to get them finished up before the sun goes down."

"You look hot. Would you like some iced tea?"

"Nah, that's okay. I have some beer at the house just calling my name."

"Oh, by the way. Do you know how to get rid of rats? I discovered some in that back room in the basement."

"Sure they're not just mice?" he asked, smiling. "I know women definitely don't like those varmints."

"Don't think so," Kyra replied. "They're about this big," she held up her hands eight inches apart, "and they had beady red eyes."

"Huh." Sam nodded. "I'll pick up some traps and fill them with cheese. That should take care of them. Why the heck were you in that back room anyway?"

"Curiosity." Kyra figured that was good enough for Sam. "If I'd been a cat, I could have taken care of the rats at the same time."

Sam laughed and stood up. "Come on, Tex. Let's leave the lady alone and get back to our pruning."

Kyra relaxed as she watched the butterflies flit from flower to flower. As the sun eased down behind the fence, she leafed through her magazine and sipped iced tea, feeling calm for the first time in days. Maybe Trudy was right and everything would be resolved.

Kyra's calmness lasted almost twenty-four hours. After a good night's sleep and a busy day of house cleaning and writing, the anticipation of

Brad's arrival began to stress her out. She needed to fill him in on all the events of the week, including the broken windows, the real estate agent's offer, and the revelations of Mr. Berchtold. Brad called around five to say he was running late. After he explained he wouldn't be there until eleven or twelve and said she didn't have to wait up, she almost shouted "hurray!"

Reprieved from the tension for a few more hours, she watched an old movie on television until ten and then headed up to bed. She meant to stay awake reading a book she found in Aunt Mary's room, but fell asleep. When something woke her about an hour later, she assumed it was Brad moving around downstairs. Drowsy, she waited for him to come upstairs and almost dozed off again. Shaking herself, she called, "Brad?" The absolute stillness puzzled her and she called again, "Brad? Brad, are you down there?"

Her bedside lamp was still on so she slid out of bed and grabbed her short robe. Unsettled now by the silence and certain she'd heard a noise that woke her, she crept across the room and quietly opened her door. Shadows blanketed the hallway and no glow of a living room light filtered up the stairway. Shaking, Kyra closed the door and fumbled with the knob. Staring at it in dismay, she remembered it didn't have a lock of any kind. Since she knew she'd deliberately left the lamp on by the sofa in the living room, someone had turned it off. Or maybe the light bulb had simply burned out, she thought, but didn't quite believe it.

With her back to the door, she looked around the room. Spying the chair sitting before the small desk, she ran across the room. She carried it to the door and jammed it under the knob. It didn't fit as snugly as she'd hoped, but it was at least a small deterrent to a forced entry. Hurrying back to the bedside, she grabbed her phone off the table as she clicked off the light. She needed to give her eyes time to adjust to the darkness.

She dialed 911 and ran to the window, pulling back the curtain to peer into the backyard. In the seconds before someone answered, she wondered if Brad was playing games with her, and he'd be angry when he discovered she'd call the emergency line.

"911, what's your emergency?"

In a low voice, Kyra gave her address and then quickly explained, adding that she wasn't certain an intruder was really in the house.

"We're dispatching a car right now," the calm voice of the operator said. "Please stay on the line."

Kyra told him about how her husband was due any time now, but she'd called out several times and he hadn't answered. As her eyes adjusted to the dark, she stared at the outline of the door, the phone held tightly against her ear. That's when she heard the squeak of the next-to-last top step of the stairs, the step that always creaked. Holding back a scream, she whispered, "Someone's in the hallway!"

Suddenly remembering the softball bat she had kept by the bedside since the window incident, she skirted around the bed to pick it up. Determined not to be a victim, she crept next to the door and waited. She set the phone down, just as the operator said something about hiding. Gripping the bat with both hands, she finally heard the distant sound of sirens.

"Hurry, hurry," she screamed in her head as the doorknob turned. She stopped breathing. The knob clicked softly and the door moved a fraction. A harder shove and it moved a fraction more. Sirens wailed and barking erupted from the front yard. Loud, excited barking. Tex! Kyra sucked in air and stared at the doorknob as it twisted back and forth. Banging against the front door reverberated through the house, and Sam called, "What is it, boy? Kyra, Kyra, you all right?"

Footsteps retreated, pounding down the stairs. Kyra shoved the chair out of the way and ran into the hall. "He's going out the back," she screamed. The flashing light from the police car entering the driveway bathed the living room as Kyra hurried downstairs. She ran to the back door, just in time to see Sam and Tex chasing the man across the lawn. They disappeared behind the rhododendron bushes for a few moments and then a form jumped for the top of the fence. He missed and jumped again as another figure grabbed onto him. Tex howled and tried to leap after him. The man hung onto the fence, pulling himself up and over just as Tex latched onto his foot. He shook the dog loose, and a crash and groan were drowned out by Tex's frantic barks. Running back and forth along the fence, Tex tried to find a way around it.

Kyra rushed to join Sam and they ran toward the gate as two policeman carrying bright flashlights rounded the corner of the house.

As she heard some scuffling and another groan, a policeman shouted, "Stop where you are! Don't move!"

Kyra turned back, saying, "I'm the woman who called 911. The man who was in my house is getting away behind this fence. Hurry!" She pointed toward the gate and Sam called Tex to heel. He obeyed reluctantly as one officer rushed to the gate, opened it, and flashed his light around the area. The other policeman stopped beside Kyra and Sam. He commanded them to return to the house and wait. Kyra felt just as reluctant as Tex to obey orders, but decided the police were only thinking of her safety.

The policeman who opened the gate shouted, "Stay facedown and place your hands on your head!"

"Looks like we'll know who your intruder was any minute now. Guy must have injured himself jumping over the fence," Sam said, huffing after all the exertion.

"Good! I'm glad." Sitting down, Kyra realized she was still wearing her shorty pajamas and light robe. Embarrassed, she said, "I'll be right back." Running upstairs, she thought about that man creeping up here only minutes ago, and it freaked her out a bit. She pulled on shorts, a t-shirt, and sandals and rushed back to the kitchen. A sudden attack of shaking hit her and she crossed her arms to try and stop it. Her teeth rattled and she clamped her mouth tightly to keep Sam from seeing.

"Hey!" Sam must have noticed her shivers because he reached for her and forced her to sit. "It's shock. Do you have some soda or something in the fridge? You need sugar."

"Gin—gin-ger ale," she managed to say.

Sam grabbed a can, popped the tab, and pushed it into her hand. "Here, start sipping."

He disappeared into the living room and came back with an afghan, which he settled over her shoulders. "That'll help ease the shakes."

As Kyra began to feel better, one of the policemen knocked on the back door. When Sam let him in, Kyra could tell right away something was wrong.

"I'm Officer Cornwell," he said. He looked down at a notebook in his hand. "I believe you're Kyra Martin?" He studied Kyra's face as she nodded. "And you are?" He frowned at Sam, who gave his name and his status as the next-door neighbor.

When the front door opened and steps came toward the kitchen, Officer Cornwell placed a hand on his weapon. Kyra stood up as Brad burst into the room, demanding, "What the hell is going on here?"

"Sir, stop right there!"

"It's all right, Officer." Kyra hurried to explain, "That's Brad Martin, my husband."

The policeman nodded to Brad before saying, "Too bad you weren't here when the intruder broke into the house."

"What? Oh, Kyra, are you all right?" He rushed to her side and pulled her against his chest. "How awful. I'm so sorry I had to stay a little late at work before driving here."

Despite his words and hugs, Kyra suspected he was still angry with her. He'd blame her because she had insisted on staying at her aunt's house. But why was it suddenly so dangerous when it had been perfectly safe for Mary to live here all those years?

"Excuse me, but I need to have Mrs. Martin come with me to see if you recognize the man behind the fence."

"Why? Won't he tell you his name?" Kyra was confused.

"Sorry, ma'am, but it looks like he fell onto his own knife. I'm afraid he's dead."

CHAPTER 9

Kyra gasped as she stared at the policeman.

"Come along, ma'am, if you're up to it. We need to know if you can think of any reason why this man was in your house tonight."

Brad grabbed her arm, saying, "You don't have to do this, honey. Let the police take care of it. That's what fingerprints are for!"

Kyra shrugged off his hand and nodded to the officer, saying tightly, "Let's go."

"You're not going alone," Brad declared, daring anyone to object.

The three of them marched across the lawn following the beam of the policeman's flashlight. The other officer stood aside, keeping them at a slight distance to preserve the crime scene. His light showed the body of a man wearing dark jeans and a black turtleneck lying on his side, his face turned sideways toward them. Kyra sucked in her breath and slowly nodded.

"Yes, I know him." Her voice sounded unusually high-pitched. She cleared her throat and said, "That's the man who came to my house last week and introduced himself as Ethan Owens." She saw Officer Cornwell using his left hand to text something on his cell phone. She added, "He said he was the son of Jasper Owens, who was my Aunt Mary's husband years ago, and he insisted this property really belonged to him."

"That's enough!" Brad pulled her away from the scene. "Can't you see my wife is upset?"

"Brad, stop it! I want to help; I want to get this settled once and for all. This man frightened me and now he's dead. It's awful!"

The shakes were back and Kyra was furious with herself. Brad placed his arm around her shoulders and despite herself, she was grateful for his solid warmth.

"Does this place really belong to him?"

Kyra shook her head. "Not according to my lawyer. The will only names me as her heir."

The sound of crunching gravel in the alley where they stood alerted them to the appearance of the crime scene van and several other vehicles.

They were sent back to the house and were eventually interviewed by a Detective Andrews. After setting up a time to sign their reports at the police station the next morning, they were finally left alone.

Sam and Tex ambled off and all Kyra wanted to do was lie down and sleep for hours. Brad had other thoughts, though.

"How did that guy get into this house, Kyra?"

"I have no idea." She sighed and moved toward the stairs. "I really need to sleep, Brad. Maybe in the morning something will come to me."

"That detective thought it was pretty strange. He thinks you let him in, you know."

"I don't care what he thinks. I woke up when I heard someone moving around the house, and at first I thought it was you. But after I shouted your name several times and you didn't respond, I realized it must be an intruder. I called 911 because I was afraid for my life. Ethan Owens frightened me from that day he used a key to get inside this house. I'd never let him in!"

"But it all seems so strange. I think we need to talk—"

"Brad! Enough! Either come to bed with me or stay down here. I need your support, not your badgering!"

Kyra practically ran up the stairs, turned on the light, and stared at the tousled bed. She replaced the chair by the desk and straightened the covers on the bed. After blowing her nose, she lay on the bed in her shorts and t-shirt and willed sleep to come. A headache had blossomed over her eyes and she reached over to turn off the lamp. Instead of dozing off, she caught herself straining to hear what Brad was doing downstairs. She couldn't understand why he had been so adamant about her not staying in Mary's house, and why all kinds of scary things had happened since she'd moved in two weeks ago. Did Brad know something she didn't know? Or could he be behind everything that had happened?

Sitting back up, she stared at the door and heard the distant murmur of voices. *Who was Brad talking to?* Forcing herself to get back up, she crept to the door and peered out just as the sound stopped and Brad came into view in the lower hallway. Glancing up, he said, "I thought you were sleeping." He moved to the stairs and bounded up, as if he didn't have a care in the world. When he placed his arm over her shoulders and turned her toward the bedroom, she cringed away from him.

"Now what, Kyra? I'm trying to help."

"Who were you talking to down there?" she demanded.

He shook his head, saying, "You've become so suspicious lately. I was simply leaving a voice mail at work for something I forgot to tell my boss."

Kyra studied his face, but between the headache and her tiredness, she had no interest in pursuing the subject. "Whatever. I'm getting a few aspirin and then going to bed."

Brad made no effort to hold her when she slipped back into bed and that suited Kyra just fine. She lay awake for an hour or so as the headache faded before finally dropping off to sleep. When she awoke again, the window curtains were outlined with bright sunlight and the smell of coffee wafted up the stairs. Kyra stretched and relaxed against the pillows until she remembered the events of the night before. Glancing at the old-fashioned bedside clock-radio, she realized she only had about an hour before her appointment at the police department.

After a quick shower and a gulp of coffee, Kyra jumped into the car beside Brad. At the station, Detective Andrews had them sign their statements separately. As he reviewed Kyra's information about the locks being changed in the house, he said, "The curious fact is that the man somehow entered your house without breaking in. Can you think of some way to explain that?"

Kyra didn't care for his accusing tone and his ice-blue eyes that tried to penetrate her defenses. She sighed before replying, "I would never have given Ethan Owens a key because he was the reason why I had new locks installed: To keep him out. And because of the recent incidents, I made sure the windows and doors were locked downstairs so I didn't have to worry about him or anyone else getting into the house."

"And yet he did find a way in." His left eyebrow quirked up as he waited for her response.

Annoyed, she tilted her head and blurted out, "Magic?" When his face turned red, she continued, "I don't know. I thought you were the detective."

"Look, ma'am, last night the police responded to your emergency call, and at the time you sounded quite frightened. And now it's all a joke?"

"No, it's not a joke. You're right, I was terrified and I still am." She hated how his disbelieving attitude made her respond. "If he could get into my house somehow that I don't know about, then maybe someone else can, too."

"And maybe you just let him in and then when things went sour, you called the police to get you out of a jam. Now you want to play on our sympathy."

Exasperated, Kyra shook her head. "No, you're wrong. I've told you the truth all along, and if it weren't for my neighbor Sam and his dog, I might not be here right now."

"Oh, don't worry. We're looking into your neighbor and his timely intervention."

"You've got to be kidding me!" Kyra stood up, knocking the papers she had just signed onto the floor. "You're going to go after the one person who was there to help me?"

The detective held up his hands in a placating way. "All right, hold on. We're not 'going after him' as you said. We merely want to know why he suddenly came to your rescue. I'm sure there's an explanation."

"Sam was probably walking his dog and noticed something unusual. He's been helping guard my house since the window-breaking incidents."

Detective Andrews nodded. "I have that information here. Before you leave, I have one more question about your situation." Kyra slipped her purse under her arm to show him she was more than ready to leave and waited. "Are you and your husband separated? He obviously isn't living with you."

Quickly, Kyra explained about inheriting the house, her writing goals, and the fact that she'd probably be putting the house up for sale in a couple weeks.

He quirked that eyebrow again and murmured, "I see. Well, that will be all for now. I might suggest getting a home protection system installed if you continue to live in the house. However, if you decide to move back home now, please keep us informed. We may be in touch again after the pathologist and the crime scene investigators have finished their reports."

Kyra walked away as fast as her dignity would allow. Frustration and anger warred within her, and she wanted to kick somebody. Preferably Detective Andrews. She bet he'd never treat his wife or mother the way he grilled her in that room. When she looked up, Brad was sitting on one of the plastic chairs in the lobby. He jumped up when she appeared, hissing, "What took you so long? I've been waiting out here for half an hour. Were you and the detective getting to know each other or what?"

"Don't be ridiculous, Brad. And if you must know, he grilled me like I was a suspect. I couldn't exactly walk away." As if Kyra wasn't upset enough, Brad had to keep it going.

"Then you should have asked for a lawyer. You have rights, you know." Brad studied her face and then glanced around the police station. "I'll bet he wanted to know how the guy got in, just like I wondered."

Kyra turned on her heel and walked toward the exit. Brad called after her, but she pushed through the doors and stomped to the car. She was desperately trying to get her key into the car door as tears trickled down her face when Brad reached around her and inserted his key.

"I'm sorry . . . again," he murmured into her hair. "This whole incident has my nerves all jangled and I know you're really upset. We need to start this whole time together all over again, and see if we can sort out what's happening to us."

As much as Kyra agreed with his words, she didn't know if she could trust Brad anymore. He'd become too controlling after their first few months of marriage, and he always wanted her to go along with the plans he'd mapped out for their lives. Her decision to stay at Aunt Mary's house after her death had created a definite wedge between them, and she wasn't sure if their rift could be healed. For now, though, she needed someone strong to lean on, and Brad had offered the olive branch of peace.

Forcing her stiff body to relax against him, she nodded. "Okay, but please, Brad, don't keep hurling accusations at me. Let's work on this together from now on."

"Sure, Babe," he said, opening the door and handing her into the driver's seat. She almost laughed then because Brad hated it when he had to ride shotgun. And he hadn't called her "Babe" since the early days of their marriage. He must be feeling repentant.

With Brad in a conciliatory mood, she allowed herself to forget the horror of the past night and focus on getting through the weekend. He'd be gone Sunday night, so she'd have time later to figure out what she needed to do.

Back at the house, Kyra ran upstairs to freshen up and Brad headed into the kitchen. When she returned, she could see him rummaging in the freezer.

"Let's cook on the grill and eat on the patio tonight." Brad smiled at her from where he stood in front of the freezer. "I just found these steaks in here and they'd be great for dinner."

Kyra hesitated, saying, "I don't know. It might be strange to look across the yard and think about what happened last night. After all, a man is dead."

"And you didn't like him, so why pretend to be upset?" Brad still had a smile on his face, but Kyra sensed he could slip into anger any moment. "Besides, why waste a beautiful patio? You might only get to enjoy it a couple more weeks."

Hearing Brad infer that he knew she still planned on staying this week weakened her resolve enough to agree to his barbeque plans. They fell into their old roles of Brad preparing the steaks and manning the grill, and Kyra as chief salad maker and dessert chef. She made a simple cheese pie with graham cracker crust and a filling of cream cheese, eggs, sugar, and lemon. It needed to cool and then chill in the refrigerator for two hours, but she had plenty of time before the steaks were thawed.

By angling her chair away from the area where Ethan jumped over the fence last night, Kyra managed to enjoy her dinner. She watched the butterflies flutter around the roses Aunt Mary had planted years ago. Brad topped off her wine glass as she discovered the steak and salad tasted better than she expected.

All went well until Tex bounded around the house and skidded to a stop when he spotted Brad. He backed up and issued a growl deep in his throat.

"Tex, it's okay, boy," Kyra said, standing up. She clapped her hands to attract his attention away from Brad, who had a lifelong dislike of dogs. It had something to do with being bitten as a boy when he visited a friend's house.

"I told Sam to keep his dog off our property," he said, his easy demeanor gone.

"And it was Sam and Tex who chased Ethan away last night." Kyra reached down to pet Tex who had slunk over beside her. "Otherwise that knife might have been sticking into me when you got home." She dared him to argue the point.

Brad's body stiffened and he stared at Kyra. Finally, he nodded. "Okay, I guess you're right. But I'm here with you now, so you don't need the dog. If you take him back home, I'll clean up this mess. We can have the cheese pie and coffee in the kitchen."

Surprised at his capitulation, Kyra smiled. "That sounds good. I'll be right back." Walking over to Sam's house, she wondered if she had been too hard on Brad lately. She kept picking out the negative side of all their interactions when maybe it was time for her to change her attitude. If she always pointed out what Brad did wrong, of course he'd respond in anger. She tended to say to Brad "you did this" and "you did that" instead of saying "what can we do to make this better?" Wasn't that what marriage counselors used as examples for couples seeking advice?

When Kyra found Sam sitting on his front porch reading the newspaper, he looked up at their approach. She patted Tex one more time and then reminded Sam about Brad's phobia.

"Sorry, Kyra, I just forgot. I'll make sure I keep Tex close to me when Brad's around. I guess I thought maybe since Tex scared that guy away last night, he would feel a little differently. But it's not a problem."

He opened his door and shooed Tex inside. "Everything okay? You holding up all right?"

Kyra smiled and patted his arm. "I'm fine, and Brad's taking good care of me. So don't worry. And thanks again, more than I can say."

"I'm just glad Tex wanted to go for a walk when he did. Usually at that time, he's bedded down for the night." Sam stood up and gave her a quick hug.

Walking back to the patio, Kyra thought about the fortunate circumstances that had interfered with Ethan Owens' plans the night before. Had he only been trying to frighten her? Or had he planned on using that knife to harm her, even kill her? But why? He hadn't hidden his face, and that seemed ominous. She hurried to join Brad in the kitchen.

The coffee was perking, but Brad wasn't in sight. Assuming he had a call of nature, she pulled the cheese pie out of the refrigerator and set it on the counter. As she sliced into the pie, it released the lemony scent and she couldn't wait for her first bite.

When Brad entered the room, she smiled as she carried the pie slices over to the table. "Ready?" she asked, and then she saw his face. "What is it? What's wrong?"

"I saw your story up on the laptop." He waited and when she frowned at him, he continued, "You know—your murder mystery. The one where the woman is being stalked and then the man ends up dead in her backyard. Sound familiar?"

Kyra felt the blood drain from her face. "But I didn't write that!"

CHAPTER 10

Kyra slammed the plates down and whirled past Brad in the doorway. Her laptop stood open on the rolltop desk, exactly where she left it. Since she knew she had shut it down when she went up to bed, she suspected Brad opened her file again. It wasn't password protected because she was the only one who used the laptop. Brad had an iPad at home.

"Did you just open this?" she demanded when he walked into the den behind her.

He shook his head. "No, it was open, right there on that page. It's where your main character finds the guy who was stalking her in her backyard, and he's dead, just like I said."

"I never wrote that! Someone's messing with my computer because my murder victim is found buried in the basement of the house."

"That doesn't sound like a good plot, either, but that's not what was written there."

They glared at each other, and Kyra's heart sank. For a few hours it had seemed like they were drawing closer again, and now this strange incident had to occur.

"Could you, just for once, try and believe me?" she asked, her voice brittle. "Why would I be so stupid as to write a murder scene and then carry out the exact crime?"

"Okay, you're right, it doesn't make sense." He studied the page and then said, "You can delete it and no one will ever know."

"Except you and me, and the next time you're angry, will you mention it to the police? Tell them how you didn't want to say anything, but it really bothered you. Then what?"

"Look, Kyra, I'm trying to help. I'm not the bad guy here." He backed away. "You do whatever you want. I'm going to the kitchen for a cup of coffee."

Kyra nodded and turned away to study her desk. "Where's my flash drive?" She shifted the laptop, looking behind and around it. "Brad? Did you take it?"

"No, I didn't touch the damn thing!" he shouted and continued walking away.

Caught between saving the pages and getting rid of them, in case she needed them for evidence or something, Kyra thought she would save the document to a flash drive before deleting the chapter. After searching the entire desk and the floor around it, she realized someone had saved it already and taken the flash drive with him or her.

Her hand hesitated over the delete button and then she sighed and picked up the phone. It was better to inform the police about the event instead of hiding what had happened. Maybe they could pick up fingerprints or some other evidence on the laptop. She regretted now that she hadn't told them about the day she'd smelled cigarettes and found cigarette ash on the laptop.

Detective Andrews was unavailable at the police station when she called, but they were sending out one of the policemen who had been first on the scene the night before. Then Kyra joined Brad in the kitchen, where he stood sipping his coffee and staring out the window at the dying sunset.

"I've called the police to report the incident," she said, expecting an explosion. Brad just nodded, saying, "I heard."

"It's too bad the police didn't check my laptop last night or take it in for evidence. You know, like they do on television all the time."

Brad laughed and slowly turned around. "Yeah, I wish this was just a TV episode, too. Then the whole mystery would be solved in one hour and we could go back to our normal lives."

"Oh, Brad." Kyra slipped across the room and wrapped her arms around his neck, as he lifted his arms to allow her in. He plunked the coffee cup down on the counter behind her and lowered his lips to hers. For a few moments, Kyra forgot all their troubles as instinct took over and she leaned her whole body into him. "Hmm. That feels good," she murmured.

Brad lifted his head and sighed, but kept his arms around her. "I planned on taking you to bed tonight and reminding you why we belong together. But—I guess it will have to wait a few more hours now." He studied her face. "That's if you feel like it after the police get done with us."

She lifted her hands and ran her fingers through his sandy-colored hair while looking into his eyes. "I can't wait. And I promise I won't let the police destroy our chance to renew our love. Maybe I should forget this writing project and put Mary's house up for sale, like you said. If you just promise me that you won't mind the hours I spend writing—"

Brad pulled her hands down and grasped them tightly. "You're not going to let someone scare you out of here, are you? That doesn't sound like the Kyra I know."

Surprised at his words, she looked down at the joined hands and murmured, "I thought you'd be happy that I agreed with you. Are you sure I'll be safe? What if . . ."

"Nothing should happen now. Ethan Owens is the man who tried to get into your bedroom and he's dead."

"Then who wrote about his death on my computer? I doubt Ethan himself wrote that to foretell his own death."

Brad dropped her hands and turned away just as the doorbell rang. Surprised at his reaction, Kyra tried to gauge his feelings, wondering if he felt inadequate at his ability to solve the puzzle. When the doorbell rang again, she had no time to continue the discussion. If she didn't answer the door soon, the police would probably pound down the door.

"Officer Cornwell, thanks for coming," she said, opening the door. "Please come in."

The tall blond policeman entered, followed by a small dark-haired woman whose badge read "Officer Jamison." Kyra showed them into the den and pointed to the laptop. They took their time reading over page 152 and then the policeman slipped on latex gloves and scrolled back and forth. The story ended at the bottom of page 152 after the victim was found stabbed by his own knife in the backyard and the next page was empty.

"Very strange," said the officer, glancing at Kyra. "And you claim you didn't write this last night or today."

Brad had entered the room as the police studied the laptop, and he said, "Kyra was with me the entire night after all of the police left, so I can vouch for the fact that she did not use her laptop last night. We've also spent the day together, trying to forget about what happened and distracting ourselves with shopping and planning our dinner. "

"And as I said on the phone, my flash drive is missing. The one I use to back up all my work."

Officer Jamison frowned as she looked at Brad. "I'm sorry, sir, but you couldn't have spent every single minute with your wife." She held up her hand when Brad opened his mouth to argue, saying, "I'm not saying she actually did this since it seems rather stupid, especially now that she's called us in. I'm just saying it's possible that she typed this page when you had to use the bathroom. I mean, we all have to go eventually."

"And my missing flash drive?" Kyra asked, staring around the room in frustration.

"A flash drive is an easy thing to misplace," she said. "And really easy to throw away and make sure it's never found again."

Cornwell nodded. "Officer Jamison will take a picture of that page and then dust for fingerprints, but I doubt we'll find anything. Unless you think something else is missing from the house, we'll have to put it down as a prank."

"It's not very funny," Brad said. "And it seems like someone has easy access to this house. My wife stays here alone during the week."

"Have you looked into a home security system? That might put your mind at rest."

Kyra agreed she'd check into that idea, adding, "I'm sure nothing else is missing, but a few strange things have happened lately. I found the kitchen window open a few inches after I was positive I closed and locked all the downstairs windows, and one day I found cigarette ash on my laptop. That was the day the window guys were here, and they denied going anywhere near the den."

"But you can't be sure they told the truth." The policeman shook his head. "We dusted for prints on your doors and doorknobs last night, and now the computer. Since we took prints from both of you last night, we can eliminate you and see what we come up with. Now that Mr. Owens is dead, you won't have to worry about him. I'm afraid there's nothing else we can do for now."

"And that's it?" Kyra saw Brad's frustration coming to a boiling point as he moved over to place her hand on his arm. When he started to say something else, she hurried to intervene.

"Thanks for coming and dusting the laptop for prints. Of course, if the person used gloves, there won't be any evidence." Kyra sighed. "Still, I feel better knowing that the incident was reported and the police now have it on record."

"I'm sure you've been through a frightening time, ma'am, and it's good your husband's here with you this weekend." The policeman reached out to shake Brad's hand, and he reluctantly responded. "If anything else happens, don't be afraid to give us a call."

"Not that it will do much good," Brad murmured under his breath. Kyra pinched his arm before escorting the officers to the door.

She found Brad in the kitchen pouring a glass of chardonnay. "Sorry, but I need something stronger than coffee. What would you like?"

"Coffee's fine. Let's have our cheese pie now since I've been waiting to eat it for the last hour or two."

Brad mellowed after another glass of wine, and they called a moratorium on any conversation about things that had happened in the last twenty-four hours. Hours later, Brad had kept his promise, and they made slow, sensuous love, rekindling some of those feelings Kyra thought were gone forever. Curled up next to Brad, with drowsiness tugging her into oblivion, she remembered her fear of awakening the previous night knowing someone was in the house. The drowsiness disappeared and she lay rigid as she listened, wondering if every creak of the house or click of the air conditioning meant something else. If she was this afraid with Brad beside her, how would she get through the next week alone?

She slid out from under Brad's arm and quietly stood up. She wrapped her short robe around her and walked over to the window. Pushing the curtain aside, she stared out at the backyard where Ethan Owens had escaped last night, only to die on his own knife at the other side of the wooden fence. Kyra wondered about it being rather convenient that he'd died and now the episode was nicely wrapped up. Too convenient?

Turning around, she studied Brad's vague form lying on the bed in the darkness. Strange how he had come last night right after the police and Owens' death. She hated herself for wondering if he'd actually been here just a little earlier than he claimed. How could she think such horrible things about Brad when they'd just made love and he'd held her so close to his heart?

She blinked to keep the tears back, just as Brad moved and murmured, "Kyra, Kyra?" He pushed himself up on his elbow and stared across the room. "Are you okay?"

She swallowed and said, "I'm fine. I thought I heard a noise in the yard, but nothing's out there." She forced herself to walk toward the bed, dropped her robe, and slipped in beside Brad. He wrapped his arms around her and she laid her head on his shoulder.

"There, that's better." He brushed her hair back from her face and kissed her lips. "I'm here, honey. Don't think about last night anymore."

She forced herself to relax against him and allowed her breathing to slow. In minutes, Brad had fallen asleep and Kyra carefully rolled away and lay on her side staring into the darkness. Thoughts tumbled around in her brain until the early morning light outlined the windows. Then, exhausted, she fell into a deep sleep.

CHAPTER 11

Somehow Kyra got through the following day, dreading the thought of Brad leaving that evening. At the same time, his solicitous behavior had begun to drive her crazy. He'd gone from being unhappy and angry about her staying at Mary's house to being overly concerned about her sticking to her project and not letting one insane man hold her back. He assured her that the danger was past and she was perfectly safe in the house.

"If it makes you feel better, see about getting a home security system installed," he'd said. "It may take a week or two, though, and by then you'll be coming back home."

The way he said it made Kyra feel like she was acting foolishly, and he was just placating her. She couldn't decide which husband was worse—the angry Brad or the rather condescending one. The temporary joy and hope for their future of the night before had faded away by the time she kissed him goodbye at seven o'clock that evening. After closing and locking the door, she walked through the whole house checking the locks on the back door and all the windows. Still, locked doors hadn't kept Ethan Owens out of the house, and the police claimed they hadn't found her house key on his person.

She finally decided she'd call the locksmith back tomorrow and have deadbolts installed on both doors. That way the doors would be double-locked and need two keys to be opened. In the meantime, she placed the dining room chairs under the doorknobs as an added precaution, hoping that would allow her to sleep. Brad called around eleven after he got home to make sure she was all right, and she finished her glass of wine before going upstairs.

After choosing a book of short stories from the bookshelf, she tried to relax in bed. Surprisingly, she found herself enjoying the first story, so she read another, slipping lower on the pillow as she read. When she finished the second story, she felt tired enough to turn off the light. At first she stared around the room in the dark, but slowly drowsiness overcame her and she fell asleep. She awoke to see the sun's early rays revealing the furniture in the room and realized she'd forgotten to place the desk chair under the doorknob. Too lazy to worry about it now, she dozed off for another hour before getting up.

That morning she set up her laptop on the kitchen table because she didn't want to work in the den. She had picked up several flash drives the day before, and she used one to save her story with the page she hadn't written and set that one aside. Then she deleted that page and rewrote it, using the second flash drive to save her ongoing work. Although she managed to write several pages, her rhythm was off. She hoped that after she met Trudy for lunch, she might be able to spend a block of time working.

The restaurant Trudy suggested was a small place specializing in Greek food, Christo's Café, and Kyra discovered her sitting in a back booth and talking animatedly with the waitress. When Kyra saw Trudy's enthusiastic wave, she wove between tables to slide into the booth seat across from her.

"Kyra, this is Marian. Her father owns the restaurant, and I've known her family forever."

Kyra smiled at Marian, wondering how old her father must be since the waitress appeared to be around seventy.

"Yeah, people always look at me that way," she said, laughing. "My father's only ninety-five. He swears working in the restaurant is what keeps him alive." She laughed again, saying, "I'll leave you two ladies to look over the menu and decide what you want. Just yell when you're ready." She tottered off to a table near the front where three men about her age greeted her with friendly banter.

"Nice place," Kyra said, grinning at Trudy. "I might need to use it in one of my stories."

"It's a great family restaurant," Trudy said. "Believe it or not, my parents always brought all five of us kids here when we were youngsters. We'd cram into this booth with my dad sitting on a chair at the end. Mom would sit on one side between the two youngest, and three of us kids on the other side. We loved coming here on Saturday nights."

Kyra followed Trudy's suggestions for their order since she wasn't that familiar with Greek food. Gyros and baklava were the only two things she recognized on the menu, but Trudy ordered chicken souvlaki and spanakopita after Kyra assured her she wasn't a picky eater. When Marian took their order she laughed about Kyra not knowing about Greek food, pointing out that her name was probably from the Greek, meaning lady, the feminine form of Kyrie, or lord.

Trudy reached across the table to hold Kyra's hand. "We have so much to talk about," she said. "I'd like to tell you more about Mary and your father."

Kyra's mouth went suddenly dry as she looked into Trudy's now serious face.

"My father? Honest, I don't think it matters anymore, as long as I know Mary loved me enough to give me to my parents who raised me. I never lacked for love, and that's all that counts."

Trudy sighed and shook her head. "That's what Mary always said, too, but I'm afraid circumstances make it obvious that it wasn't enough. Something happened after Mary's death and I don't want your life in danger. You need to know the background to protect yourself."

Kyra looked around her at the comfortable family atmosphere of the restaurant and shook her head. "I can't believe this is happening." She studied Trudy's face and saw her troubled gray eyes returning her steady look without flinching. She took a deep breath and asked, "Exactly what are you talking about?"

"I saw the news, and I know about Ethan Owens. I'm sorry you had to go through that ordeal."

"But it's over now. He accidentally fell on his own knife trying to escape." Kyra desperately wanted Trudy to agree with her because she hoped to put the whole incident behind her. Even Brad believed it was over—after all, he'd left her alone in the house last night.

Just then Marian arrived with their food and set it on the table with a flourish. "Enjoy!" She smiled at both of them. "And save room for dessert. I'm holding two servings of galaktoboureko for you!"

After she left, Trudy said, "Sorry, Kyra, I didn't mean to get into this discussion before we had a chance to eat lunch. Maybe you're right, and I'm just an old lady worrying about nothing. Let's forget about it for now and maybe you can tell me about your book."

Kyra frowned and murmured, "I don't know . . . everything is so strange." The scent of lemon and spices wafted up from the chicken and her stomach growled. "Umm, that smells good."

"Please, enjoy the food. Marian will be devastated if we don't eat every bite." When Kyra laughed, Trudy smiled back at her. "Believe me, you'll love it."

"What's that dessert she was talking about?"

"I don't even try to pronounce it, but it's a custard pastry that's absolutely delicious. If we're too full to eat it, we'll take it home."

As soon as Kyra took her first bite of souvlaki, she decided Trudy was right and she didn't want to ruin it by worrying. She gave Trudy a quick synopsis of her novel without mentioning the added-on page from the night before. Trudy asked questions about the plot and even made one or two thoughtful suggestions. When they finished, they opted to take the dessert with them and relocate to Kyra's house for coffee and a more private talk.

Before they settled in the kitchen, Kyra used the flash drive to show Trudy the page they'd found on her computer last night.

"Oh, my!" Trudy shook her head as she read the words. "I can't believe the police thought it was a prank."

"I don't even know when it appeared since I hadn't looked at my book since Friday afternoon. And I hardly think Ethan wrote that before he ran outside and fell on his knife to fulfill the story plot." Kyra shivered after saying those words and shook her head. "Sorry, I didn't mean to sound facetious. It really was frightening that night to know someone had gotten into the house." She moved toward the window and stared out at the backyard. "Still, I saw him jump over the fence and heard him groan in sudden pain. That was horrible, too. Maybe I could have done something . . ."

"Kyra, don't do that to yourself." Trudy crossed the room and hugged her. "For whatever reason, Ethan Owens chose the wrong path and he paid the price. Maybe if I tell you more of Mary's past we can sort out some of his motives. Remember that I mentioned Ethan was Jasper's son, but he was illegitimate and his mother died in childbirth. "

"That's sad," Kyra said. "Did Mary know him as a baby or young child?"

"No, his maternal grandparents took over his care. Jasper either didn't know how or didn't want to care for his son."

"I guess sometimes that might be better," Kyra said, doubt in her voice. "Especially if Jasper wasn't a good father."

"That's true. From what I saw of him, he wasn't a loving man."

Kyra frowned. "It also sounds like he drank a lot from what I read. I can't understand why Mary would be attracted to him."

When Trudy suggested they settle down at the table, Kyra moved her laptop aside and brought them each a cup of coffee.

Taking a deep breath, Trudy said, "Mary was madly in love with your father long before you were born. Although they were compatible in so many ways, they discovered they couldn't live with each other. But in the beginning . . ." Trudy hesitated and closed her eyes. When she began again, she chose her words carefully. "In the beginning, too many problems reared their ugly heads. Both Leonardo, or Lee as he was known, and Jasper vied for Mary's affections, and Jasper fought dirty."

"But why didn't that make Mary turn away from him?" Kyra cradled her coffee cup in her hands. "I don't understand."

"Jasper wasn't rich, but even though he was young, many people already owed him favors. He did little odd jobs for people to smooth out their lives, but in return, he expected favors."

"Oh, you mean he killed people or stole things?"

"Umm, more like threatened their lives or made sure they didn't get the money deals they expected, unless they agreed to do something for him."

"And he threatened to hurt this Lee?"

"Sadly, yes. He showed your mother exactly how easy it would be for his bullies to catch Lee and make sure he never walked again." Trudy sighed and rubbed her eyes. "The next day, Mary announced she would wed Jasper Owens, and Lee Napoli packed up and left town. It wasn't until many years later that we realized he'd moved to Italy."

"That's a terrible story. I can't believe the Mary I knew went through such an awful experience, and even my father never said anything." Kyra finally took a sip from her cup and set it back down.

"You have to remember that Mary's brother, Scott, the man who raised you, was quite a few years younger than Mary. He was only around 8 or 9 when all this happened, and I'm sure your grandparents didn't even know most of it." Trudy managed a small smile. "Parents then didn't involve themselves in the lives of their children like they do now. They were too worried most of the time about everyday survival."

"I guess you're right." Kyra stared down into her coffee, thinking of her closeness to Aunt Mary for all those years, and yet she was discovering now that she knew very little about her. "After Jasper died, why didn't my father, my biological father, come back to marry Mary?"

Trudy shook her head and sighed. "I'm not sure, but I think he decided to make a life for himself in a small town in Tuscany. He immersed himself in learning Italian and adapting to the country of his ancestors. Eventually, though, he emerged from his hideaway when his mystery books became popular."

Kyra looked up from the contemplation of her cooling coffee. "I did look up Leonardo Napoli on the internet, but I find it hard to believe that person is actually my father. I think I was happier not knowing anything about him."

Trudy glanced at Kyra's laptop sitting on the back of the table and gave it a slight nod. "And yet you said you're writing a mystery novel right now. As they say, the apple doesn't fall far from the tree." Trudy patted Kyra's arm where it rested on the table. "Even when the apple didn't know the tree existed for most of her life."

"Why didn't Mary tell me sooner? She had many opportunities over the years . . ."

"If it's any consolation to you, I know Mary was planning on telling you everything soon. She'd discussed it with me and said she thought you'd be ready to accept the reasons why she'd given you to Scott and Beth thirty years ago." Trudy bit her lip. "She just never expected to die in her sleep that night, even though she knew she'd been diagnosed with a heart condition." She held up her hand when Kyra started to interrupt. "The reason she didn't act even sooner was that she had already named you in her will long ago as the one to inherit her money and property. She knew you'd be protected."

"Protected? Protected from what?" Kyra asked sharply.

"Maybe I said that wrong. I don't necessarily mean protected. I guess I mean that Mary wanted to be sure you'd have something of your own if life didn't turn out the way you planned." She looked around the kitchen before smiling at Kyra. "As a young woman, Mary tried to make her own way as a secretary. Her parents were poor and raising an unexpected change-of- life baby after losing several children at birth or shortly thereafter. She didn't want to be a burden if a marriage opportunity didn't come along."

"And yet she suddenly had two men fighting over her when she reached her twenties." Kyra tried to imagine Mary as a young woman forced to choose a husband she didn't like in order to save the man she loved. "That was fortunate for her that Jasper died falling down the stairs not long after they married."

"That's what the police thought at first, too," Trudy said. "They figured Mary had pushed him down the stairs, and she lived under a cloud of suspicion for months. They even looked into Lee Napoli, but he was already in Italy by then. Mary struggled to hold onto her job so she could keep the payments up on the house. I think she would have gladly sold the house, but no one wanted it after rumors flew around that it was haunted. So I guess Mary remembered those early years and wanted to spare you that kind of struggle if things went wrong in your life."

Kyra nodded. "So much went on here that I never knew. And yet my dad left me with my 'aunt' every summer after mom died. Evidently, he wasn't worried about ghosts or Mary being a murderer." She pushed her hands through her hair. "This is all so confusing. I keep talking about Mom and Dad and I mean the parents who raised me, Scott and Beth Wyndham. And yet Mary and this Lee or Leonardo Napoli were my 'real' parents."

"I know the perfect antidote to all your confusion," Trudy announced, getting up and walking to the counter. "Let's try some of this Greek custard we brought back with us."

"At this point, I'm willing to try anything." Kyra placed the custards wrapped in phyllo dough on plates and brought them over to the table with forks and napkins, while Trudy poured them each another cup of coffee. After the first bite, Kyra sighed with delight as Trudy said, "I told you so."

Not until the last bite of dessert and last drop of coffee were gone did Kyra ask, "Is Lee Napoli still alive?"

Trudy turned pensive. "Actually, yes he is. I'm afraid you mustn't expect much from him if you plan on contacting him. After he left America, he chose to immerse himself in Italian culture and concentrate on his writing career. Mary knew that and knew he would have no interest in becoming a father."

"That's okay. Mary would have done something if she really wanted me to know him as a father, and she never did."

"One other thing you should know about Mary and Lee. They continued to maintain their friendship over the years when she occasionally visited him in Italy." Trudy studied Kyra's face to see the effect of her words.

"Really? That's odd. I wish we'd had a chance to talk more before she passed away."

Kyra realized that Trudy looked worried and wondered if she knew an even darker secret. "What's wrong? Is there something more I should know?"

"When I was talking to Marian today, she told me an old customer had dropped in yesterday. They talked about the old days, and he was quite shocked to learn—"

"No," Kyra whispered. "I don't believe it."

"Yes, I'm afraid so," Trudy said. "Leonardo Napoli has returned to Stonecliff after forty years!"

CHAPTER 12

After Trudy left that afternoon, Kyra sat for a long time thinking about Leonardo Napoli returning to Stonecliff. What did it mean for her? Or did he return to see Mary, and now that he knew she had passed away, he'd turn around and go back to Italy? Kyra's feelings wavered between wanting to meet the man who had fathered her, and hoping she'd never have to deal with him since he hadn't cared enough to be her father.

To distract herself, she called the locksmith and set it up to have double locks placed on both doors. She was fortunate that someone was available to come the next day. As she started falling asleep that night, Kyra recalled the detective's grilling of her after Ethan Owens' death. His accusations sounded eerily familiar to what had happened to Mary when her husband fell down the stairs. The police tried to put the blame on them both for a death on the property because it resolved a problem for them. *We were both innocent,* she thought in their defense; although how could she be absolutely sure Mary didn't give a little shove to her abusive husband? *I don't even care if she did!*

Sitting at her laptop the next morning and feeling groggy, she stared at the blank screen and tried to force her mind into writing mode. At first she'd patted herself on the back for returning to the den after everything that had happened. She sipped her coffee and fiddled with the pens, scribbling meaningless words on the writing pad on the desk. Then she stared out the window at the back fence and wondered if she was too spooked to write after all.

Sighing, she decided to run the vacuum sweeper and dust the furniture instead of wasting time doing nothing. As she dusted the knick-knacks on the living room shelves, she noticed several items were missing. Frowning, she studied the various statues and keepsakes until an interesting idea for her novel distracted her. The best way to exorcise the problem of a "father who was not a father" would be to write him into the story.

Leaving the living room half dusted, she hurried into the den, reread the last page of the previous chapter and began typing. The man in her story had walked away from his family when he lost his job and left a wife and two children to fend for themselves. When the son became a thief and ended up in jail, he blamed his father. After he got out of jail, he searched everywhere to find his father to make sure he paid for all his problems.

Jennie was attracted to the son when they meet at the library where he tried to discover more about his father's past. She failed to mention that she knew his father and was determined to persuade him to meet the man who made so many mistakes years ago. She wanted to show the son he had lots of potential and should focus on what skills he had and not live in the past. She had already located the father and wanted them to meet and resolve their differences. The fact that she and the son had become lovers complicated the plot.

Kyra's story had taken on a life of its own and now she had plenty of plot twists to work on in the immediate future. She just hoped her own life didn't develop as many problems. When she heard the knock on her door, she nearly fell out of her chair in her haste to jump up. It wasn't until she remembered it must be the locksmith that the pounding in her chest resumed its steady heartbeat. She forced herself to take deep breaths all the way to the front door, but cautiously looked out the peephole before opening the door. She recognized Josh Parkins, the same locksmith from Bryant Locksmith Services who had come before.

As he worked on the front door, she had a sandwich in the kitchen and emailed a few friends from home. It had been ages since she'd been in contact with anyone, and she felt guilty when she realized she had let her friendships dwindle away. Thinking about it further, though, she realized that wasn't exactly true. Because Brad didn't care for her friends, it was easier to meet them less and less so that she didn't have an argument with him. Instead they'd begun to have dinner or drinks with guys Brad worked with and their wives. Kyra pushed aside the last few bites of her sandwich as she recognized the fact that she didn't actually like any of them, particularly the wives. When had she begun to allow Brad to make her choices and close her off from her friends?

Grabbing her notebook, she put Brad's name at the top of a page and drew a line down the middle. On one side she put Brad's good points: works hard, even though he often likes to change jobs, takes out the garbage, good lover, sometimes clears the table and fills the dishwasher. Tapping the pencil on the table, she waited for more ideas. Since her brain didn't cooperate, she went on to list the bad points on the other side: likes his own way, doesn't believe in my writing, thinks his job is more important than mine, never sweeps or dusts, never does the laundry, doesn't like my friends, starts arguments when I don't agree with him, doesn't want me to keep Mary's house. She stopped there when it became obvious the bad side looked to be the winner.

Kyra frowned as she tried to decide if she was being fair to Brad. They hadn't celebrated their second anniversary yet so maybe she should consider that they were still working things out. Compatibility didn't happen overnight, and he was a good lover. *When it suits him*, the devil on her shoulder whispered in her ear. *If he's unhappy with you, he turns a cold shoulder to you. Literally.* She stared down at her hands, trying to remember when they'd made love before this past weekend. He'd been upset about her writing time, even before her decision to keep Mary's house temporarily, so it had been three or four weeks. She knew that was a long time without sex for a young married couple. Should they see a marriage counselor? But the bigger question was: Did she even want to?

Reading over the list again, Kyra calmly pulled the page out of the tablet and tore it up into tiny pieces. She'd known the answer to that question before she made the list, but she couldn't deal with the ramifications right now. She had too many other problems tugging her into different directions, and she needed to deal with those first. After a slight hesitation, she returned to the email she was writing to her friend, Sandy, and typed a few sentences about inheriting her aunt's house and the writing she was doing. She ended by saying she'd be in touch soon when she returned to Pittsburgh. After hitting the "send" button, she cleaned up the kitchen before checking on the locksmith.

"Just in time," he said, pointing to the door. "Lock's all done. Come and check it out."

Kyra smiled as he gave her a demonstration and then he followed her into the kitchen. She left him there to go about his job, and she returned to the den. Since she was determined to finish the first draft of her novel by the end of next week, she studied her outline, trying to fit the story of the runaway father and his angry son into her main plot. She decided to tie it together by having a second murder occur in the public library where Jennie worked. Her fingers flew over the keyboard and the next thing she knew, the locksmith stood clearing his throat in the doorway.

"Excuse me," he said in a loud voice.

Kyra looked up in surprise, and for a few seconds, she couldn't quite remember who he was. "Oh, sorry, I was off in another world. All finished?" she asked, smiling to let him know she didn't mind the interruption. She wondered how long he'd been standing there.

"Yep, all done. Let me give you a demonstration. Then I'll give you the keys and be off."

When she followed him back to the kitchen, she felt rather disconcerted to think she'd forgotten all about the locksmith being in the house. What if he'd walked out and left the door open? Anyone could have walked in and she wouldn't have known about it until it was too late. Or he could have been a serial killer or . . . she realized her imagination was running away with her. She sounded foolish even to herself and gave the locksmith another bright smile.

After he gave her the keys and reminded her she had to lock the door with the key from the outside, he packed up his tools and left. Kyra stared at her bright shiny new lock and breathed a sigh of relief. Right now no one had a key to these double locks, including Brad, and it made her feel secure. Still, she wondered why she needed to feel she was locked up tight in her fortress. All the years she'd lived with Mary they'd never overly worried about the house being locked as they wandered in and out to the front yard and the back garden. Only at night did Mary check to make sure they'd remembered to lock the doors. What had happened to change things after Mary died?

Kyra returned to the den and decided to make another list, showing a timeline of events since Mary's death. She puzzled over Ethan Owens' first appearance, his surprise visit inside the house, and his subsequent death, but could find no reason for what happened. Why didn't he just consult a lawyer and pursue the legal channels to claim his inheritance? Or did he know he had no rights at all and thought he could just frighten her into agreeing to give him what he wanted?

Kyra threw her pen down and sighed. Since she didn't have any better idea, she decided to ask Sam to look over the back basement room for her. Maybe he could recommend someone to lay down a concrete floor and add lighting to the room. If the area was bright and clean, and the rats exterminated, it would no longer look like a spooky dungeon. Before she changed her mind, she jumped up and headed over to Sam's house, locking her shiny new double lock behind her.

When Sam opened his door, Tex barked a greeting and ran over for a pat on the head.

"Come in, come in," Sam said as he waved her inside. Kyra felt her whole body relax as she stepped into the house. "I just made some of my special recipe oatmeal muffins, and you must try one out." Sam patted her arm and led her into the kitchen.

Over tea and muffins, Kyra explained her errand, and Sam agreed to check out the basement for her. "I tried to get Mary to let me ask a friend who runs a cement business to take a look at that room a couple years ago, but she said she never used that area anyway. I thought maybe she just didn't want to pay for the work, so I didn't bring it up again."

Kyra sipped her tea before replying, "I guess I don't want to pay for it, either, but it might make sense if I am going to sell the house soon. Seeing that dreary room might turn buyers off."

Sam set his cup down carefully and murmured, "I'd really hate it if you sold the house. I think you'd make a great neighbor, and Tex and I would miss you."

"Oh, Sam, thanks for those words, but you know I'm married and my life with Brad is in Pittsburgh." When she smiled at him, she saw his face tighten and he looked away.

"Yes, of course, you're right. Well, if you change your mind, just remember we'd be happy to have you living next door." He got up and began clearing the table of their plates and napkins. Turning back toward her, he said, "How about if I take a quick look at that basement room now and do some measurements? Then I'll get in touch with my contractor friend to come check it out."

"That's great; I really appreciate your help." Seeing Sam's smile, Kyra wondered if she'd imagined his unhappy look right after she mentioned Brad and her life in Pittsburgh. Could he be jealous of Brad? But that didn't make any sense unless he was mistaking her friendliness with something more affectionate. Was she relying on Sam too much?

Walking back to her house with Tex at her heels, she worried if she should tell Sam that she changed her mind and she didn't need his help. As they stepped onto the back porch, Sam exclaimed, "Oh, good, you got the double lock put in. That should ease your mind a bit at night from now on." Kyra smiled because it sounded so much like the Sam she'd known for years, and that helped her shrug off her worries. He was simply an older man thinking about Mary's niece, and in his mind she was probably still that young girl who needed protecting.

When Kyra opened the basement door, Tex charged down the stairs as if he were on a new adventure. Kyra laughed at his enthusiasm, even as Sam called out for him to sit until they could get downstairs to join him.

"I don't want him getting into anything he shouldn't," Sam said as Tex sat wagging his tail and waiting for them. Once released, Tex ran from corner to corner, sniffing and giving an occasional woof. "He probably smells mice." Sam grinned at Kyra's frown. "You'll never see them because they make themselves scarce when that light comes on."

"I hope it's just mice in that back room and not rats. The light barely penetrates in there since it's probably a 25-watt bulb in the middle of the ceiling."

When Sam said he could fix that if she had a higher watt bulb, Kyra dug around on a shelf with miscellaneous objects and handed him a 100-watt replacement. With the door open, shedding more light, she decided the back room looked even creepier. Spider webs adorned all the corners, and the two small glass block windows hadn't been cleaned in many years. The musty smell almost made her gag, and every movement Sam made produced a little puff of dust. A few alarmed squeaks had greeted the opening of the door, and she tried hard not to look at the small dark shadows scurrying around the edge of the floor. Tex ran hither and yon, emitting excited little yips.

Sam took out his tape measure and calculated the length of all the walls so he could give his friend the approximate total square feet of the room. Kyra watched as he walked around, apparently unperturbed by the smell and dirtiness. Shaking her head, she told her helpful neighbor she'd wait for him upstairs and he responded with a nod.

Fifteen minutes later, Sam joined her in the kitchen where she was emptying the dishwasher. "It's nothing a scrub bucket and a new floor can't fix," he announced, heading for the sink to wash his filthy hands. "If you want, I'll be glad to do some of the scrubbing for you. It will be something to fill in my days now that I'm retired."

"I can't ask you to do that," she said. "I'll just have to don one of those face masks and a pair of boots, and get the job done. I only hope your friend is available in the next two weeks. After that, I'll have to get back to work, and I'm not sure when I can stop by again."

"How about you and I do the clean-up together?" Sam's eyes twinkled. "It will make the job go faster that way," he added persuasively, making Kyra laugh.

"I guess I'll have to agree when you put it that way."

Sam dried his hands on the towel Kyra handed him, and then looked around. "Did you see Tex come upstairs?" When she shook her head, Sam crossed the room and opened the basement door. "Tex, here boy!" Tex bounded up the stairs and headed into a corner of the room. Lying down, he started crunching on something he had dropped between his paws.

Kyra watched as Sam leaned over and reached down. Tex growled a little, but Sam shushed him with a wave of his hand. When he stood up, Kyra gasped at the long white bone he held in his hand.

CHAPTER 13

"Sam!" Kyra's voice came out in a squeak. Clearing her throat, she asked, "Could that be a human bone?"

Frowning, Sam studied the bone before saying, "Could be, I guess. Or maybe a deer or some other large animal."

"But what would a deer be doing down in the basement? What about a large dog, somebody's family pet? You know, they didn't want to bury it outside . . ." Kyra didn't finish the thought, knowing how silly it sounded. She just didn't want the bone to be human, the worst scenario.

"Now, don't jump to conclusions. Let me go back down there and take a look. You wait here and keep Tex with you since I don't want him digging up anything else."

Tex whined at the basement door after Sam left, and Kyra stood paralyzed at the kitchen counter. What possible reason could explain why Aunt Mary had a skeleton in her basement? Mary had lived here ever since her marriage to Jasper Owens more than fifty years ago, but maybe the bones were way older than that. Jasper had a reputation as an enforcer, a man who'd stop at nothing to get what he wanted, so maybe someone had crossed him at one time.

She jumped when Sam opened the door and quickly shut it behind him. "I'm sorry, Kyra, but I think we need to call the police."

"No! Not again. Didn't you say it could be a big animal? How can you be sure—"

Sam held up his hand. "Just believe me when I say I'm sure. It looks like it's been there for years, so I doubt if they'd say it has anything to do with you or Mary."

"Of course it doesn't! I think I should go check for myself before calling the police. That way I'd know exactly what to say." Kyra placed her hand on the door knob, but Sam stopped her from opening the door.

"There's a human skull, Kyra, just tell them that."

"Oh!" Staggering backwards, she eased herself down onto a kitchen chair, and Sam asked if she wanted him to make the call. Shaking her head, she pulled her cell phone out of her pocket. Taking a deep breath, she called the local police number. It was hardly an emergency call at this point.

After Kyra convinced the police that she wasn't imagining things, a patrol car showed up within minutes. She recognized Officer Cornwell from his earlier visit, and he nodded politely as he and his partner followed her through the house to the basement door, and Sam joined them in the trip downstairs. They instructed Kyra and Sam to stay out of the room while they checked into the bones. Even from where Kyra stood, she could see the skull in the glare of their flashlights.

"Damn, she's right!" exclaimed Cornwell's partner, a tall young woman around Kyra's age. "We need to call the forensic team."

Cornwell sneezed and then sneezed again. "Allergies," he mumbled. "There isn't anything we can do in here anyway."

Herding Kyra and Sam upstairs, they took down their information about finding the bones. Kyra felt disoriented and angry at the same time because she kept reliving a similar bad event time and time again. None of it made any sense, either, because Mary had lived in the same house for years without these things happening. She worried the police would bring it up again about Mary possibly killing Jasper Owens now that there was another body in her home.

"How long ago did you say you moved out of this house?" the woman police officer asked.

Rubbing her forehead, Kyra said, "I lived here summers through college, and then moved back into my family home in Pittsburgh around eight years ago when I got a job. After that, I visited for a week here or there or for long weekends. Sometimes, Mary visited me instead."

"You never suspected your aunt was having any problems? She never acted suspiciously in any way?" Officer Cornwell looked up from his notebook.

"No, of course not! My aunt was not a murderer." Ignoring a shakiness that threatened to shatter her apart, Kyra took several deep breaths and said, "And for the record, Mary was my mother, not my aunt."

"What?" Both police officers stared at her in surprise. "That was never discussed the last time I was here." Cornwell frowned at Kyra.

"It wasn't important, that's why. But you keep saying my aunt, and I wanted to clarify it. I just found out recently that she gave me up for adoption to her younger brother and his wife, and they raised me as their own."

The woman officer narrowed her eyes. "It sounds like Mary Wyndham had a lot of secrets."

"What are you trying to say?" Sam demanded, his face red. Kyra put a hand on his arm to keep him calm. She didn't need Sam to explode and end up getting carted off to the police station.

A loud knock on the door interrupted their conversation, and the forensic crew stood at the front door. Kyra and Sam were told to stay out of the way in the kitchen, so Kyra brewed a pot of coffee and dug out some oatmeal-raisin cookies from the freezer. Since there was nothing they could do, they might as well try to be comfortable.

A little later, Officer Cornwell stopped by and she offered him some coffee. He shook his head. "Sorry, but I've got to be off. When the work is done downstairs, they'll seal off that room and leave with the evidence."

Kyra shivered at those words, but she just nodded. As she tried to think of a way to ask about the results before he walked away, Sam saved her by demanding, "And when will we know who the hell that skeleton belongs to?"

Cornwell shook his head. "It could take weeks. They'll try DNA, if there's anything to match it to once they figure out how long the body's been down there, and then dental records. They can always look into the records for missing persons."

"I see." Kyra felt her heart plummet. The answer could take weeks or months, and during that time people would be whispering behind their backs about Mary and all kinds of horrible suspicions.

"I don't know if it helps, but the pathologist believes it's a man from the size and shape of certain bones . . . I mean, the evidence." He frowned and stood up taller. "Sorry, I shouldn't have said anything. I'll be on my way now."

After he left, Sam patted Kyra's hand. "Don't get too worked up. In all my sixty-some years, I've realized I spent too much time getting upset over things that didn't matter in the long run."

She tried to smile back at him, but she knew it was a poor effort. "I know you're probably right, but I don't want Mary to be remembered as a killer. She was a good person and a wonderful 'aunt' to me all my life."

Sam went from patting her hand to awkwardly rubbing her back. When she realized she was upsetting him by her lack of response, she forced herself to tamp down her emotions. "Of course, you're right; no use getting too overworked about the situation. There must be some logical explanation, and I'll have wasted all this worry for nothing."

Sam started talking about plans for his fall garden, and Kyra knew he wanted to distract her from the voices downstairs and sounds of shovels scraping through the dirt. Just when she thought she couldn't continue small talk a minute longer, she heard plodding steps on the basement stairs. The door opened, and two men appeared, carrying a gurney with a large zipped plastic bag between them. She quickly averted her eyes, trying not to think about the bones it held. A young woman followed them with a camera around her neck and lugging a container filled with the tools Kyra assumed they'd used to loosen the bones from the soil. The tech explained that she'd placed crime scene tape on the back room door, and they'd have to leave it until the coroner said otherwise.

Finally, Kyra stood up and gave Sam a big hug. "Thanks so much. I don't know what I'd do without you these past couple weeks." Then she firmly pointed him toward the door. "Now it's time for you to go home and relax." As he started to protest, she shushed him. "I'll be all right now. I lived here before when a skeleton was in the basement, so I guess I'll be fine now that it's gone. Besides, I have writing to do, and I'm getting way behind. I'll be busy the rest of the day, and I always know where you are if I need you."

After he studied her face to be sure she was okay, he nodded. "I'll go home, but I won't relax. I want to trim my roses and do some weeding before it gets dark."

She smiled and ushered him out the door with a reluctant Tex who had settled down in the corner for a little nap. When they were gone, Kyra returned to the den, ignoring the door to the basement. She needed to recalibrate her brain and become her character Jennie again; it was the only way she'd get anything done.

To her surprise, she found the words flowing easily and she finished up a chapter on a suspenseful note. Without stopping, she continued onto the next chapter as Jennie got into more and more trouble. Even as she wrote about the danger surrounding her main character, Kyra hoped her own life didn't ever become so frightening again.

As the slanting sun settled onto her keyboard, Kyra realized it must be near dusk and she was starving. Eight o'clock already! She finished her sentence, saved her manuscript to a flash drive, and headed into the kitchen to figure out what to have for dinner.

After eating a salad and two of the oatmeal muffins Sam had insisted she take home, she walked around the house checking the doors and windows. She hated her constant anxiety, but so many alarming events had happened that she couldn't just ignore her feelings. When she heard a loud knock on the front door, she almost fell over the coffee table behind her. She crept to the door and peered out the peephole.

At first all she could see was the figure of a man dressed in a suit. After she flicked on the porch light, the young man standing there squinted in the brightness, and that's when she recognized Mr. Berchtold's nephew, Peter Craig. Wondering why he would be visiting her at this hour, she opened the door partway.

"Hello," she said, looking behind him for her lawyer. "Did Mr. Berchtold send you with some information?"

Peter Craig smiled and introduced himself again, in case Kyra didn't remember him. "I'm sorry to bother you this late in the evening, but I wanted to ask if you could sign some forms my uncle forgot to give you the other day."

"Why now? Can't I go into the office tomorrow?" Kyra could hear the distrust in her voice, but she didn't care.

He deepened the smile to show his sincerity and murmured, "I had to pass by this way on an errand tonight, and I offered to do this for Uncle Simon. He didn't seem to think you'd mind."

When she hesitated, he added, "If you'd rather come in tomorrow, that's fine."

Taking a deep breath, Kyra opened the door wider. "Please, come in."

Kyra motioned to the living room, and Peter sat on the sofa and opened his folder onto the coffee table. He pulled out several forms and a pen before offering them to her.

"I'll need a few minutes to read over everything before signing," she murmured.

"I'm also a lawyer, in case you have any questions. Soon I'll be a full partner, and then you'll be dealing with Berchtold and Craig."

When she didn't respond, he glanced around the room to show he wasn't in any hurry to leave. As Kyra shuffled through the papers, she tried to watch him without looking obvious. He seemed to be looking for a specific item, but Kyra couldn't imagine what.

"I hear you had some trouble in your basement today." Peter settled his gaze on Kyra's face.

"And how did you hear that?" she demanded, wondering what that had to do with signing forms.

The look he gave her was rather sheepish. "A bad habit of mine—a police scanner. I heard about the body in the basement." He laughed a little. "That sounds like a good book title."

When she tried to ignore him and focus her attention back on the forms, he asked, "Was it scary finding that skull? Oh, sorry, that was a stupid question." He got up and peered down the hallway. "I don't know how you'll have enough nerve to sleep here tonight. Maybe you should stay at a motel for a night or two. I'll bet Uncle Simon could extend some money from your inheritance, if you wanted to do that."

"Mr. Craig, please sit down while I finish studying these pages. And I'd appreciate it if you'd stay quiet while I do so."

"Oh, of course." He sat down and stared at the shelves holding Mary's curios.

Frowning, Kyra flipped through the forms again and then set them back on the table unsigned.

"Excuse me, but I've already signed these same forms in the office. These must be copies. I'd like to know why—"

Peter exclaimed, "What? That doesn't make any sense. Uncle Simon told me they still needed done, and I can't believe he'd make a mistake like that."

"Perhaps we should call him right now and see what he says." Kyra reached for the cell phone in her pocket, but Peter grabbed her hand.

Kyra snatched her hand away and jumped up. "Don't do that again! Now, please, get out of my house."

"Sorry, sorry. I was only trying to stop you because I think Uncle Simon is getting forgetful and I didn't want him embarrassed." Peter raised his hands in a placating gesture before reaching for the forms. "I didn't mean to upset you."

"Just leave," Kyra said. "I believe you only came to talk about what happened earlier today. Make sure you tell your uncle that I'll only do business directly with him from now on."

Peter moved toward the door, but kept talking. "Didn't you hear what I said? He's getting forgetful and making mistakes at the office.

That's why he'll need me to be a full partner at the practice. I'm trying to protect him, not cause trouble for him."

"Go!" Kyra followed him closely to the door and slammed it in his face when he turned back to say something. Locking and double-locking the door, she leaned against it and took a deep breath. "Now what was that about?" she wondered aloud.

She hurried to the living room windows in time to see his car pull away from the curb. Then she dialed Mr. Berchtold's private number because she had no intention of keeping a secret with Peter Craig.

"What?" Mr. Berchtold sounded angry and upset with his nephew, but certainly didn't sound confused. "I'll take care of this problem, Ms. Martin. I can't imagine what came over my nephew, but I can guarantee you it won't happen again."

Exhausted from her roller coaster ride of a day, Kyra decided nothing could keep her awake at this point. As she said to Sam, she'd lived here all that time with a skeleton in the basement, so it didn't make sense to feel spooked now that it was gone. Still, she ignored the basement door as she checked all the windows and doors making sure everything was locked. When she crawled into bed, she had a few misgivings about her ability to sleep so she started counting down from one hundred. She woke up with the light creeping in her window and the number seventy-six lodged in her brain.

CHAPTER 14

The morning flew by as Kyra worked at a frantic pace on her book so that she wouldn't have to think about yesterday. Fresh ideas had filtered through her brain overnight, and she tried to keep her focus on how to tie them into her plot. Finally, she got up to refresh her cup of coffee, and she thought about the night Brad showed her that page on her laptop about the body being found in the backyard. Now she was sorry she called in the police since she insisted she'd really written about a body in the basement. It would look like she had already known about the skeleton buried in the basement and that's why she used it in the plot of her book. She was sure Detective Andrews had been told all that information, and he didn't seem to believe anything she said.

Frustrated, but knowing she couldn't change the past, she packed up her laptop and headed to the local library to do some research. She wanted to take notes as she delved into the history of Jasper Owens and anything that might have a bearing on Mary's past before Kyra knew her. Her other motive was her curiosity about Leonardo Napoli and his life as a writer of detective novels in Italy.

The Cartwright Library in Stonecliff was located off the main street in a neoclassical building. It was larger than most visitors would expect from a relatively small town because Thomas Cartwright had funded the entire construction of the library from his extensive business holdings. Kyra remembered spending many hours here in the summer, choosing books to read on the patio of Aunt Mary's house.

When she asked the petite gray-haired librarian about where she could find information on a man named Jasper Owens from around the 1950's or 1960's, the woman looked startled for a moment.

"My, you're the second person to ask me that in two days. How odd."

It was Kyra's turn to be surprised, and she wanted to know who it was or at least what they looked like. Trying to seem casual, she smiled and said, "Maybe that was my friend. He's medium height, brown hair, and smiles a lot." A rather bland description, but it fit Peter Craig with his artificial manner.

The librarian shook her head. "Oh, no, it was an older gentleman, rather serious, but quite polite. I suggested the newspaper archives in the back room. We keep hoping to transfer everything to computer files, but it's just so costly. A small library like this just can't afford to do everything we'd like, even with funding from the Cartwright legacy."

Kyra nodded and then asked, "How do I access those files?"

It turned out she had to use the microfiche machine, and the librarian, Mrs. Perry, brought her several films for her to review. If the information wasn't on those films, she'd get Kyra a few more. It looked like it could be a long day.

"I've started with the two rolls of film that the gentleman from yesterday seemed most interested in," Mrs. Perry said, as she showed her how to use the cumbersome machine. "It might save you some time and eye strain."

Kyra thanked her for her help and sat down to search through the newspaper files. Scrolling through page after page of interesting news from long ago, but not anything about Jasper Owens, she almost missed his name in a story about a car accident.

Mr. Owens had evidently hit and killed a pedestrian, and he was accused of being drunk at the time. The police were looking into the matter. Kyra thought it all fit in with what she'd heard about Jasper

Owens. She continued to scan the news articles to see if there was a follow-up, and suddenly there it was. The editor of the paper wrote an editorial on the surprising new evidence about the accident showing the pedestrian had walked right out in front of the car. Rumors were that Mr. Owens had paid off the police and the victim's family to withdraw all charges, although nothing was proven. Kyra shook her head. It added more evidence to the likelihood that Jasper Owens had threatened Lee Napoli's life, which was the reason Mary gave in to his demands for marriage.

The rest of that film didn't show anything else of interest, so Kyra tried the next one. Almost immediately, she saw Mary's name headlining a story about the possible murder of Jasper Owens. Kyra sucked in her breath and nearly cried to see her aunt's frightened face next to a photo of her husband. Gaining control of her emotions, she forced herself to study the grainy black-and-white picture of Jasper. He had dark hair slicked back and a neat mustache above thin lips. Even in the grainy photograph, she could see his eyes staring out of the page as if daring anyone to cross him. She read the article, taking down notes, although she discovered that no real evidence was provided. Everything was supposition.

Then she went back and studied Jasper's photo one more time, trying to see Ethan's resemblance to his father. No matter how she looked, though, she couldn't pick out anything in particular. The shapes of Ethan's eyes, nose, and mouth were completely different, so she concluded that he must have taken after his mother.

Kyra quickly scanned through more pages of the newspaper, but didn't find anything else of interest. After the initial flurry of possible charges and finger-pointing, the police must have decided they had no real proof that Mary pushed her drunken husband down the stairs. Kyra assumed too many people had been hurt by Jasper Owens to pursue charges against Mary. Still, the case was never completely resolved, and some people might have believed Mary had gotten away with murder.

Bleary-eyed from the strain of staring into the microfiche machine, Kyra returned the tapes to Mrs. Perry with thanks.

"Did you find what you were looking for?" she asked.

"Yes, I think so." Kyra smiled, but didn't elaborate.

The librarian seemed disappointed not to be taken into her confidence, but she smiled back. "I keep thinking you look familiar. Did you come here years ago as a young girl?"

Nodding, Kyra realized that the woman looked familiar to her, too. "Oh, you used to work in the children's and young adult section of the library. But I think your name was Miss Duncan then and you had long blonde hair." She felt herself blushing. "Sorry, I didn't mean . . ."

Mrs. Perry waved her hand. "Don't worry. I tried to stay blonde for a while, but it was just easier to go gray. I've gotten used to it by now."

"My name's Kyra Martin, but it was Kyra Wyndham, Mary Wyndham's dau—um, niece. I just loved coming here in the summers when I stayed with Mary."

"Oh, my, so sorry to hear of your loss. Mary was a great contributor to the library, and she'll be missed by many people in this community."

"Thanks, and she was a wonderful aunt to me, too. I sometimes can't believe she's gone." Kyra suddenly found herself close to tears and blinked hard. Struggling to change the subject, she asked, "So did you know the gentleman you mentioned earlier who wanted to look up the same information I did?"

The librarian shook her head. "I didn't, but I keep thinking I've seen his picture somewhere. It's odd how that happens sometimes. Of course, we can't actually give out information about people anyway. Normally, we'd have you apply for a library card, but I didn't bother with either of you since you didn't ask to take out any books."

"If I decide to stay in town much longer, I'll definitely get another library card. I'm sure my old one expired long ago." Kyra laughed lightly as the incipient tears faded away.

A few minutes later, she stepped outside onto the steps of the library and wondered what she should do next. She needed to work on her writing, but she found herself walking aimlessly down the side-walk. Since Brad hadn't picked up the phone when she called late last night, she was worried that he'd given up and gone to bed. It meant her call this evening would be even more difficult when she had to tell him about the skeleton in the basement. Sighing, she turned toward home—time to lose herself in her writing and forget about her problems.

That's when she saw the newspaper box with the afternoon's issue of the *Stonecliff Times* displayed showing the front page news. A photo of Aunt Mary's house was highlighted by a headline proclaiming—Skeleton Found in Home of Recently Deceased Mary Wyndham. Under that, in smaller print, it read, Niece Claims to Know Nothing about It. Even worse, a photo of her taken at the funeral accompanied the article.

Standing frozen in front of the box, Kyra was jostled by a young woman wearing a track suit.

"Excuse me," she said. "If you're not buying a paper, then please move." As Kyra moved back, the girl looked up and realized who she was. "Wow! Aren't you lucky? You'll be famous overnight." She put in her three quarters and grabbed two papers. Keeping one, she handed Kyra the other one. "Here, you can have a freebie," she said, laughing. "What the newspaper people don't know won't hurt them. Now tell me all about it. Aren't you creeped out living in that house? Did you ever notice ghosts wandering around? I'll bet . . ."

Kyra turned and hurried down the street, her mind in turmoil. How did the news about the incident get in the paper already? She hadn't seen any reporters around the house and no one had phoned her. So who had leaked the story? It had to be the police. Angry, she crossed the street and headed for the police department. Before she got there, she was startled by the ringing of her phone. She whipped it out and checked for the caller. It was Trudy.

She answered, saying, "I guess you saw the newspaper."

"Oh, Kyra, why didn't you call me yesterday? I could have given you some support."

Sighing, Kyra replied, "Sam was with me, and unfortunately, he was the one who found the skull." She went on to explain quietly to Trudy as she checked around to see if anyone was looking at her. By the time she reached the red brick building proclaiming "Stonecliff Police" in large block letters, she said she'd call back about getting together sometime tomorrow.

She marched up the steps and into the lobby, crossing to the desk, and glared through the Plexiglas at the policeman sitting there.

"Yes, miss, may I help you?" he asked, his attention distracted by something on his computer.

"I'd like to make a complaint about improper police conduct."

"Oh. And what kind of complaint would that be?" When he looked up, his face was guarded.

As Kyra began her explanation, he held up his hand. "Maybe you'd better come back and speak to the detective assigned to that case."

Sighing, Kyra said, "And I guess that would be Detective Andrews."

He nodded, and after a brief quiet conversation on the phone, he motioned for her to follow him down a hall to the office where she'd spoken to the detective last week. When he knocked and opened the door, Kyra stepped into the room, selected the least uncomfortable chair in front of the desk, and sat down.

"Why is the story of the skeleton found in my basement last night in the newspaper today?" she demanded.

Detective Andrews quirked his eyebrow and said, "I believe I'm the one usually asking the questions."

"Not when someone in this squad leaked news to the media," she said, refusing to back down.

He shook his head, saying, "We don't leak news around here. I would suspect one of your neighbors would be the most likely culprit. What about your nosy neighbor, Sam? He always seems to be around when something exciting happens."

Kyra clenched her fists. "Excuse me, but Sam is the only one who's helped me so far. He and his dog chased off the man who tried to attack me, and he was in my basement at my request when the skeleton was discovered."

"Like I said, very convenient." The detective stared back at her with a calm expression, as if he'd proven his point.

"So, are you saying that Sam found the skeleton, so he put it there?"

"Hmm, never thought of that. No, what I was saying is that Sam is the most likely person to have called the newspaper." He frowned. "However, if we did discover that he was responsible for the body in the basement, then it would leave your aunt off the hook. I think maybe you're worried that your aunt killed that person."

"No, I'm not." Kyra floundered, afraid no matter what she said she would hurt someone she loved or cared about. "I don't believe she knew a thing about it. How could she continue to live in that house for years thinking about that body?"

"And where were you seven or eight years ago?" he demanded, leaning forward on the desk.

Kyra blinked and felt the anger coursing through her veins. Just before she said something she'd later regret, she took a deep breath and said through gritted teeth, "Let's get back to discussing how the media knew about what happened at my house last night."

Detective Andrews stood up and leaned against the edge of the desk. Looking down at her, he said, "Okay, let's call a truce. I'm pretty sure no one here leaked the news, but many people must have seen our police cars and the forensic van in your driveway. Any neighbor could have called someone else they knew, and eventually the press caught on. If no one has bothered you for more information yet, I'm afraid they will now."

Kyra groaned. "Just great. I don't need this aggravation. I have a book to finish and a job to get back to in less than two weeks."

"Oh, that's right; you're a writer. Convenient that all this excitement has happened since you inherited your aunt's house. Didn't your book have something to do with murder?"

Kyra stood up. "It's none of your business, but I can guarantee you it's not about a woman who inherits a house where a man falls on his knife and a skeleton is discovered in her basement!" She turned at the door. "Just make sure your police officers aren't talking to the media!"

He frowned at her, but Kyra could swear he was holding back a smile. "Even if you don't trust us, remember that if you need us, we're here to protect and serve."

She marched away without saying another word, but she wondered if his comment was meant to be sarcastic or heartfelt. Was he worried about her? Shaking her head, she found her way out of the building and stood on the steps outside taking a few deep breaths.

Walking home, Kyra tried to work out plot lines in her head so that she wouldn't think of her own problems. As she crossed the main street, she heard someone calling, "Miss, miss!" but she paid no attention since several other young women had crossed with her. When a man called out, "Kyra Wyndham!" she stopped in surprise and turned around. The light had changed, but an older man stood on the opposite side of the street waving to her.

He stepped off the curb just as a car zoomed up the side street and made a right turn without stopping at the red light. A couple of women behind the man grabbed his arms and pulled him back just as the car whizzed by. He stumbled and nearly fell as the women helped him stay upright.

Kyra felt herself shaking as she stared at the neatly dressed man with a gray mustache staring back at her. When the light changed, she walked back across the street and stood in front of him, saying, "It's nice to meet you at last, Mr. Napoli."

CHAPTER 15

"Please, just call me Lee," he said, reaching out to take her hand. As several people walked around them, he asked, "Would you like to have a cup of coffee?"

She nodded, not sure how she felt about finally meeting Mary's lover and the man who had fathered her. Odd, she decided, as if her whole world had tilted on its axis.

"How about Christo's Café?" he asked.

Kyra started to nod again when she realized what that would mean. They'd be in a restaurant where he was known, and none of their conversation would be very private. Marian, Trudy's friend the waitress, would love to know they were father and daughter, and the news would spread faster than any late-breaking news on television.

"Um, don't get me wrong. I like Christo's, but it's not the place to discuss family history." She stopped to gauge his reaction, only to see him roll his eyes and grin.

"You're right about that. Then where . . .?"

"If we stop by Mary's house, I'll pick up my car so we can drive to a restaurant out of town. It would give us more privacy while we talk over dinner."

He nodded and they crossed the street and headed toward Kyra's temporary home. When Mr. Napoli retreated into silence as they walked, Kyra wondered what thoughts of the past were going through his mind. Was he remembering the happy days in his relationship with Mary before Jasper Owens interfered? Or was he thinking about finally coming home to visit Mary and finding out he'd waited too long?

"Your," he hesitated before saying, "your aunt was a beautiful woman. I shouldn't have allowed her to convince me to leave for my safety all those years ago."

Kyra slowed her pace to look directly at him. "You mean my mother, don't you?"

He sighed and returned her frank look. "Yes, I'm sorry. Your mother. So you do know I'm your father. You must think me a terrible person not to have acknowledged you . . ." He stopped and murmured, "Isn't that Mary's house at the end of the street?"

Kyra turned to stare at the turnaround circle filled with vehicles where nicely dressed men and women hovered around, including a man with a huge camera on his shoulder.

"Oh, no!" The news media had shown up in full force. "We've got to turn around. Hurry, Mr. Napoli, if you don't want every spotlight on you."

"But why?" he asked, but obediently changed direction and started walking back the way they had come.

"Wait! Ms. Martin! Stop! We'd like to hear your version about the body in your basement."

Footsteps pounded toward them and Kyra discovered that Mr. Napoli must have been used to walking or biking around the cities of Italy because he had no trouble keeping up. As they came to a side street where one of her playmates used to live, Kyra remembered a section of overgrown woods beyond her house. Praying it wouldn't be long gone by now, she found it even more overgrown than in her childhood. Before the news people rounded the bend, she pulled Mr. Napoli into the shady area behind a large tree trunk.

They stood there trying not to pant as the news hounds rushed by, and eventually trickled past again when they realized they'd lost their prey.

"Must have ducked into someone's house," one disgruntled voice said. They slowly trooped back to their stakeout, as Kyra and the man beside her grinned at each other.

"I expected to find Mary's neighborhood drowsing under the summer sun. Instead, it looks like there's a story here that I could use in the plot of one of my books." When she opened her mouth to explain, he held up his hand. "No, later. Where do you suggest we go now?"

Kyra bit her lip before saying, "Sam, who lives next door, would be a great help, but unfortunately we can't go there. How about Trudy Dawson's house? I'll call and see if she's home."

"Trudy, hmm. I remember she was one of Mary's best friends. You think we can trust her?"

"Yes, I do." Kyra held her breath until her friend answered. She briefly outlined their problem and moments later, they checked to be sure the way was clear. Stonecliff was such a small community, Kyra could walk to most places, especially since her car was being held hostage. Still, she'd slowed her steps partway through their walk when Mr. Napoli began huffing a bit. Not surprising when she realized he had to be around eighty years old. In fifteen minutes they were at Trudy's house.

Trudy flung open the door before they even reached it and welcomed them in.

"Lee, you look great!" she exclaimed. Smiling, she wrapped him in a big hug, and then hugged Kyra next. "So glad you called me. Please, come into the kitchen. I have coffee and banana bread waiting."

When they started down the hall, Kyra said, "I'll be right there, but I need to call Detective Andrews first. I want those news reporters out of my yard and away from the house."

Half expecting the call to go to voice mail, she was surprised to hear the detective's voice. "What may I do for you now, Mrs. Martin?"

"Get those reporters off my property!" Kyra listened as he explained they could do that, but not stop them from camping in the street. He suggested she use the back alley to her house since it was already marked private, for residents only. Any violations could be reported.

As she entered the kitchen, she saw both Trudy and Mr. Napoli looking a bit teary-eyed. Trudy jumped up to pour Kyra a cup of coffee and give her a slice of the bread.

"We were just sharing a few far-off memories," she said to Kyra. "But those times are gone, and I know we have present problems to solve."

Kyra had no idea she was hungry until she took her first bite of the walnut-studded banana bread on her plate. "Oh, my, this is delicious." She smiled at Trudy. "Problems will have to wait until I've eaten every crumb."

Conversation about the sunny skies and fragrant breezes filled with the scent of roses wound down at the same time as their snack, even second helpings, disappeared. Kyra sat between Trudy and the man who was her biological father, and she found herself tongue-tied. Mr. Napoli turned to study her face, hesitated, and then began to speak.

"I guess I should start first because I think everything began when Mary and I became lovers." He closed his eyes and brushed his fingers across his mustache, and Kyra was reminded again that he was an old man, despite his full head of gray hair and his sturdy build. When he opened his eyes, he looked at Kyra, saying, "Mary was a wonderful woman and we cared about each other very much. Sadly, Jasper Owens practically ruled this small town then, and he wanted Mary for himself. When she turned down his marriage proposal, he went about it another way. He threatened to make sure I'd never walk again, and he had the ability to make bad things happen to people. The townspeople lived in fear of him, and the police only managed to make it to the scene of the crime after the damage was done."

"Couldn't they prove it was Jasper who committed the crimes?" Kyra asked, frowning. "There must have been evidence pointing to him."

"He and his cohorts controlled everything," Trudy explained. "No one dared cross them or testify against him. If you did get up the nerve to testify, he made sure someone in your family got hit by a car or your store was vandalized."

"Sounds like the Mafia." Kyra frowned as Mr. Napoli went on.

"Exactly. So Mary caved in and agreed to marry Jasper. At the time I was furious with her because I felt she didn't believe I was capable of taking care of myself. It seemed like an assault on my manhood, so I packed up and went to visit relatives in Italy." He shook his head at Kyra's sad look. "I know; I was an idiot. I should have packed Mary up with me and taken her along."

"Still, what about her parents and her young brother?" Trudy said. "Jasper might have harmed them." She stopped talking, an introspective look on her face. "No, I don't think Mary would have gone with you. Not with that worry about her family."

"I agree, Mr. Napoli," Kyra said, patting his arm. "You were put into a bad position, just like Mary."

He smiled at Kyra and placed his hand over hers where it rested on his arm. "You really don't have to call me Mr. Napoli, you know. I know it's rather late in the day for you to recognize me as your father, and that's all my fault. It's just less formal to use my nickname, Lee."

The odd feeling hit Kyra again, and at first she couldn't decide what to say. As he studied her face, he moved his hand away from hers, and said, "Of course, you don't have to. I didn't mean to make you feel uncomfortable."

"No, it's not that." She struggled to say the right words. "I never expected to meet you and I feel overwhelmed. I only discovered 'Aunt Mary' was actually my mother a few weeks ago."

Trudy stood up and murmured, "I think you two need a little bit of time alone together." When Kyra and Lee tried to tell her it was okay for her to stay, she demurred. "No, I have a few calls to make for the bake sale coming up with the Women's Guild, and I'll do that now. If you need coffee or more banana bread, feel free."

After thanking her for her thoughtfulness, Kyra turned to Lee.

He sighed, saying, "After going to Italy, I spent years trying to establish my writing career. I pursued my goal with the single-minded purpose of forgetting Mary. I'd heard about Jasper's death, but I assumed Mary would put those early years behind her and move on with her life, probably marrying again and having a family." He shook his head, gazing into the past. "And then I got a letter from Mary saying she had planned a two-week trip to Rome and hoped she could visit me."

Lee looked back at Kyra and smiled sadly. "Mary flew to Florence instead of Rome and stayed with me for two weeks. When we met again, it was as if no time had passed, and we were still young lovers. Before she parted, we made plans to meet again soon, but Mary called two months later to say she was pregnant. I reacted badly, I'm afraid. I immediately asked her to have an abortion and said I'd find a doctor in France, if it wasn't possible to have it done in the States. She refused, of course, and she was right." He looked off into the distance. "I was a selfish man, and my career writing detective novels had finally taken off with editions in English and Italian. Since I enjoyed living in Italy, I had no desire to move back home. Not only had I thought she should come live with me, but I couldn't imagine raising a child. That's when Mary told me good-bye and I lost her for the second time in my life."

"So she came home, had the baby, and gave me to her brother and his wife." Kyra searched his face. "Did you miss Mary when she was gone?"

"I thought my heart would break. At first, I kept thinking she'd change her mind, but she didn't. When my second chance at love dissipated, I threw myself completely into my work, producing a book a year for several years. Then I got an invitation to my fortieth high school reunion, and since I had a book conference in New York at the same time, I decided to attend. My ulterior motive, of course, was to sell more books, but I went and there was Mary." He smiled. "And so our relationship began again, only this time we settled for those occasional visits together. No more talk of marriage—just happy times without any stress."

"Until you heard of Mary's death." Puzzled, Kyra wondered why he had bothered to return now.

"No, that's not true. I was shocked to hear the news when I got to Stonecliff. Why would anyone alert me? As far as the people in this town knew, we hadn't met in many years."

"But your visits?"

He shook his head. "No, I never came here. Either Mary came to Italy, or we arranged to meet at various vacation spots in the United States. That was Mary's wish," he added to forestall any questions.

"Oh, I see." Kyra's eyes filled with tears. "How horrible for you. What a terrible homecoming."

He sighed and slumped forward a little. "That's the story of my life. Always afraid to make commitments. I thought that maybe, even at this late stage, I'd offer marriage to Mary and come home to live. That maybe we'd have a few years living like any other old couple."

Kyra watched his face and how he struggled to maintain his calm exterior. She reached across the table and offered him both her hands. He met her halfway and gripped her tightly before the tears slid down his face. "I was a fool for too long, and now my chance is gone."

Ignoring the tears gathering in her own eyes, Kyra whispered, "No, Mary loved you the way you were, or she never would have continued meeting you. She was quite happy here, you know, with me, her friends and neighbors, her work for many years, and her gardening. She didn't lack for love, although you obviously held a special place in her heart."

Lee took a deep breath and squeezed her hands before releasing them. "Thank you, Kyra. Thanks for knowing the exact words to ease my mind, and I can see now the reasons why Mary loved you so much."

"She talked about me to you? I didn't think . . ."

"Oh, yes. All the time. And that brings me to the other reason I returned home now. Mary said you had hopes of becoming a writer one day, which pleased me, as you can imagine. The apple not falling far from the tree and all that."

"Well, I hope it works out for me. I'm in the middle of writing the first draft of a mystery story right now. But you know I wasn't trying to copy you since I had no idea you were my father, let alone knew that you wrote mysteries."

"Of course not." He smiled. "However, I wanted to add that you and Mary are really my only family, so . . ."

Kyra interrupted, saying, "Oh, I'm so sorry. Don't you have any brothers or sisters?"

Lee shook his head. "My parents and brother passed away years ago when I was still a young man. My cousins own a catering business in New York and they do quite well on their own. Besides, we haven't had anything to do with each other in years. They didn't approve of my career writing in what they called 'detective novels featuring foreigners.'" He reached for Kyra's hand. "And have you forgotten that you *are* my family?"

CHAPTER 16

Just then Trudy bustled into the room. "Goodness, I didn't realize the time. Here it is, six o'clock, and I haven't offered you dinner."

"Oh, no, that's all right," Kyra said. "We didn't mean to intrude for so long. I'm sure Lee has other things to do, and I'll sneak in the back alley to my house."

Trudy frowned. "But you haven't even told me what happened in your house yesterday. I'll just take out some frozen spaghetti sauce and warm it up while we make a quick salad. I have angel hair pasta that only takes a few minutes to boil. Please stay." When she looked hopefully at both of them, Kyra said, "Well, if that's okay with you, Lee."

Lee stood up, saying, "I don't think we have any choice. Now, where's your salad fixin's?"

By the time dinner had been eaten and the dishes cleaned up, Kyra had recounted the discoveries of the day before to Trudy and Lee. Since Lee hadn't known about Ethan Owens or anything else that had happened in the past few weeks, Kyra filled him in on all those events, too. When she finally said she was ready to go home, Trudy insisted on driving them back.

As they approached the back alley, Kyra could see a few reporters standing around, hoping for someone to interview. Trudy drove right past them, turning into the alley where a large sign saying "Residents

Only" was posted. When the reporters hesitated, obviously debating whether to obey the sign or chase down the car, Trudy stopped at Kyra's back fence, giving Kyra a moment to jump out and dash onto her property before being accosted by a reporter holding a microphone. Hurrying across the backyard, she shoved her key into the back door and whipped the door closed behind her. She stood breathing heavily, thrilled to have made it safely into Mary's home. Before she could decide what to do next, the phone rang.

"Oh, for Pete's sake! The reporters are already calling." Shaking her head, Kyra turned on the kitchen light and decided to have a glass of wine. The answering machine clicked on, and she heard Sam's voice say, "Kyra, are you okay? I saw you running away earlier with an older man, and I hoped you were all right. Those damn reporters have been making a nuisance of themselves all day."

Quickly picking up the phone, Kyra said, "It's me, Sam. Yes, I'm fine. I've been hiding out at Trudy's house most of the afternoon."

She spoke in a soothing tone to Sam because she could hear how worked up he was, and she hated to think he might have a heart attack worrying about her. When she explained how she talked to the police earlier and they promised to keep the reporters off her property, he calmed down a little. Then she gave him the short version of meeting Leonardo Napoli on the street and asked if he knew anything about him.

"Sure, he was the guy Mary was really in love with, not that jerk Jasper Owens. But she said that was a long time ago."

"Well, sort of." Kyra hesitated, suddenly not so sure she wanted to share the information about her paternity. "She, um, continued to see him on and off for years."

"Oh, I see." Now Sam hesitated before saying, "So . . . I guess that's why she got kind of quiet when I asked why she didn't ever think about marriage again. Still, I can't say I ever saw that Napoli guy around here."

"That's because they met in other places and sometimes in his villa where he lived in Lucca, near Florence, Italy."

"Rich guy, huh?"

"Actually, he's a writer of detective novels."

Sam laughed. "Hey, that's great. Maybe he can give you some tips since you're writing a mystery book. Oh, wait a minute!"

In the abrupt silence, Kyra could tell Sam was connecting the dots and coming up with one possible conclusion. "Yes, Sam, Leonardo Napoli is my father. I just never knew it until recently. In just a few weeks, my whole world has tilted on its axis."

"Jeez, Kyra! That's unbelievable. I don't know what to say."

"Don't say anything, Sam. I think I'm just exhausted after the events of this day, so I'm having a glass of wine to calm down and then I'm going to bed." Before he could try to offer any kind of help, she added, "Why don't you come over for breakfast tomorrow about nine? We can discuss all the latest happenings then."

Kyra was sure he could hear the exhaustion in her voice because he quickly agreed and hung up. Breathing a heavy sigh, she poured a glass of sauvignon blanc and carried it up to her bedroom. Sipping the wine as she changed into her nightgown, she barely made it through a hasty wash and lotion routine in the bathroom before brushing her teeth and heading to bed.

Sometime in the middle of the night, Kyra jerked awake. With her eyes opened wide, she strained to hear whatever had awakened her. All was quiet as she sat upright and stared across the shadows to her bedroom door. As her eyes adjusted to the darkness, she realized she hadn't shoved the desk chair under the doorknob again. Now that she had the double locks placed on her doors, she hadn't felt the need. Still, what if someone had broken a window?

This can't be happening again, she thought, sliding out of bed and reaching for the baseball bat she'd hidden under her bed. When she heard a strange clicking noise, she focused her attention on her window. It sounded like someone or something was outside in the backyard, and she wondered if it was one of the reporters snooping around her house. Slipping across the room, she parted her curtains and stared down onto the lawn sparsely lit by a waning half moon. At first nothing moved and then she caught sight of a figure directly below her. It crouched outside the basement window and the beam of a flashlight swung out into the yard before shifting away again. Then she heard the click again followed by a flash.

Some reporter was taking pictures through the basement window! Without thinking, Kyra grabbed the potted plant on her desk, quietly opened the window, and dropped it out. Dirt, African violet, and flower pot rained down on the unsuspecting housebreaker, followed by a clunk and a loud yelp. She watched in satisfaction as a man staggered back from the house and limped across the lawn, holding his head. After she was sure he'd left her property, she closed the window and went back to bed.

Thinking she probably should call the police, she decided against it. She hated to talk to the police if the problem was resolved, and she was tired of having suspicious policemen asking her questions. She lay in bed, but her eyes wouldn't stay closed. Finally, she got up and dragged the desk chair across the room and jammed it under the doorknob. This time she fell into a fitful sleep and only woke up when she heard Tex's excited bark, the one he did when he spotted a rabbit. Glancing at the bedside clock, she saw it was already 8:30.

After a quick shower and dressing in shorts and a t-shirt, she measured coffee and water into the coffee maker, started frying sausage links and mixed fresh blueberries into her pancake batter. By the time Sam knocked on the back door, fresh from his own shower, Kyra was dropping batter onto the sizzling griddle.

"Umm, smells good," Sam said. "You need any help?"

"Just put out the napkins and silverware and pour the coffee." Kyra flashed him a grin as he sniffed the fragrant air.

"Did you ever notice how coffee smells better than it tastes?" Sam wondered as he reached for the coffee carafe. "Don't get me wrong—I still like my coffee, but you know what I mean?"

"I do," Kyra said, sliding berry-studded pancakes and browned sausage links onto each plate and setting them on the table. "I can't explain that phenomenon, so I'm not going to worry about it," she added as she handed the syrup to Sam.

They avoided talking about any of the incidents of the past few days, and Sam regaled Kyra with accounts of his youth when he worked as a fishing guide in Maine. In his late twenties, he went back to school and became a park ranger in Ohio and Pennsylvania. After an injury during a fall helping to rescue some hikers on a steep hillside, Sam retired and moved to Stonecliff.

After breakfast, they lingered over a final cup of coffee, and Kyra gave Sam an account of yesterday's events.

"So your real father is in town now. That's amazing." His forehead furrowed in thought. "Oh, sorry. Are you all right with everything? It must be a difficult situation for you."

"Don't worry. I'm fine." When he looked uncertain, she assured him, "Really, I mean it. He seems to be a pleasant man and obviously, Mary loved him enough to continue their relationship."

"Okay." He glanced around the room before saying, "Maybe he could buy this place and live here. Then you can visit any time, and he could give it to you when he passes away. Then you'd be able to keep it as a vacation home."

"Oh, Sam! I don't think you want me to leave." Kyra laughed and then saw the sad look on Sam's face. "I'm so sorry. You must be missing Mary so much."

He sighed and tried to smile. "You're right, but I understand you have your own life to live. It's been good having you here to fill in the gap Mary's death made in my life. But I'll adjust. Don't you worry." He reached over to pat her hand before standing up. "Now let me take care of these dishes so you can get back to your writing."

Kyra tried to stop him, but he insisted. When Sam left, he gave her a quick peck on the cheek as he thanked her for a delicious breakfast. She watched him go and tried to push aside the worried feelings she had for him. Brad would throw a fit if she said she wanted to hold onto the house a little longer because it would upset Sam if she sold. Shaking her head, she settled in the den and opened her laptop. It was time to concentrate on her story and forget about the present problems in her life.

Hours later she only resurfaced from Jennie's problem dealing with a disbelieving policeman when her cell phone rang. Kyra pushed her papers around, trying to locate the phone. At last she realized it must be on the kitchen table and hurried into the other room. Grabbing it, she gasped, "Hello."

"Well, it's about time! I thought something had happened to you. Where the hell have you been?"

"Brad? Why are you calling now?"

"In case you haven't checked, it's five o'clock on Friday. I needed to talk to you about this weekend." Before she could say anything, he continued, "And why didn't you call last night?"

"I did." Then she remembered she'd been so exhausted last night that she'd forgotten to call. Quickly, she added, "No, that was the night before but you never picked up. Why didn't you answer on Wednesday?"

"Forget about it, Kyra. I called now because I have to work this weekend, and I'm sorry, but I won't be able to drive out to Stonecliff."

He didn't sound sorry to her; he almost sounded glad, which she found strange after all his insistence on seeing her every weekend. "Oh, Brad, and I have lots to talk to you about."

"Well, it will have to wait until next weekend when you come home."

Kyra sat down abruptly and stared down at the phone in her hand. Next weekend? Going home? That couldn't be right; she wasn't ready.

"Kyra, are you there?" She heard Brad's voice squawking away and she sighed with impatience. Finally, she said, "Yes, I'm here. Well, I guess I'll see you then." She clicked off the phone. Fully expecting him to call back, she waited for several minutes, but nothing happened. Just as she got up, the phone rang again.

Checking the phone, she saw with relief that it wasn't Brad's number so she picked up.

"Lee, how nice to hear from you," she said.

"I hope you haven't eaten yet. I wanted to take you out to dinner this evening."

Peeking out the front window, Kyra saw two cars and several reporters lounging around talking to each other. It was a smaller crowd than yesterday, and she imagined other more important news was edging out the discovery of an old skeleton in her basement.

"I haven't eaten, but there are still a few reporters out front. I guess some of Stonecliff is still abuzz with the skeleton story."

"Don't worry," Lee said. "I have ways around that. I rented a car and I've made reservations in the Diamond City Restaurant in Jefferson. How does that sound?"

"It sounds wonderful. What time will you be here?"

Lee picked her up in the alley at 6:30 with his rented SUV. Relaxing in the passenger seat, she told him she had expected to introduce him to her husband, but he wouldn't be coming this weekend, as he usually did. She explained about her vacation time running out and how she'd have to return home to Pittsburgh after next weekend.

"What about Mary's house?" he asked.

She hesitated, not sure what she wanted to say. "I haven't made up my mind yet. I'd like to keep it, but it doesn't make sense. But maybe, at least for another few months, I'll hang onto it."

"Perhaps I could—"

Kyra shook her head, saying, "No, please, don't offer help right now. I need to make some decisions myself about where I want my life to go."

He glanced over at her before turning his eyes back on the road. "Of course, I understand."

After Kyra asked a few questions about Lee's career, and Lee told her a few funny stories of life in Italy, their talk faded away. Kyra sat back and marveled at Lee's profile that looked like it belonged to a much younger man. His driving was competent and nothing about him suggested a doddering old man, although he'd admitted he was eighty years old. Seeing him so involved in life made Kyra sad that Mary hadn't lived long enough to spend a little more time with him. She quickly turned to look out the window so Lee wouldn't see the tears that threatened to fall.

"It's okay," he said quietly. "Don't be afraid to show your grief. It's the only way to come to acceptance and understanding. Believe me, I know." When he reached for her hand, she hung on for several minutes before wiping the tears away.

"Thank you," she whispered. She felt so confused about her acceptance of this man she'd never known until yesterday. Yes, he was her biological father, but that didn't automatically create a bond. Too many people could prove the opposite.

When her cell phone rang, she jumped. Grabbing it out of her purse, she saw an unlisted number and said, "Yes?"

"Ms. Martin, it's Detective Andrews. May I meet with you tomorrow morning at your house? I have some surprising information to talk over with you."

"Why can't you tell me right now?" Her tears dried instantly and she could feel her irritation grow at his abrupt manner.

"Because I won't discuss it on the phone and I want to watch your face when I do. Is ten o'clock convenient?"

"What if it isn't?"

"Well, is it or isn't it?" he demanded.

Huffing a little, she replied, "Fine. I'll see you then."

CHAPTER 17

When Kyra opened the front door the next morning, Detective Andrews held out a white paper bag with a name along the side, "Margie's Bakery."

"Peace offering," he said. "And don't tell me you're dieting. Their muffins are fantastic."

Kyra couldn't help herself—she laughed. Even when the detective was trying to be nice, he couldn't stop himself from telling her what to do. Then she suddenly realized the street was empty and no reporters shouted at the detective to know what was going on. The only vehicle in sight was his car sitting in her driveway.

"Where is everybody?" she asked in surprise. "Did you wave your magic wand and make them disappear?"

He smiled. "Something like that. May I come in?" When she stepped away, allowing him entry, he added, "It might have had something to do with a ten-car pileup on the interstate, including the bus carrying the local winning baseball team." She gasped and he quickly went on, "No one is seriously hurt, but it involves lots of parents and kids, so it's a big deal."

"Oh, thank goodness. I knew that eventually something would come up to get the reporters away from my house." She led him toward the kitchen, all the while wondering why in the world he wanted to meet at her home. Sighing, she motioned him to a seat at the table and set the bakery bag on the counter. She'd already had her morning cup of coffee, but she couldn't manage to eat anything until she knew the detective's purpose in visiting her today. Sliding the muffins onto a plate, she inhaled the fresh-baked scents of banana and something else, cinnamon?

Detective Andrews still hadn't said anything when she sat down across from him after placing the muffin plate, small plates, coffee mugs, cream and sugar on the table.

He poured cream into his coffee and smiled at her. "This is an unofficial-official visit," he said.

"And what exactly does that mean?" She frowned back at him.

"It means I think it's unofficial, unless I learn something that makes it official."

"I see," she said, studying the muffins and deciding on the blueberry one with the streusel topping. She wanted him to think she wasn't very interested in what he had to say.

"Good. I was hoping you'd take that one. I'm not crazy about blueberries. I like banana-nut best." He rambled on a few minutes more, explaining what flavor the other four muffins were and why he liked each one.

Finally, Kyra raised her hand, palm out in a stopping motion, and said, "Enough! I'm sure they're all delicious. Now tell me why you really came here today."

He sat back, looked directly into her eyes, and said, "The man who died in your backyard wasn't Ethan Owens."

Kyra shook her head a little before managing to say, "Wh—What?" When the detective just sat there without saying another word, she murmured, "I don't understand. What do you mean?"

"His fingerprints matched those of a small-time thief and con man named Max Keller. He wasn't Ethan Owens."

"But that doesn't make any sense. He said he was Ethan Owens. He talked about his father being Jasper Owens, and he knew all about my

Aunt Mary. He wanted to get his share of this property. He . . ." she stumbled over words and fell silent. She realized she was babbling and stared down at her hands.

Silence filled the room until Detective Andrews said quietly, "And you had no reason not to believe him."

She jerked her head up and saw what she thought was an understanding look. "Yes, that's right. I believed him because all the pieces fit together, just like a puzzle."

He nodded and his face broke into a genuine smile. "You can call me Dave when we meet informally like this."

"So you don't think I'm lying to you all the time, and you believe I didn't let that man into the house the night he died."

He nodded again. "That's correct. I'm thinking someone's trying to pull a scam of some kind and you're caught in the middle."

Kyra stood up and grabbed their cups to refresh their coffee. She needed to do something while she comprehended this latest development. Returning to the table, she nearly spilt coffee all over the table as she set the mugs down.

"Sorry," she said. "I'm still trying to figure out this whole mess. If that's not Ethan, then where is Ethan? And whose body has been buried in my aunt's basement all these years?" She fiddled with her spoon, but couldn't look back up into the detective's face.

"I was afraid you'd ask that question." He sighed and then Kyra did look up, right into his serious blue eyes. "We think that body may belong to the real Ethan Owens. They found partial dentures in the skull, so they're searching for a dentist now."

"I see," Kyra murmured, placing her spoon down carefully by her cup. "So now you're thinking my aunt might have had something to do with Ethan's death."

"We don't know." The detective looked across the table at Kyra and frowned. "We just can't be sure of anything until we know the identity of the body, and how long it's been in the basement."

"So when was Ethan Owens last seen? Does anyone know?"'

"Good question. We're trying to ascertain that right now. It will be important to the whole investigation to know the answer to that question." He studied Kyra's face before adding, "I don't want you worried before we know anything definite."

"That's nice of you," she said, and couldn't quite keep an edge of sarcasm from her voice.

He started to reach across the table for her hand and then pulled back quickly. "We don't believe the man who introduced himself to you as Ethan Owens is smart enough to be the mastermind. That's why we're worried you might be in danger because his death isn't the end of the scam. There's something else they want from you."

"But what?" Kyra shook her head. "I can't imagine what they expect from me." She rubbed her hand over her face and murmured, "All this happened after Aunt Mary died. Why not before? Why wasn't Aunt Mary in danger?"

The detective's head jerked up and he studied her face across the table without saying a word. Kyra suddenly realized that he thought everything had begun when Mary died, too. That maybe her death wasn't natural.

"No, no, no!" Kyra jumped up and stood beside the back door staring out at the yard without seeing it. The horrible thought of Aunt Mary dying as she fought for her life nearly made her throw up. Tears threatened, but she refused to cry because she wasn't ready to trust the detective yet with her feelings.

She sensed him moving across the room before he said quietly, "Is your husband on his way? Do you want me to call him?"

The thought of Brad murmuring worthless words of comfort at this time wouldn't help her at all. She knew he didn't care about Mary or her house; all he wanted was for Kyra to leave here and come home to be his wife. After all, he had pretended he didn't even see Ethan or whoever that man was in the bar that night, and he acted like he didn't believe anyone had really approached Kyra at the house with threats of taking the house away from her.

"No, he's not coming this weekend," she said. "And I don't really want to bother him. He'd rather I just went home and forgot all about my aunt, this house, and my writing."

"And why is that?" he asked.

Kyra turned quickly to give him the "it's none of your business" speech, only to find him standing directly behind her. He backed away with his hands in the air.

"I didn't mean to pry. Honest, I won't say another word."

Kyra couldn't seem to get a handle on her emotions. She managed to take a deep breath and say, "Another cup of coffee?"

"No, I think it's time for me to go, but I need to make one thing clear." He studied her face before continuing, "I don't believe you have anything to do what's going on, and I'm hoping your aunt died a natural death, just as it was ruled. But I want you to think about one way we might be able to find the truth, once and for all."

It took a moment for Kyra to understand what the detective meant and then she didn't know what to say. She'd watched enough detective shows on television to realize he wanted to do an autopsy on her aunt. The thought was abhorrent to her, but at the same time, part of her wanted to know the truth.

"I need to think about it and talk to a few people first."

"No problem. It may not ever come to that, anyway," he said and reached out to shake her hand. She hesitated before grasping his hand and offering a firm handshake. He smiled and added, "I believe you have my card, but here's another one. If you need anything, anything at all, call me."

"Even if I want to order a pizza?" she asked, trying to lighten the mood.

Laughing, he nodded, saying, "Even that."

Kyra saw him to the door and then leaned against it for a minute with thoughts swirling around her brain. Finally, she decided to call Lee. His cell phone rang and rang before Lee's voice asked her to leave a message. Thinking that maybe he was taking a shower or just forgot to carry his phone with him when he went out, she cleaned up the kitchen and moved into the den.

After sitting in front of her laptop for fifteen minutes without writing a word, she tried Lee's cell phone again. No answer, but she left another message. Sighing in frustration, she forced herself to begin typing a page. Rereading her words, she deleted the whole page and tried Lee's cell again. Still no answer. Worried, she called the front desk of his hotel and asked to be connected to his room. She was surprised when the clerk asked her name.

Taken aback by her question, Kyra said, "I just want connected to his room. I don't know why you need my name."

"I'm sorry, ma'am, but there's been an emergency, and I need to know your identity."

"Oh!" Kyra's heart suddenly pounded and all she could think about was the phone call she'd received from the hospital telling her that Aunt Mary was dead. "I'm his daughter," she managed to say. "Now connect me to Mr. Napoli."

"Sorry, Ms. Napoli, but your father collapsed in the lobby about an hour ago, and he's been taken to the Stonecliff Community Hospital. We didn't have your name listed on the registration form or we would have called you."

Kyra grabbed hold of her chair and slowly lowered herself into it. "Is he all right? Was he conscious before going to the hospital?"

"Please, I think it's better if you go to the hospital. I'm sure they can give you the information you need."

Frustrated, but understanding the clerk's predicament, she said, "Yes, okay, thanks for your help."

Hurrying to the garage, she hopped into her car and opened the garage door. Looking into the rearview mirror, Kyra saw a reporter jump out of her van and run toward the driveway. Obviously, one of the reporters had returned from the interstate accident. She gunned the motor as she backed down the driveway, scaring herself and the woman as she nearly clipped her outstretched arm holding the microphone. Driving down the road, she couldn't help feeling victorious about thwarting the woman.

By the time she reached the hospital, her nerves had gotten the better of her, and she worried that she might be too late. Maybe he'd had a stroke or a heart attack. She forced herself to enter the emergency room and ask for Leonardo Napoli at the front desk.

The nurse looked up as Kyra identified herself as Mr. Napoli's daughter. She studied her face before asking, "May I see some identification? You look rather young to be his daughter."

Kyra dug around in her purse for her wallet to show her license, explaining Martin was her married name. Once the nurse reluctantly accepted her identity as the person on her license, she led her back to a curtained-off room where Lee lay connected to a machine showing his blood pressure and heart rate. His eyes were closed, but he opened them immediately when he sensed Kyra's presence.

"Sorry, my dear," he murmured hoarsely. "Didn't mean to scare you like this."

Seeing that Lee immediately knew Kyra, the nurse withdrew.

"Oh, Lee, don't worry about it. I couldn't figure out why you didn't answer your phone, but it's okay now." She reached for his hand and was relieved when he gripped her hand tightly. "How are you feeling?"

He smiled a little. "Better now. I guess they say I just keeled over. Don't remember it, but evidently someone happened to catch me before I slammed into the ground. I must remember to thank that Good Samaritan."

Pulling a chair closer without letting go of Lee's hand, Kyra settled next to him. Her eyes teared up when she thought about losing Lee now that they'd finally met. Not only was he a direct link to Mary, but he'd loved her for many years. They had so many memories of Mary to share with each other. When Lee asked her to help him sit up higher, Kyra hurried to shift the pillows behind his head.

"That's better," he said. "I needed to make you do something to distract you from getting teary." His eyes twinkled, making Kyra laugh. "I'm not dying yet," he promised.

Before they could say anything else, a white-coated woman entered the cubicle. She picked up the clipboard at the end of the bed and perused it for a moment before looking up and nodding to them.

"I'm Doctor Madison, the ER doctor. I see you had a little episode awhile ago, Mr. Napoli."

"You could say that," Lee replied. "I don't normally faint in the middle of a lobby." He smiled, but the doctor just nodded again.

"Any health problems that you know about?"

"High blood pressure and some knee problems. My doctor said I'll need knee replacement one of these days."

"I see. No heart or lung problems?"

"Nope. I'm afraid if you want access to my health records, they're in Italy where I live now."

She shook her head. "I don't think that's necessary at this point. We've checked your blood and done an EKG and chest x-ray, and everything looks normal. Did you have breakfast and lunch today?"

"I always remember to eat," Lee said, winking at Kyra.

"That would seem to eliminate low blood sugar, then." Dr. Madison frowned at the chart and then said, "If you're staying with someone, then you can leave now or we can keep you overnight for observation. I'd prefer that you'd not go back to your hotel, if you're alone."

Lee's face turned red as he said, "I'm perfectly capable of taking care of myself . . ."

"He's coming home with me," Kyra interjected, placing a hand on his shoulder as a warning. "I was calling to have him stop over when I discovered he was in the hospital."

"Good, then that's settled." The doctor held up the chart, adding, "Let me fill out your discharge papers and you can be on your way."

When she left the room, Lee groused, "Why did you have to side with the doctor?"

"Because I need to talk with you, and I don't want to be alone tonight." She sighed. "Please, Lee, come home with me?"

He studied her face and finally nodded. "I guess it's the least I can do after being a derelict father all your life. As soon as they disconnect me from the infernal machines, I'll get changed and be ready when they let me go home."

"Good." Kyra leaned back in her chair before asking, "Do you have any idea why you keeled over if nothing's wrong with you?"

"Hmm. You'll think I am getting old and senile, but when I glanced around the lobby this afternoon, I saw a young man staring at me and, well, you know that saying 'if looks could kill?'"

"And that startled you so much that you felt faint?"

A far-off look came over Lee's face. "I can't explain it—it was like looking into Jasper Owens' eyes that day he threatened to kill me if I didn't leave Mary alone!"

CHAPTER 18

Much later, when they were settled in the living room at Mary's house, Kyra asked, "I still don't understand, Lee. Are you telling me that young man looked like Jasper Owens?"

Lee frowned. "No, that's just it. It wasn't his face; it was his eyes. Did you ever hear of the malocchio?" When Kyra shook her head, he continued, "It's an Italian word for the evil eye given by someone who's jealous or envious. Believe me, I've never forgotten that day when Jasper forced me against the wall and demanded I leave his girl alone. The evil intent of his eyes was branded in my memory, and I hoped I'd never see anyone look at me that way again."

She tried to imagine Lee looking up to see someone glaring at him with absolute hatred in a town where he hadn't lived in many years, but she couldn't think of any reason for it.

"You probably think I'm an old fool for getting so upset, but it seemed like my body responded before I could control it." Lee stared down at his hands resting on his knees. "I must be getting old."

Kyra patted his shoulder. "I'm sure it would have terrified me, too, to suddenly see someone so angry at me in a crowd of people. Maybe it's a good thing you needed immediate help, and scared the man away. Or maybe it was all a case of mistaken identity."

Lee leaned back and sighed. "Okay, we'll let it go for now. I doubt even the police would bother looking into such a ridiculous claim of someone giving me the evil eye." Lee smiled and asked, "So why did you try to get in touch with me earlier today?"

"I'm afraid we'll have to stay on the subject of Jasper Owens," Kyra said, as she explained the point of the visit from the detective earlier in the day.

"And the man you met calling himself Ethan Owens was actually a petty criminal?" Lee's brow creased in thought. "So then where is the real Ethan Owens? I'm afraid he couldn't be the man I saw because he was much too young."

Hesitating, Kyra suddenly wondered if Lee was more fragile than she'd realized after his frightening incident earlier in the day. She took a sip of iced tea and studied his face.

"I'm fine, Kyra. Really. So what is it?" he asked.

Kyra told him about the likelihood of the skeleton in the basement being Ethan, and the police working with the dental records. She saw he understood the implications right away; after all, he was a mystery writer.

"Don't worry, my dear. Mary would never be involved in anyone's death." He reached across the coffee table to give her hand a reassuring squeeze. "So put your mind at rest."

She smiled back at him, but knew she had to bring up the detective's other theory. "There's more," she managed to say. "The police are considering that Mary's death might be suspicious."

"Oh, no!" Lee's face drained of all color. "No! I should have been here. Why did I wait so long to come back? Mary needed me and all I could think about was the comfortable life I'd made for myself in Italy."

Kyra hurried to sit beside him on the sofa. "Don't do this to yourself! If Mary felt in danger, she would have let someone know. And maybe the detective is wrong, so until we know differently, we have to treat her death as natural since her doctor signed off on the certificate."

Lee rubbed his forehead as he stared down at the floor. Finally looking up at her, he asked, "Are they thinking of doing an autopsy?"

She nodded, saying, "Possibly, but they'd need my permission, of course. They'll let me know in a few days." Suddenly, Kyra realized how odd it sounded that she needed to talk to this man she'd only known for three days, and she'd never thought to call Brad, her husband, the person who should be closest to her. She saw Lee studying her face and shrugged. "Sorry, my thoughts were getting sidetracked."

"No problem," he said. "But I'm sure you don't need my opinion to make a decision."

Sighing, she said, "Of course I don't. I know that, one way or the other, we need to know the truth. I'll talk to Detective Andrews in the morning." She hesitated before explaining that she slept in her old bedroom, and she only had Mary's bedroom to offer Lee for the night.

"Don't worry, dear, I'll be fine. It upset me to think Mary might have needed me, but sleeping in her bed is comforting. Maybe I'll dream of her and the times we shared together."

Kyra slept surprisingly well that night, maybe because she felt comforted having Lee sleeping across the hall from her. It was good that her night passed peacefully because she woke up to the sound of pounding on her front door. She sat up, confused, and checked the time: 6:30.

"Kyra Martin! Open up; it's Detective Andrews." Grabbing a pair of shorts to add to the t-shirt she had slept in, she hurried downstairs. Peering through the front window, she saw the detective and several other policemen. Her heart thumped as she opened the door, wondering what could possibly have happened.

"What's going on?" she asked.

"Sorry, but we need to know if Leonardo Napoli is in your house." The detective's face was impassive as he stared down at her.

"Yes, I brought him home from the hospital last night. I don't see why it's any of your business, though."

"We need to talk to him, Ms. Martin." His voice was frosty.

"I don't understand why you need all these men to talk to one old man, but I'll go get him now."

"No!" he shouted, and Kyra nearly jumped a foot in the air. "Is he upstairs?"

Kyra took a deep breath and began, "I don't know what your problem is, but this is my house and . . ."

"It's all right, Kyra," Lee spoke from the top of the stairs. "I'm coming down right now."

She noticed Lee was already dressed as she hurried over to wait for him at the bottom of the stairs. Lee patted her arm and murmured, "It's all right, Kyra. Whatever the problem is, I haven't done anything."

She nodded, but felt frightened anyway. She didn't want to lose Lee now, not when they were finally getting to know one another.

Detective Andrews cleared his voice, saying, "Mr. Napoli, we'd like you to accompany us to the police station. We have a few questions we'd like to ask you."

Her uncertainty with the situation gave her the strength to demand, "Is that cop lingo for 'you're under arrest'?"

"It's just questioning for now," the detective said smoothly as one of the policemen escorted Lee away to a waiting police car.

"Then I'm coming, too," she stated.

"Perhaps you'd like to get dressed first." He glanced up and down at her before turning away. She thought the corners of his mouth had turned up before he strode off to his car. "I'll see you when you get to the station," he said.

Furious and upset, Kyra sped through her normal morning routine. She was just getting into her car in the driveway when Sam traipsed across the lawn toward her.

"What's with the police?" he asked, a worried frown on his face.

She sighed because she wanted to get to the police station, but she could see how concerned Sam was. "It's about Mr. Napoli. He was unwell yesterday and he was staying with me. Now, for some reason, the police carted him off to the station. I need to hurry up and see what's going on, but I promise that I'll call you as soon as I can."

"Oh, okay. Just let me know if I can be of any help." He stepped away from the car, but Kyra saw his puzzled confusion. She'd be sure and explain all the details to him once she knew what was going on herself. He'd been a good friend to her and she wouldn't leave him in the dark too long.

By the time Kyra reached the police station, she had decided to call Mr. Berchtold, just in case Lee needed a lawyer for any reason. Since it was Sunday, she'd have to bother him at home. After long minutes, a woman answered the phone, her voice so hushed Kyra could barely hear her.

"This is Kyra Martin. I'd like to speak to Mr. Berchtold, please."

"He's not available." As Kyra began to insist on speaking with him, the woman whispered in a teary voice, "I'm sorry; that's all I can tell you right now. He's not available!" Surprised, Kyra sat holding the disconnected phone in her hand.

Wondering what could possibly have happened to make the poor woman so upset, all she could think of was that Mr. Berchtold had some kind of health emergency. She slowly replaced the phone in her purse and decided to first find out why the police wanted Lee and then try the lawyer's home again. Maybe everything was already settled and Lee would be ready to come home and have breakfast with her.

The sergeant at the desk told her Detective Andrews was busy, but he was expecting her and he'd be with her as soon as possible. Rolling her eyes, she stomped across the waiting room and settled into one of the uncomfortable plastic chairs against the wall. She studied the wanted posters for something to do and then was sorry she did. *What a nasty bunch of people*, she thought. Instead of looking for them, the police were hounding one old man because he used to have a relationship with someone who lived in the house where a skeleton was found.

Distracted, Kyra looked up in surprise when a voice said, "Ms. Martin, follow me, please. I'll escort you to the detective's office."

She followed the broad sergeant's back to the office she'd been in before. He knocked, opened the door, and waited for Kyra to enter before closing it again. Detective Andrews stood up from his seat behind the desk and Lee sat directly across from him.

"Lee, are you all right?" she asked and rushed to his side, ignoring the detective.

"I'm fine," Lee said. "But there's been an unfortunate incident, and you might want to sit down while Detective Andrews explains."

Kyra rubbed his shoulder and looked up at the detective. "Whatever it is, I can't imagine it has anything to do with us, and I really think I need to take Mr. Napoli home now. He's recovering from an accident yesterday, and as you can see, he's not young anymore."

"Please, Ms. Martin, sit down," he said.

Kyra glanced down at Lee, who nodded his agreement. Kyra sat as cold tendrils of fear touched her spine. "What is it?"

"Well, now that you're here, could you tell me if you've ever met Mr. Simon Berchtold's nephew Peter Craig?"

"Yes, of course. I met him in the office once and then he stopped by one evening and asked me to sign papers." She fiddled with her purse strap as she continued, "It was weird because I'd already signed those forms for Mr. Berchtold, and all Peter did was ask questions about the skeleton in the basement. When I got upset about his nosiness, he insisted his uncle was getting forgetful and had told him get the forms signed."

"You thought he was deliberately trying to get information from you?" Detective Andrews asked.

"Yes, and I called Mr. Berchtold and complained about Peter's unprofessional attitude."

"Hmm. I see. So I can assume you didn't particularly like Mr. Craig?"

"That's right, and I doubt he liked me after I called and complained to his uncle."

The detective drew in a deep breath, and then said, "Then I guess you won't be particularly upset if I tell you that Peter Craig was found dead yesterday afternoon in his apartment."

At first, Kyra couldn't process what the detective had said, and her purse slipped from her grasp onto the floor. Leaning over to pick it up, she struggled to control her voice before asking, "You mean as in murdered?"

"That's what it looks like. Just for the record, may I ask what you were doing yesterday afternoon between eleven and one o'clock?"

"Well, considering you didn't leave my house until a little after eleven, I think I had just settled down to do some writing in the den."

"You didn't go out anywhere?"

"Not until about two when I drove to the hospital after discovering Lee had been taken to the emergency room. I nearly ran over a reporter from Channel 7 on my way out of the garage, so I'm sure that woman can testify to that."

He nodded, saying, "We'll check into it, although I guess you could have slipped out the back alley without anyone noticing and returned again before two o'clock."

"Don't be ridiculous," Lee interjected. "There's no way she could have gotten all the way to Mr. Craig's apartment and back in that time frame without a car."

The detective held up his hand. "We won't go into that any further until we get the report back from the autopsy and the crime scene. In the meantime, Mr. Napoli, I don't want you leaving town and going back home to Italy."

"Of course not! I'd never leave Kyra while someone is killing people all around her."

Lee sat quietly on the ride back to Kyra's house until she finally asked him why the police had picked him up that morning.

"Sorry, my dear, I forgot that you didn't know that part. Unfortunately, I was seen arguing with Mr. Craig yesterday morning outside of the hotel. He had the nerve to stop me and ask if I'd like him to be my legal representative for my estate now that I'm in the States." Lee grinned at Kyra with that twinkle in his eyes. "He got quite upset when I told him to buzz off!"

"Oh, my! I wonder whatever gave him the idea you needed a new lawyer."

"I'm guessing he was thinking of a big fat lawyer's fee." Lee shook his head and the grin faded from his face. "Not that I'm happy to hear he's dead, but I had nothing to do with his murder."

"Did you have an alibi so the police will quit bothering you?" Kyra glanced at him and was afraid she knew the answer.

"No, sadly I was reading a book I'd bought in the gift shop and must have nodded off. Before I knew it, it was one o'clock and I went down to the hotel restaurant for some lunch. That's when I had my little episode and ended up in the hospital."

They had just sat down at the kitchen table for coffee and bagels when Kyra heard Tex barking. A moment later Sam appeared at the back door. Kyra went to let them in, and Sam hesitated when he saw Lee.

"Sorry if I'm intruding, Kyra. I'll come back another time."

Before he could turn away, Lee said, "Don't be ridiculous. There's plenty of coffee and I know Kyra has more bagels in the bag over there. Come and join us."

Kyra reached for Sam's arm and drew him into the kitchen. After introducing him to Lee, she insisted Sam sit at the table while she put another bagel in the toaster. Tex roamed around the kitchen, sniffed Lee, and curled up in the corner. Within minutes, Lee had put Sam at ease and they were discussing Italian food and whether angel hair pasta or linguine tasted better in marinara sauce. Eventually, the topic turned serious as they discussed Peter Craig's death and how it might relate to the fake Ethan Owens' death.

"Have you talked to your husband?" Lee asked.

Kyra looked at him blankly, surprised she hadn't even thought of calling Brad. "Um, no, it's been so crazy, I haven't had time. And I know he's working a lot of hours this weekend."

Lee sent a look her way, but didn't say anything. Sam's forehead furrowed in a worried frown as he said, "You got us now, so don't bother your husband. By the time he comes next weekend, maybe it'll all be over."

Next weekend? Kyra couldn't believe she'd be going home so soon. She picked up her coffee and sipped at it, all the while thinking that she wasn't ready to go home yet. Somehow, despite all the frightening and strange incidents and the tangles with police, Mary's house felt like her home. Sam, Trudy, and Lee, even Simon Berchtold, made up her little circle of friends, giving her a feeling of belonging.

Sam was telling Lee all about the broken window episodes and how he and Tex had chased the intruder away. Kyra suddenly realized that the group of people she viewed as friends might harbor a person who was her enemy. After all, she didn't really know Lee, except the friendly persona he'd shown her and the fact that he said he was coming home to offer Mary marriage. Sam and Trudy both had been very helpful, but what if they were plotting to protect Mary from some crimes she'd committed, and they wanted to keep Kyra from discovering the truth? Mary had trusted Mr. Berchtold with her finances and the knowledge that Kyra was her daughter, but maybe he had used some of Mary's money and didn't want Kyra to find out. When Lee and Sam fell silent, Kyra stared up at them with new eyes and for the first time, she didn't know who to trust.

CHAPTER 19

"What is it?" asked Lee.

Kyra shrugged, trying to find something noncommittal to say. "I was just thinking about how far behind I've gotten on my book, and I really need to work on it today."

"Hmm. Speaking of your book, would you like me to take a look at it?" Lee smiled at Kyra, and she almost agreed before remembering her fears.

"I appreciate your offer, but I'd like to finish the first draft before letting anyone read it." She touched his hand lightly so he wouldn't sense her unease. "Then I'll let you read the whole thing, and you can give me suggestions for revision." When he nodded, she added, "At the same time, I'll start reading your books because I think I've read one or two of them, but it was several years ago."

"That sounds like a plan. And don't buy any of my books; I'll have my publisher send me copies of the complete series of the Inspector Mario books."

Sam smiled at both of them as he got up. "Thanks for the breakfast and the update, but I'd better get my shopping done for the day. I sure hope you stay around after next week, Kyra, because I'm getting spoiled having breakfast at your house." He laughed as he called to Tex and let himself out the back door.

"I guess I'd better head back to the hotel today, if you wouldn't mind giving me a lift," Lee said.

"Oh, Lee, I didn't mean you had to leave, too. I think the hospital expected you to stay with someone for a few days."

He shook his head, and Kyra worried that he'd noticed her uncertainty when she'd stared at him and Sam a few minutes ago.

"You need some quiet time with your book, and I understand that completely. You don't want to be worried about ignoring your guest when you should be concentrating."

Kyra tried to object again, but Lee insisted she needed peace and quiet, so she gave in and waited while he went upstairs to gather together the possessions he'd left in Mary's room. After he came back down carrying the plastic bag given to him at the hospital, she drove him back to his hotel. He promised to call if he needed her for any reason and refused her assistance in getting up to his room.

When Kyra finally sat down in front of her laptop again, she sighed and tried to force her mind into writer's mode. Instead, she kept wondering how she could resolve the events around her, and not the imaginary ones in her story. She decided it might help address her fears if she figured out the possible motives of the people around her. Grabbing her tablet, she started writing down all the key incidents that had happened since she learned she was Mary's daughter and moved into Mary's house three weeks ago.

Her list included:

Ethan Owens had a key to Mary's house, one day he paid for my lunch without me knowing, and before that I saw him at the bar in the restaurant, but Brad didn't believe me.

Living room window is broken. Later, when another window is broken, Sam's dog Tex chases man and gets stabbed, but not seriously.

Real estate agent has buyer for house, but I turn her down.

I discover Mary's husband Jasper Owens died falling down basement stairs, and for a while Mary was considered his killer.

I search closed-off basement room that is considered source of some mystery in house.

Ethan Owens is Jasper's son, but not with Mary, from a former relationship. He's two years old when Mary weds Jasper.

Intruder shows up in house before Brad comes home one Friday night. Sam and Tex scare him away, and he falls on his knife jumping over the backyard fence. I identify the body as Ethan Owens.

I call for locksmith to place double locks on doors. Later that day Trudy tells me Mary's lover and my father, Leonardo Napoli, a detective mystery writer, has returned from Italy.

After deciding to have the dirt floor in the back basement room concreted over, Sam takes measurements for me. Tex finds a long bone buried in the floor, and when Sam looks around, he discovers a human skull.

Police pathologist takes skeleton of a man away. That night Peter Craig shows up with papers I already signed with Mr. Berchtold—he keeps asking questions about skeleton and wants to see basement.

I go to Stonecliff library to look up info on Jasper Owens. Ethan Owens doesn't look like Jasper in microfilm photo. Older gentleman had been to library looking into the same archived material, and later Leonardo Napoli calls out to me on the street. He almost gets run over.

Lee explains how he planned to visit Mary and only discovered she had passed away when he returned to Stonecliff.

Detective Andrews visits me and explains that the man who introduced himself as Ethan Owens was actually a petty thief named Max Keller. Now the dental records from the skeleton in the basement are being checked to see if they're a match for Ethan. The detective suggests possibly doing an autopsy on Mary to rule out murder.

Lee has an episode and faints in hotel lobby. I go to the hospital to see him and he says he saw a man giving him the evil eye. It reminded him so much of the day Jasper Owens threatened his life if he didn't leave Mary alone.

Detective Andrews takes Lee in for questioning from my house the next morning because Peter Craig is found dead and Lee was seen arguing with him on the street earlier that day.

When Kyra finished her list, she read over it several times, trying to find the common link between all the incidents. If Peter Craig hadn't been killed, she thought he could have been the one. She couldn't picture Lee breaking the windows and then running away fast enough to get away from Tex. And Sam was right here when the man broke the windows. Did that mean the window smasher had nothing to do with any of the more serious crimes? She supposed it was possible.

But—the window smasher and Max Keller both had knives in their possession, so maybe Max broke the windows and later fell on his own knife. Talk about poetic justice, she thought. Kyra tapped the end of her pencil on the tablet, trying to make sense of Max's part in the pattern. There obviously had to be at least one more person involved in the events of the past couple weeks. She kept circling back to Peter Craig, but he was now dead, too. Did that mean three people had embarked on this plan, and one of them was slowly eliminating the other two? But why?

If one criminal was left, he or she had to be the mastermind. Kyra suspected that person wouldn't make any mistakes, and she also believed that person was the most dangerous of all. Fear crept along Kyra's spine and she shivered. As desperate as she was to have time alone to write, she now wished she had convinced Lee to stay at the house with her. How dangerous could an eighty-year-old man be? Rubbing her forehead where a headache had begun to stab behind her eyes, she realized how silly that thought was. Even if Lee didn't present any danger to her, how much safety could he provide if someone attacked them?

Suddenly, an idea almost smacked her in the face. If the person who identified himself as Ethan Owens was a fake, why did she believe Leonardo Napoli was who he said he was? She had assumed the old man calling her name was Lee because Trudy had told her he was in town. So far only Trudy had verified he was Leonardo Napoli. Turning to her laptop, she connected to the Internet and typed in Lee's name. She found lists of his books, but no photo, not even on the back covers of his books. She discovered several photos of men named Leonardo Napoli, but none of them was the correct age.

Then Kyra remembered Lee had been in the hospital and at the police station, and he'd certainly have to show his identification. Of course, the police would have no reason to think he was anyone but Leonardo Napoli, so maybe they had no reason to check if he had given them a fake ID. She debated about calling Detective Andrews, but decided to do her own sleuthing first.

First, she searched the box of correspondence belonging to Mary since she hadn't yet disposed of it. She sifted slowly through page after page, but found nothing. Then she ran upstairs and stood in the doorway of Mary's room, noticing that the bed was neatly made, before taking a deep breath and stepping into the room. She'd avoided violating the privacy of Mary's bedroom, but now she forced herself to look through the dresser drawers and the closet, fighting back tears the whole time. Everything she touched brought back a different memory of Mary. When she opened the jewelry box, she saw the fake pink pearl necklace she'd given Mary for Christmas the year she was twelve. It sat in the place of honor on top, glowing in the reflection of the mirror. Reaching for the necklace, Kyra held it tightly to her chest, and allowed herself the time to mourn again the woman she'd loved so much.

A little later, she checked the small antique desk in the corner. Mary had used it mainly in the early morning or late at night to write her to-do lists or letters to friends. She told Kyra it was handy when she had trouble sleeping, and she didn't have to bother going downstairs to use the larger desk in the den. Now Kyra wondered if this is where she liked to write her letters to Lee in the intimacy of her bedroom. The desk only held two narrow drawers at the top, but she still hesitated before pulling open the first one. She almost laughed at her deflated anticipation when she discovered it held all the usual stuff found in a desk drawer— pens, pencils, paper clips, notepads, a box of stationery, address labels, stamps, and a small pair of scissors. Anticipating that the other drawer might hold more important items, she pulled it out, only to discover it was completely empty.

Surprised, she pulled it out all the way to check the back corners, and it almost fell onto the floor. There was nothing. When she tried to fit the drawer back onto the runners, she rubbed her hand across something scratchy on the underside. Flipping in over onto the desk, she saw an envelope taped there, its edges coming loose from the dried-out tape.

Unbelievable! It's just like in a mystery story. With shaking hands she pried off the envelope to reveal a black-and-white photograph. She saw a very young Mary smiling up at a good-looking, dark-haired man with his arm wrapped around her shoulders. It didn't take much imagination to guess they were madly in love. Turning the photo over, she read: Me and Lee Napoli, May 14, 1954. She couldn't believe she was looking at Leonardo Napoli as a young man.

Setting the photo on the desk, she checked to see if there was anything else in the envelope, but it was empty. As she replaced the drawer, she wondered if Mary had hid that picture away from Jasper Owens so he would never find it. Maybe Jasper had destroyed all her keepsakes from Lee and this was the only thing she had managed to save after her marriage. But the most important question now related to the reason for the empty drawer. Kyra doubted it had lain empty all the years Mary lived here.

Lee had stayed overnight in this room. Did he check around and find things he didn't want people to know about? Maybe personal letters from him to Mary? She frowned then, remembering how Lee had gone upstairs when they'd gotten back from the police station, bringing down the plastic hospital bag. Had it looked rather overloaded for carrying just a few personal items? Kyra couldn't be sure because she really hadn't paid attention to it.

Hearing a faint ringing tone, she cocked her head, and realized it was her cell phone. She touched her pockets before remembering she'd left it on the desk downstairs. She held onto the photo as she hurried down the stairs, and naturally the ringing stopped before she reached the den. Huffing a little, she grabbed the phone and saw the call was from Brad. *Now what?* She debated about returning the call, but the decision was taken out of her hands when the phone rang again. She gritted her teeth and answered.

"Where were you?"

"Hello, Brad. How's work going?" She ignored the accusatory note in his greeting.

"Busy," he said. "How come you didn't pick up at first?"

"Brad, for Pete's sake. I was upstairs in Mary's room, um . . . cleaning, and I left the phone downstairs."

The line went silent on the other end and Kyra was just about to check if he was still there when he said, "Are you sure you were upstairs, um . . . cleaning? Or was someone upstairs with you? Like some guy?"

Anger over Brad's certainty that she only wanted to stay at Mary's house to cheat on him left her speechless. She finally forced herself to say, "Don't be ridiculous."

"You've gotten pretty chummy with that Sam next door. Maybe you like them old and grateful for any attention."

"If that's all you called to talk about, I'm hanging up."

"Don't you dare! And while we're on the subject of Sam, if you would've sold the house sooner and not let him fool around in the basement, nobody would know about that moldy old skeleton down there! That damn dog causes more trouble!"

Kyra blinked in surprise, trying to understand Brad's sudden attack. "You're saying Sam and his dog caused the whole problem? As if they made the skeleton appear?"

"Look, just forget what I said. You always get me all worked up." His tone softened. "I really called to check and make sure you're all right."

Kyra stared at the phone in her hand, debating whether to throw it across the room or not. Sighing, she said, "Then you have a funny way of showing you care about me. And I do not get you upset; you do it to yourself with your insane ideas. "

"All right, all right. I can't wait to see you next weekend. At least all this craziness will be over and you'll be coming home where you belong."

Kyra sat down hard in the chair and clutched the phone tightly. *Do I belong with you? Right now I feel like it's the last thing I want to do.* "Okay, see you then," she managed to say, but her voice must have betrayed her real feelings.

His voice came sharply over the line. "You don't sound okay. You sound kind of funny. What's going on?"

"Brad, enough already. I'll see you Friday night." Without giving him a chance to respond, she broke off the connection. Fully expecting him to call back, she dropped the phone on the desk, and then carefully slid the envelope with the photo into the inner pocket of her purse. Afterwards, she wandered out to the patio.

There was no way she was going home when her book wasn't finished, and she still didn't know who was responsible for the frightening events all around her. Why was Peter Craig murdered? And why did someone named Max Keller have a key to her house, and who was buried in the basement? She knew there had to be a connection behind all these crimes, and she felt like she was the bull's eye in the middle of a target. What linked her to Mary, Lee Napoli, Max Keller masquerading as Ethan Owens, and Peter Craig?

Frustrated, Kyra sat on the patio chair and stared out at the garden and the pink blossoms of the rhododendron bushes Mary had planted years ago. Thinking of Mary's kindness to her over the years, she tried to relax and let her mind wander back to happier times. Reminiscing, Kyra never heard the knock on the front door, so when Detective Andrews walked around the corner of the house, she jumped up in surprise, wondering what the bad news was now.

CHAPTER 20

"Sorry to barge in on you, Ms. Martin," the detective said, "but you didn't answer your doorbell or my knock."

Kyra stood, her fingers gripping the edge of the table, afraid of his next words. "Is everything okay? Don't tell me someone else has been murdered . . ."

He waved his arms to calm her down. "Everyone's fine, as far as I know. That's not why I came to see you." He looked around the backyard and studied the fence. "To tell you the truth, I was a little worried about you when you didn't answer the door."

"Oh." Kyra frowned, her heart still beating a little faster. "Is something going on I should know about?"

He shook his head. "No, it's just that after that incident in your house last week and then Peter Craig's death, I get a little leery when odd things happen. Like people not opening doors when I'm pretty sure they're home." He motioned her to sit back down and pulled out the chair across from her.

"It sounds like you're concerned about my well-being." Kyra found that a little confusing after he originally seemed to think she was involved in the death of the man she'd assumed was Ethan Owens.

When he didn't respond immediately, she finally asked, "So why are you here today?"

"I have news about the skull Sam found." He studied her face before looking out into the sunlit yard. "You know, sometimes I hate my job. I mean, here we are, with the sun shining and the bees buzzing around on all those flowers, and we could just sit and enjoy the peace. But I have to talk about a skeleton in the basement."

Kyra found herself smiling at his sentiment. Sometimes he even sounded like a human being, although she doubted that would last. "I thought it would take awhile before any of the testing came back."

"Normally, that's correct, but we put a rush job on the teeth. It seemed the quickest way was to identify the body. Because we had a possible victim right away, we checked dentists in this area, and sadly, we got our answer." He sighed. "Strangely enough, you thought Ethan Owens was in your house the other night, and he was, but not as the man who broke in."

"He was the skeleton in the basement," Kyra said, stating the obvious. When he nodded, she asked, "So what comes next?" She wondered what the ramifications would mean for Mary and if she would now be under suspicion for murder again.

"We'll have to find out how he got here and who killed him. It's a cold case file, but there's not much info on him. Nobody really seemed to care when he disappeared, and it was assumed he left town on his own and didn't want to be found."

"Do you have any proof Mary had anything to do with him? I thought he was raised by his mother's parents."

"He was. I can't give you confidential information, but it doesn't look like he ever had any inclination to live in this house. I'm sure you can find out nearly as much as we know by talking to some of Mary's old friends."

"Don't worry; I will." Kyra thought it was time for a lunch date with Trudy again.

Detective Andrews slapped his hand down on the patio table. "That doesn't mean I want you running around trying to solve this case. If there's somebody out there committing murder, the police don't need you endangering your own life. We'll take care of the detective work."

Kyra narrowed her eyes at him and smiled. "I hear you. I'll be the good little citizen and just concentrate on writing mysteries, not solving real-life mysteries. Okay?"

"I know you think you're being funny, but I mean it. Maybe it's time to cut short your stay here and go back to your own home for now."

"Oh, not you, too! Don't even start that. My husband's bad enough!"

The detective stood and backed away. "Okay, I'm not touching that comment. Just make sure you stay safe and keep out of police business." He nodded one more time and added, "Don't bother seeing me out; I'll just walk back around the house to my car."

Kyra sat outside for a few more minutes, thinking, and then she went into the house to look for her cell phone. It was time to have a crime-solving meeting with Trudy.

❖ ❖ ❖

Trudy was already there when Kyra reached Christo's Café the next afternoon. The lunch crowd was thinning, and within minutes Marian stopped at their table.

"You'll have to fill me in on all this gossip I'm hearing about the identification of the body found in your house. Just wait until I get rid of these last stragglers," Marian said, motioning toward the other customers. She marched away with a spring in her step as she anticipated a good gab fest.

Kyra groaned. "I don't believe it. I just got the news from Detective Andrews yesterday. How in the world could everyone in town already know about it?"

Trudy smiled. "Maybe not everyone. Marian has an inside connection at the local newspaper named Justin Farrell. He's her sister's son."

"In that case, maybe I should be milking her for information. Detective Andrews didn't exactly expand much on the basic facts."

Trudy laughed then, before becoming serious again. "How are you handling the news that Ethan Owens was buried in Mary's basement for many years?"

"I don't know. It feels odd to think about it, especially at night when I'm all alone in the house." Kyra rearranged the silverware where it lay on the napkin in front of her. She finally looked up and studied Trudy's face. "Did Mary ever say anything about Ethan to you?"

Trudy shook head. "I'm sorry, Kyra, but she rarely ever mentioned her marriage at all. She said once that those years were like a bad dream to her, and she was glad Jasper's son was being raised by his own people."

"You never heard that he'd contacted her or expected to inherit the house?"

"No, not at all. I think she assumed his family was just as happy to be rid of Jasper as she was."

"Are you speaking of that devil Jasper Owens?" Marian stood over their table, her hands on her hips. "I couldn't help overhearing your words."

"Who are you kidding?" Trudy demanded. "If I know you, you were straining to hear every word we said."

"Okay, you're right. Hold off just another minute, and I'll get your lunch. Then I can sit down with you and discuss this problem properly."

Kyra never expected to have Marian join them, but it turned out she was a fountain of information. After half an hour, she was pretty sure she knew more than Detective Andrews and his team did about Ethan Owens, and most of it was a sad story. Ethan had been raised by his mother's parents and they were very strict with the boy. When he was old enough, he rebelled, and started stealing and running with the wrong crowd. The day he turned eighteen, they washed their hands of him and kicked him out of the house. He lived in his car for a while, and then fell madly in love with a sixteen-year-old girl he met at a corner drug store in a small town in Pennsylvania. When Natalie ended up pregnant, her family insisted they marry and live with them. His love lasted through several years as they raised their child, and he accepted a job with his father-in-law working at his construction firm.

When Ethan later decided he wanted to move to California and work out there, his wife's parents refused to allow him to take their daughter and grandson away. One morning he was just gone, and Ethan wasn't seen by his family for more than twelve years. The next time Ethan showed up, he was nearly dead from exposure and malnutrition from hopping trains across the continent. Natalie dutifully nursed him back to health, and Ethan was thrilled to entertain his fifteen-year-old son, Ford, with tales of his adventures in California.

"How do you know all this?" Kyra finally asked when Marian took a long sip of the cola drink she'd brought to the table for herself.

"Got relatives and friends all over the place." She winked at Kyra. "Anything you want to know about anybody, just give me the heads up. I'll consult the Greek grapevine."

"Is that the end of the story?" Trudy asked, shaking her head at her friend.

"Not quite. Of course, Ethan wasn't the best person for his son to meet at an age when he was getting tired of being smothered by his mom and grandparents. The good thing was he was smart enough to know he didn't want the nomadic life his dad seemed to love. Ethan worked odd jobs, but disappeared again right after the boy graduated from college. Then his son left town and no longer kept in touch with his family."

"How sad. Did you ever hear that they got together again?" Kyra asked.

Marian shook her head. "Don't feel too bad for Natalie. She had divorced Ethan before he disappeared the second time, and a year later married the widowed banker in town. I don't think she tried to find her son or ex-husband after that."

Several customers came into the restaurant and Marian sighed. "I guess I'd better get to work. Are you two ready for dessert?"

After ordering the custard dessert to take home, Kyra and Trudy finished up the last few bites of their lunch and said goodbye and thanks to Marian. Sam was standing with trimmers outside her front windows when Kyra pulled into the driveway. He turned quickly when he heard them and raised one hand in greeting.

When Kyra got out of the car, she called, "Is something wrong, Sam?" He had seemed so intent on staring at something in her living room.

"No, no. I was out trimming in the garden and saw your azaleas looked a little ragged. I didn't think you'd mind." Sam smiled and walked toward them. "You ladies have a nice luncheon?"

"Of course we did. The food is always great at Christo's," Trudy said when Kyra didn't immediately respond.

For a few seconds, Kyra found herself staring at his long pointy trimmers and a tremor of fear shot down her back. Then she looked back up at Sam's kindly face and shook that ridiculous notion away. This was Sam she was thinking about—the guy who'd taken such care to protect her those nights after her windows had been broken. She forced herself to say, "Would you like to come in and share the dessert we brought home?"

"Nah, you ladies enjoy your little chat. I'll just finish these azaleas and get back home. Didn't sleep too well last night and I feel a nap coming on."

After they entered the kitchen, Trudy turned to Kyra and asked, "What happened back there?"

"What?" Kyra smiled at Trudy and tried to pretend she didn't know what she was talking about. "I'd better get the coffee going."

"Kyra! I'm not blind. For a moment there you were terrified of Sam."

"That's not true." She breathed in and let the air back out slowly. "All these frightening incidents crowded into my brain when I saw those sharp pointy trimmers. But it wasn't Sam, not really. It was the idea that danger lurks everywhere around us, even in the most mundane objects. Then I snapped out of it and realized how silly I was acting."

Trudy took the dessert bag out of Kyra's hands and set it on the table. She placed her hands in Kyra's and held on tightly. "Now look me in the eye and tell me truthfully that you don't fear Sam."

"I do not fear Sam," she said, enunciating every word. "He and Tex have saved me too many times for me to think anything else."

"Okay, good," Trudy said, dropping her hands. "Now we can make coffee and relax on the patio."

Much later that evening Kyra took a break from working on her book. After Trudy left, she'd felt calm enough to reread the last ten pages and move onto a new chapter. Her heroine Jennie discovered that the father of the man she loved wasn't the nice guy he had convinced her he was. He didn't want reconciliation with his son at all; he wanted the property the young man owned. If the father owned the property on the bay, he could sell it to developers for millions. But the son wanted to keep it because that's where he'd been happiest growing up. Suddenly, Jennie was all that stood between the greedy father willing to kill and the son who believed his father was dead.

As Kyra made a sandwich for her belated supper, she mulled over how Jennie would explain to her lover that she'd known for some time his father was alive, but neglected to tell him. She'd planned on making it a happy surprise, but now she'll have to tell him his father is plotting to kill him. Kyra sipped her iced tea as her thoughts shifted to the events happening around her. A man walked into her house with his own key, trying to claim he was the inheritor to Mary's house, and then he showed up at night frightening her before he ran away and fell on his own knife. That story sounded more made up than her own plot.

She frowned, thinking of her long lost father showing up after Mary's death, and his interest in becoming part of her life. Should she trust Lee? Was the idea of finally meeting her father making her accept him too easily? She'd suspect some kind of possible scam, but he obviously was Leonardo Napoli from all the evidence she had. That included the photo she'd found under Mary's drawer, which certainly looked like a young Mary and Lee.

And how did Peter Craig fit into the story? Kyra decided to call Mr. Berchtold tomorrow and offer her condolences. Maybe she could find out how close their relationship was and something about Peter's background. She'd soften it by saying how hard it must be, and how she understood since she'd just lost Mary. Kyra looked down and realized she'd finished her sandwich while all these thoughts whirled around in her brain. The sad thing was that she did miss Mary, and she wished Mary was here to help make sense of the latest happenings.

When the phone rang, she sighed, expecting it to be Brad. Instead it was Lee, and she picked up quickly.

"Are you okay?" he asked, his voice breathless.

"I'm fine, Lee. What's going on?"

"I've found out some interesting background on Peter Craig, and I'm a little worried. You'll think I'm a sentimental old fool, but when I left Italy, I brought along some of Mary's letters to me from this past year. I was sitting here reading them when she mentioned Peter Craig. It didn't mean much to me at the time, but now I wonder."

Kyra leaned against the counter and asked, "Was it something about him working with Simon Berchtold?"

"So you've been thinking about that, too? See, it didn't seem important at the time, but she talked about how she didn't like his nephew much. Then one day Simon let slip that Peter was actually Peter Craig Cartwright, the grandson of Thomas Cartwright."

"Oh, the library in Stonecliff is named after him."

"Right. It seems the grandfather was a strong believer in making it on your own. He paid for Peter to go to college and law school, but when he died, he left the bulk of his estate to the library. Peter was furious, and legally dropped the Cartwright from his name. That man went around with a chip on his shoulder and fought for years to have the money returned to him."

Kyra rubbed her forehead, trying to figure out why Lee sounded so upset about this information. "But Peter's dead now, so he's out of the picture."

"That's true," said Lee, "but Mary thought he was scheming with someone else to get money, one way or another. She worried that Peter had access to her account and other people's at Simon's law office. He could have been stealing from clients or maybe even trying to blackmail some of them."

"And you think that's why he ended up dead? It was either a falling out among thieves or a victim decided to stop the blackmailer. Or maybe Peter had something to do with the skeleton in the basement."

"Exactly. And now I'm worried that another person is involved in his activities."

Kyra thought about the mysterious happenings since she moved into Mary's house, trying to make sense of everything. She stared out into the darkness beyond her kitchen windows, and whispered, "It sounds like you're accusing Mr. Berchtold, but so far all they've done is try to frighten me out of this house. So what are they after?"

CHAPTER 21

They talked for several more minutes, but didn't come up with a real solution. Kyra was certain that Mr. Berchtold wasn't the man who broke her windows, although they decided that could have been Peter. Lee had tried to insist on coming over to stay with her, but she assured him she'd be fine. He was too old to be running around late at night, and Kyra wasn't sure how much he'd be able to protect her if she did need help. So after she checked the doors were double locked and the windows were closed and locked, she went to bed. And here it was, morning again and all was well. She tried not to think about how long it had taken her to fall asleep, or the fact that her phone sat on the night stand right beside her, the bat on the floor below it, and the desk chair jammed under her bedroom doorknob.

She sipped her coffee and decided she still needed to talk to Simon Berchtold. However, when she called his home number, no one answered, and when she tried the office, a recording simply stated that the office was closed due to a death in the family, and would reopen in a week. Foiled on that front, she settled on going back to the library. Maybe she could dig up more information on the Cartwright family and talk to the librarian, Mrs. Perry.

When Kyra asked the young woman working behind the desk about the section for local history, she was pointed to small room in the back. Entering the room, she discovered Mrs. Perry working on several books on a large wooden table.

"Hello, there," Mrs. Perry said, smiling. "How nice to see you again."

She smiled back. "I've decided to study more of Stonecliff's history before I return home next week."

Mrs. Perry waved her hand to indicate the bookshelves on three sides of the room. "You've come to the right place. If you need any specific help, just ask. I'm in the middle of fixing some of the pages in these books published in the early 1900's."

Kyra wandered around the room, trying to look as if she wasn't sure exactly what she wanted to read. Eventually, she homed in on several books titled "The Cartwrights of Stonecliff" and "Thomas Cartwright, Founder of the Cartwright Library." Taking the books to the other end of the long table, she browsed them, looking for a list of Thomas Cartwright's children and grandchildren. Finally, she found what she wanted on a page showing a family tree.

Thomas Cartwright was the only son of Gregory and Matilda Cartwright. Thomas married Allison Mercer, and they had two sons and one daughter. Thomas Cartwright Jr. died at the age of three, and Gerald married Donna Larson and they had one son, Peter Craig. Gerald had some kind of accident, and lived in an expensive nursing home. The daughter, June, married Simon Berchtold, and she passed away about eight years ago. They had no children. Peter was Thomas's only possible heir and he would be thirty-four now, if he hadn't just died. In some ways, Kyra understood why Peter had been so angry at not inheriting anything from Thomas Cartwright as his only living family member. On the other hand, maybe Thomas had judged Peter's character and found him wanting.

Looking up, Kyra found Mrs. Perry studying her.

"Oh, sorry, I didn't mean to bother you," she said, flustered. "It's just that you seem to be searching for specific information about the past, and I wondered if there was any way I could help you." When Kyra didn't answer right away, she added, "You know, to possibly save you some time."

Kyra wasn't sure how she felt about her offer, or even if she felt comfortable taking another person into her confidence. On the other hand, it might save some research time, and she needed answers.

"Okay," she said, nodding. She grabbed the books about the Cartwright family and moved to sit beside Mrs. Perry. "I'm trying to find more in-depth info on Thomas Cartwright and his relationship to his grandson, Peter."

"I see." The librarian sat back and looked around the room as if trying to organize her thoughts. "As you know, Thomas Cartwright founded this library. That was back in the 1970's, a little before Peter was born. When his own children either died before he did, or became incapacitated like his son, Gerald, Thomas looked to Peter to become his heir. However, he didn't believe in automatically passing down wealth to family members. He wanted Peter to work hard and show that he could build up a business on his own first."

"And I assume Peter didn't show he could do it," Kyra said, thinking of the young man who'd come to her door that night last week.

"Sadly, no. Thomas got him a job with Simon Berchtold, and even there he didn't shine. Mr. Berchtold had several meetings here with Mr. Cartwright, and Thomas always had a frown on his face afterwards." She sighed. "Still, I was surprised several years ago when we heard the library was getting all the Cartwright money as a donation when he died."

"I understand Peter tried to fight the provisions of the will to no avail."

Mrs. Perry nodded. "I'm afraid Mr. Cartwright had several lawyers working for him at all times, and he made sure the will couldn't be broken. I felt sorry for his grandson, in a way, because it did seem rather unfair. He could have at least split the money and given half to the young man."

Kyra nodded. "I guess Mr. Cartwright had his reasons, but it angered Peter Craig so much that he dropped the Cartwright from his name." She hesitated and then asked, "Did you ever meet Peter?"

Mrs. Perry shook her head. "No, I guess Peter wasn't raised around here, but even when he moved here, I never saw him." She looked around the room with its shelves of books as if surprised someone could live in a town and not go to the library.

Since Kyra decided she had nothing more to glean from the librarian, she asked a few questions about book plotting. When Mrs. Perry discovered she was writing a book, she happily suggested several library books she thought might help. After signing up for a library card, Kyra walked out of the library a half hour later with three books in her arms, and several ideas to strengthen the storyline of her novel.

It had started to rain while she was in the library, so Kyra hurried to her car. Juggling the books while she tried to pull her keys out of her purse, she ended up dropping them. As she leaned over, something slammed into her back and she fell onto the ground, scraping her hands and knees. Before she could look up, a cloth bag was shoved over her head and she was pushed flat against the ground. A rough voice said, "Get out of town and don't come back."

She struggled against the pressure on her back and then suddenly it was gone. She staggered to her feet and dragged the bag off her face. Looking around wildly, she saw the parking lot was almost empty. She couldn't see anyone at all, let alone someone running away, although a van and a sedan sat about ten spaces down from her car. Shaking, Kyra watched for another minute before grabbing her books, purse, and keys from the ground. Quickly inserting the key in the door, she jumped inside, locked the doors, and started the car. Her hands burned from the scrapes and she was thankful she had worn jeans to the library, although her knees still hurt.

She drove past the van, discovered the license plate was missing, but wasn't brave enough to get out of the car to look inside. The gray sedan was empty. Quickly, she drove in front of the library and parked in the No Parking zone. With her keys in hand, she locked the car and ran up the steps. Mrs. Perry stood by the reception desk and she turned in surprise as Kyra burst into the room.

❖ ❖ ❖

Later that afternoon Kyra sat in her living room, trying to understand what had happened to her that day. Mrs. Perry had taken her back and bathed her hands and knees before the police came to take her report of the incident, including a description of the van. Her hands stung the most, but she still tried to write down everything she remembered. Although Mrs. Perry had offered to come home with her, Kyra explained that she'd call her father and he'd come right over. Only Kyra hadn't done that. Instead she decided that she needed to deal with this problem on her own without bothering Lee.

Over and over in her head she repeated the words the person who attacked her had said, "Get out of town and don't come back." The rough voice was probably disguised so it could have been anyone. She tried to place any accent or odd figure of speech, but nothing stood out. Anyone could have hurried off and hidden in that van before she struggled to her feet and dared to look around. By the time the police came, the blue van and the car had gone, but the police were checking to see if a blue van had been involved in any other crime.

Looking around the cozy living room, Kyra yearned to hear Mary's sympathetic voice and feel her arms around her. Tears threatened, but she sniffed and forced herself to sit still and concentrate on the problem at hand. She thought of the people who surrounded her now, and couldn't think of any reason any of them would want to harm her. Trudy had been Mary's friend for years, Lee had a relationship with Mary extending back almost fifty years, and Sam had been Mary's neighbor for the last ten years. Even Simon Berchtold had been Mary's lawyer for about ten years. The people Kyra had trusted the least were Peter Craig and the fake Ethan Owens, and they were both dead.

Maybe it was time for Kyra to call Brad and have a long heart-to-heart talk. Perhaps he could see this whole mess with a clearer viewpoint. Kyra sighed. She had ignored Brad every time he suggested she come back home, but it looked like she'd be much safer if she did. Frowning, she tried to figure out why it had never been dangerous to live in Mary's house until after her death. Remembering her list of incidents, she walked back to the den to find it. Sitting down at the desk, she studied the printout.

No matter how she reviewed her notes, she always came up with the initial incident related to Mary's death and Kyra's inheriting her house. Was it something about the house? The skeleton discovered in the basement? But if it was the skeleton, then why did she get attacked today? No, everything wasn't over yet. If her attacker wanted her to leave town, then it sounded like he did want something in the house. Or was the property valuable for some reason? After all, she had been approached by the real estate lady with a big offer of money a few weeks ago. Maybe she should give her a call and talk to her again. Scrambling though the papers on her desk, she had about given up finding the business card when she discovered it pushed to the back of one of the cubbyholes.

"Marsha Taylor," she read. "Matthews and Taylor Real Estate, Buying and Selling the Finest Homes in Stonecliff." Kyra raised her eyebrows and wondered how Mary's house fit into their motto of a finest home. Her modest two-bedroom house hardly fit that description. Before she changed her mind, Kyra dialed the number on the card. A nasal voice answered and asked her business. When she gave her name after requesting to speak to Mrs. Taylor, she was almost immediately connected.

"Ms. Martin, I didn't expect to hear from you," Mrs. Taylor said, and her voice held an edge.

"No, I guess you didn't after my definite refusal of your offer." Kyra smiled, thinking about how she'd almost kicked the woman out of her house. "However, I'm now having second thoughts."

"Well, I'm not sure the offer is still on the table. I warned you at the time—"

"Yes, yes, I know. But surely as the owner of one of the finest homes in Stonecliff, I might still have a home of interest to other buyers."

"What? I hardly think your home qualifies . . . oh, yes, I see. You're looking at my card." She gave a little laugh. "Not all homes fit into that special category, but they can still be the perfect home for the buyer."

"And in my case, that buyer would be?" When Mrs. Taylor remained quiet, Kyra asked, "He didn't happen to be a lawyer, did he?"

"No, nothing like that. Believe it or not, he was a writer, but that's all I'm saying."

Kyra nearly dropped the phone and sat there, stunned, as Mrs. Taylor babbled on about talking to the person again. Without saying another word, she clicked off and carefully set her phone on the desk. Lee! Lee had tried to buy the house before he'd ever introduced himself to his daughter. But why? Upset and confused, she wandered around the house. She'd thought the buyer was Peter Craig, who wanted to buy the house before the skeleton was discovered in the basement. Although she wasn't sure what he had to do with it, she was willing to believe he was the bad guy in the story, along with the false Ethan Owens.

After a half hour of indecision, she decided to drive to Lee's hotel and talk to him, face to face. Backing out of the garage, she looked all around to make sure no blue van sat on the road, but nothing looked out of place. She reached the hotel and drove around for a couple minutes trying to find a parking space near the entrance. Just as she was about to give up, a young man trotted out of a side door and jumped into a sporty-looking car right in front of Kyra.

She parked and slipped inside the same side entrance, thankful it was unlocked during the daylight hours. Taking the elevator to the fourth floor, she walked down the carpeted hallway and knocked on the door to room 428, hoping she would catch Lee by surprise. When the door wasn't answered after her second knock, she sighed in frustration. Lee wasn't there. As she turned away, the door opened. Kyra couldn't help it—her mouth dropped when she saw Trudy standing there.

Then she blushed crimson, murmuring, "Oh, sorry, I didn't mean to interrupt . . ."

Trudy laughed and pulled her into the room. "Kyra! It's not what you're thinking, although I appreciate the thought. I'm afraid I'm a little past having assignations with handsome men in hotel rooms." She turned to look back at Lee sitting at the table with his laptop in front of him. "Not that I mean your father isn't a handsome man, but it's not why I'm here today."

Lee stood up and strode across the room, enveloping Kyra in a bear hug. "That's my daughter, the writer, thinking creatively," he said, chuckling. "No, we were just working on some local history."

Kyra felt silly having misconstrued Trudy's presence in Lee's room. "I really think I should come back later," she said, slipping out of Lee's embrace. "I wanted to talk to you about something personal and I don't think this is the time."

The mood in the room shifted and Lee turned her to face him. "Something's wrong. You're obviously upset, my dear. Maybe we'd better clear the air right away before it festers."

Trudy picked up her purse where it lay on the bed. "I need to get going anyway. I'll call you tomorrow, Kyra, if that's all right?"

"Oh, Trudy, I don't want you to leave. Perhaps it would be better if I come back later."

Kyra heard voices coming down the hall, and Lee stepped to the door and closed it. "That's better. Now what's on your mind? I'm sure it's okay if Trudy stays since we've informed her of everything that's been happening."

Kyra took a deep breath and said, her voice shaking, "I'll bet she didn't know that you tried to buy my house out from under me. Even before I ever knew you were my father."

CHAPTER 22

Trudy looked at Lee in surprise. "Really? Is that true?"

Lee put up his hands as if to ward off a blow. "You misunderstand me. I did offer to buy the house, and I was willing to pay a half-million dollars. I wanted Kyra to be set up with money and didn't think she'd want to keep the house. No one else would offer that kind of money."

"But why not come to me first?" Kyra asked.

Lee motioned to the chairs by the window and Kyra shook her head, but Trudy took her arm and walked her over to a chair. "I'd like to hear this, too. Let's give the man the benefit of the doubt."

With a heavy sigh, Lee said, "Mary always made a point of telling me about you, Kyra. Over the years I heard all about your exploits, how good you were to Mary, and how you loved each other. I'd been a bachelor all my life and never really had a deep commitment to someone, so I didn't fully understand." Kyra felt as if he'd slapped her in the face, and Lee tried to reach out to her.

"Don't!" she murmured, shaking her head. "You've been pretending all this time."

"No, please, hear me out first." Lee sat on the edge of the bed before continuing, "The last time Mary visited she said she wouldn't be coming again." He caught his breath as he said those words. "Of course, she didn't mean she would die because she had no idea. At the time, it was an ultimatum. She said it was because I couldn't make a commitment to her or to our daughter. All those years, she kept meeting with me, sharing vacations together, and hoping I'd finally come home with her. After she left, I took a long hard look at my life and realized how selfish I'd been."

"You could have your cake and eat it, too, as the saying goes," Trudy said. "Mary kept telling me you'd change, but this year she finally gave up."

Kyra stood up. "I really don't care, Lee. I'm leaving now and please don't contact me again."

Trudy reached for her and gently pulled her back. "Let him finish, dear. You may not believe me, but Lee was on his way to talk to you this evening when I stopped by."

Kyra studied Trudy's face and decided she was speaking the truth. She turned back to Lee, saying, "Evidently, Mary was right and you waited too long. And now it can't be fixed."

"No, no, Mary did know. I called her a week before she died. I told her I had my plane tickets and I was coming home. I had to stop in New York to see my publisher first and then I flew here. But when I got here, I heard the terrible news." He hesitated, his face agonized. "I wasted all those years and when I finally came to my senses, Mary was gone."

He looked down at his hands and Kyra knew he was fighting tears. She didn't care. He had no right to his tears because he'd made the wrong choice years ago, and he had only himself to blame.

"So you wanted to make some grand gesture of restitution by buying Mary's house and giving me the money."

"You won't believe me, but I was too afraid to approach you and introduce myself as your father. It was easier for me to provide money for you instead. When you turned down the offer, I suddenly saw Mary in you." He half smiled. "I felt so proud of you then."

Kyra didn't know what to say. Leonardo Napoli had angered her, then surprised her, and now, just maybe he had made her happy. If she could believe him.

"After that, I decided I had to bite the bullet and finally introduce myself to you. I knew it was what Mary expected of me." When Kyra started to say something, he held up his hand. "But more than that, it was also what I expected of myself. Here I am, eighty years old, and I'm finally acting like a responsible adult." He sighed and shook his head.

Uncertain of her feelings, Kyra remained silent. Trudy touched her arm, saying, "Are you all right, dear? Would you like me to leave?"

"No, I'm not all right, but I need time to think. Will you walk downstairs with me?"

Lee followed them to the door. He didn't try to hug Kyra even though she could see he wanted to. "Let me think about all this, Lee. I've seen two sides of you, and now I must decide how I feel about everything you said and if I believe you. Please don't get in touch with me for now." She walked away without looking back, but she knew he stood at the door until she entered the elevator with Trudy.

Kyra led Trudy to a quiet alcove in the lobby to talk to her for a few minutes. She told her about the attack at the library, and Trudy couldn't believe it.

"What sense does that make?" she wondered. "You've already told most people you'll be returning home soon and probably selling the house."

"I don't know. I guess someone wants to make sure I don't keep the house and come back on a regular basis. But why would it matter?" She rubbed her forehead as she added, "I tried calling Mr. Berchtold to see if he had any information about someone who wanted to buy my house, but no one answered at his home or the office. Then I called the real estate lady who had approached me, but she didn't want to say who the interested buyer was. When I asked if it was a lawyer, thinking about Peter Craig, she laughed and said no, it was actually a writer. Then she clammed up, realizing she shouldn't have said anything. That's what led me to confront Lee."

Trudy tapped her fingers on the arm of her chair before saying, "I understand why you're upset now, and you should take a night to think about everything. However, since you never knew until last month that Mary was your mother and Lee your father, nothing has really changed for you." When Kyra looked at her in surprise, Trudy frowned. "No, that came out wrong. What I meant was . . . before last month, you didn't know any of this, so your life was different. Your parents had passed away and you lived with your husband in Pittsburgh and you worked there. That was your life."

Kyra nodded. "True. So you're saying that finding out Mary was my mother and Lee my father is a bonus. It's something extra and I'm fortunate, but I shouldn't have any particular expectations."

Trudy thought for a moment and then smiled. "Yes, I think that's what I meant. Just remember that Lee is trying and he thought he was doing what was best for you. He's feeling his way in this new life, just like you are, and you must give him time to adapt."

Kyra studied the dusk that was quickly falling outside the windows and wasn't sure how to respond to Trudy. Finally, she said, "You're saying I have to be the bigger person and give Lee room to grow into our relationship. But I'm the daughter, and he's the reason I'm here. I think the ball should be in his court." When Trudy didn't say anything right away, Kyra sneaked a peek at her face. She was smiling. "All right. Fine. But I still need time to think about it. Maybe I'll call him tomorrow."

Trudy reached down and pulled Kyra up. "I know I've mentioned before that Mary was always so proud of you, but it's true. I'm only sorry I didn't make any effort to know you better when you visited every summer. But we're lucky and we still have time to enjoy each other's company." She pointed to the restaurant adjoining the hotel. "Now, how about dinner and a glass of wine? I'm starving."

Kyra allowed Trudy to convince her to stay for dinner and realized she hadn't eaten since breakfast. She toasted Trudy with a glass of sauvignon blanc and ate every bite of her chicken picatta. She didn't remember her fear of being attacked until they walked outside and started toward the parking lot. It was fully dark now and the lot only had intermittent lighting. When a middle-aged couple left the hotel behind them,

Trudy asked if they would watch and make sure she and Kyra got into their cars safely. The gray-haired man was glad to oblige.

When Kyra reached the house, she checked all around before pulling into the driveway. Because her house was directly under a street light, the driveway was well illuminated. She drove directly into the garage, closed the garage door quickly, and finally felt safe. She hated living in fear all the time, but she didn't want to keep relying on someone else, either. Since she had left in the daylight, she hurried into the kitchen and flicked on the lights. After checking the front and back doors and finding everything secure, she made a cup of tea and relaxed on the living room sofa.

Finally, she reached for her cell phone to call Brad because she didn't want to put it off any longer. Expecting him to answer immediately and ask why she hadn't called last night, she was surprised when the call went to voice mail. She shrugged, left a message, and finished sipping the last of her tea. Thinking Brad must have stepped outside or had gone to the bathroom, she waited for his return call. Leaning back, she closed her eyes and dozed off. Hours later, she awoke to the sounds of whining and scratching at her front door. She stumbled down the hall, turned on the porch light, and peered through the curtain beside the door.

At first she didn't see anything and then she realized she could see a brown tail flicking back and forth. Tex! She hurried to unlock the door and Tex immediately barked and danced around the porch. She noticed he looked like he'd been crawling through the bushes, but she didn't have time to check him out.

"What's up, Tex? Where's Sam?" At the sound of Sam's name, Tex barked louder and turned toward Sam's house.

Kyra hesitated before grabbing a flashlight out of the hall table drawer and following Tex, worried someone was trying to lure her away from the safety of the house. Tex's yips and cries convinced her something was drastically wrong, so she locked the door behind her and hurried after the dog. He ran into Sam's driveway and stood there, waiting for Kyra. She went to the front door and tried to open it, but it was locked. Banging on it, she called Sam's name, over and over. He didn't answer. Frustrated, she ran around to the back door and tried to open it, but she didn't have any luck there, either.

Tex ran to her, nipped her jeans and barked several times before running toward the front yard again. That's when she remembered the garage and hurried after Tex. As he barked at the garage door, she realized she could hear Sam's car running. Grabbing the garage door handle in the middle, she pulled with all her strength and the door slowly opened. When it reached waist level, she ducked under it with Tex at her side.

Using the flashlight to find the wall switch, she clicked it on and flooded the room with light. To her horror, she could see Sam slumped over the steering wheel. How long had he been sitting in the car with the engine running? Panicked, she pulled on the door handle, but it was locked. A quick tour of the car found all the doors locked. Calling Sam's name and banging on the window didn't awaken him. Then remembering the dangers of carbon monoxide poisoning, she grabbed the garage door again and yanked until it opened all the way. Fresh night air flooded in.

"Is everything okay?" someone called, and Kyra saw a dark form standing in the driveway. She gasped before realizing it was the teenager who lived across the street.

"Call 911 and tell them there's a case of carbon monoxide poisoning at Sam's address."

"On it!" he shouted and immediately whisked his cell phone to his ear.

Kyra hurried to Sam's tool chest and desperately tried to find something to break the car window. She needed something pointy to pound into the window, at least that's what she'd always read. When she found a screwdriver, she tried to smash the passenger side window, but at first nothing happened. The teenager joined her and said the police were on the way. Then he suggested forcing the screwdriver between the corner of the window and the door jamb and wiggling. Within a minute or two the window shattered, glass falling all over the floor.

Wrapping a cleaning rag on her hand, Kyra pushed broken glass aside and unlocked the doors before running around to the driver's side. The teenager followed and helped drag Sam out and laid him on the driveway. The sound of sirens pierced the air as a police car and an ambulance raced down the street and slammed to a stop in the driveway. The emergency technicians rushed to Kyra's side and then motioned her back so they could take over. Tex lay on the driveway whining with his nose touching Sam's head. When a policeman tried to push him away, Tex growled.

"Wait! Don't shove him away," Kyra said, her voice shaking. "He's the reason why I knew Sam was in trouble. I only hope I found him soon enough."

Kneeling down on the concrete, Kyra petted Tex and murmured soothing words. Finally, he allowed her to wrap an arm around him and move him back so the EMT's could do their work. The neighbor boy crouched down beside her and asked, "Is there anything else I can do? My name's Darren. My family only moved in here a few months ago."

"Hi, Darren. My name's Kyra, Kyra Martin. Thanks so much for your help tonight, but I don't think there's anything else you can do."

"Will Mr. Atkins be all right?"

The EMT's had brought out the gurney and loaded Sam onto it. He had an oxygen mask and an IV line connected to him. Kyra commanded Tex to stay and then she followed them to the ambulance. When she asked, they told her they were taking him to Stonecliff Community Hospital, and she said she'd follow them.

"Are you family?" The older tech studied her with sympathy. "It sounded like you were a neighbor when you talked to the policeman."

Kyra shook her head. "Not family, but we're close friends. I'll need to know how he's doing."

"I see. Look, why don't you let his next-of-kin know about his episode? Then they can keep you informed of his progress."

"Let's go!" shouted the other EMT and the man turned away from her, closed the back doors, and hopped into the driver's side of the ambulance. With a wail of sirens, they disappeared down the street.

Frustrated, Kyra looked at the young policeman still standing in the driveway. "I don't know any of Sam's family members. He's never talked about them in all the years I've known him."

The cop shook his head. "When he regains consciousness, then he can explain everything and you'll be allowed to visit. In the meantime, could you give me a brief rundown of what happened this evening?"

"Should I stay?" Darren asked, his voice hopeful.

"No need. Just give me your name and phone number and we'll be in touch tomorrow. Then you can go home."

Kyra thanked him again and then responded to the policeman's questions. Before the policeman accompanied her to her door, he looked down at Tex. "What about the dog?" he asked.

"Oh, Tex will come home with me. He's the hero of the evening. I'll set him up in the kitchen with an old blanket and a water bowl."

Exhausted as she was, Kyra took a few minutes to pet Tex and murmur promises to him that he'd see Sam soon. When he settled down on the old blanket, she dragged herself upstairs to bed. Before she could get comfortable, though, her cell phone trilled. It was Brad. Sighing, she picked up just as Tex began barking.

"Kyra, is that a dog? Why is Sam at your house at this time of night?"

CHAPTER 23

Brad's anger throbbed through the telephone wires. Kyra hurried to explain how Sam had nearly died and probably would have if Tex hadn't come to Kyra's door.

"That damn dog! He causes more trouble!"

"Brad! What are you talking about? He was the hero of the hour." Kyra couldn't understand his fixation on hating dogs.

He still insisted she get rid of the dog, but she wasn't going to abandon Tex now. Finally, she explained it would only be temporary and she was too tired to argue. When he hung up on her, she was surprised, but relieved.

With her thoughts in so much turmoil trying to figure out what had happened to Sam, and why Lee felt the need to buy her house rather than simply introducing himself to her, she didn't have much energy left over for Brad. Just because he'd been bitten by a dog when he was a child didn't mean every dog was dangerous. Besides, she felt safer with Tex guarding the house tonight. Thoughts continued whirling around in her brain, but sometime after two in the morning, she fell asleep. She didn't awaken until light hit her eyes from the open curtains and she heard a woofing from downstairs.

Sitting up in alarm, she realized it was Tex. He must be hinting he'd like to go out, but didn't want to break into a full-throated bark. Kyra pulled on shorts and a baggy t-shirt and hurried downstairs. Tex sat by the back door and turned to give her a baleful look, but couldn't stop his tail from wagging. She patted his head and opened the door. He flew outside and hurried over to the oak tree and lifted his leg. Kyra thought that was a great idea and sped back upstairs to the bathroom. Afterwards, she grabbed a quick shower and dressed before sharing her breakfast of scrambled eggs and ham with Tex.

When she called the hospital, they said Sam was still in ICU, but wouldn't give her any details. Frustrated, she got ready to leave and saw the crime scene tape was up around Sam's garage, with a van parked in the driveway. She knew it was no use asking questions, so she drove to the hospital after assuring Tex he'd be fine staying at her house for a day or two.

At the hospital, Kyra was greeted with the good news that Sam was alert and had been moved to a regular room. The police were questioning him now, but if she waited, she'd probably be able to talk to him soon. Following the nurse's directions, she found the waiting room and poured herself another cup of coffee from the complementary stand. It didn't taste great, but it was hot and warmed her in the overly air-conditioned hospital. She glanced furtively at the other people sitting around the room, imagining what health problems their loved ones had to cause the worried look on their faces.

"Ms. Martin!" a voice boomed, and Kyra immediately recognized the voice. Detective Andrews stood beckoning to her in the hallway. Everyone else glanced up, too, but when they saw it wasn't a doctor, they turned away in disappointment. "Could you please step over here for a few minutes?"

Sighing, Kyra got up and followed him down the hall. "I came here to talk to Sam, Detective, so please ask what you want and let me go."

He motioned her into an alcove leading to a storage closet, and asked, "Are you okay? I was worried you saw something last night that might put you in danger. Sam says he has a hazy memory of someone hitting him on the head, and he's darn sure he didn't try to kill himself. His words, exactly."

"That sounds like Sam," Kyra said, a half-smile forming on her lips before she got serious. "I don't think he tried to commit suicide, either! I'm guessing he was attacked and left to die in that car. Tex was frantic to get help and barked loudly at my door, and I ran over to see what the problem was. It's a good thing, too, but in hindsight I realize I could have been in danger."

Detective Andrews paused until a nurse walked by before saying, "If Sam is telling the truth, then the problem now is that you saved Sam. Whoever tried to make sure Sam died won't be particularly happy with you."

"But why Sam?" Kyra frowned. "What does he have to do with anything?"

"Maybe he knows something about Mary he's not telling anyone. Some secret that the killer doesn't want anyone to know."

Kyra shook her head before murmuring, "But again that doesn't make any sense. Sam's lived there all this time without anyone trying to kill him. No, everything started after Mary died."

He stared at Kyra and then slowly nodded. "You're right, but we're still in the dark about what changed at her death. I think we need to see her attorney and review her will. Did she leave all her money and property to you? Did Sam get something? Maybe something you didn't realize was worth money?"

"The money and house went to me." She put her hand up. "And before you ask, no, there's not much money. After probate, it will probably be about $25,000." She hesitated, trying to think of reasons for the attack on Sam, and then added, "Maybe the killer didn't like Sam and Tex helping me out? He figured that if they weren't around to help, maybe I'd go home and he could get into the house. Only I don't know why the house is so important."

"Possibly, but it could still mean you're in some kind of danger and we don't know why. I think the safest thing to do is get out of your house. How about moving into the hotel where Lee Napoli is staying?"

"No, I don't think so. Not right now."

Her tone of voice made the detective stare at her. "Why? What's going on? Do you suspect him?"

"No, no, it's not that. It's personal; it doesn't have anything to do with him being dangerous."

When his eyebrow quirked up, she shook her head. "And, no, I'm not explaining myself. Besides, tomorrow is Friday and my husband will be here for the weekend." She sighed, murmuring, "Although that will open another whole can of worms."

He opened his mouth to ask, and again she shook her head. "It's none of your business. Now I need to talk to Sam and I think we've discussed enough for now."

As she turned to walk away, he placed a hand on her arm. "I hope you realize you can't leave town when we're in the middle of an investigation."

Kyra knew he said that to irritate her, but she just smiled. "Good. That's the excuse I'll use when my husband expects me to go home this weekend." She strode away, imagining the look of surprise on his face.

When she entered Sam's room, he was lying in a semi-reclined position, his eyes closed, with an oxygen mask on his face. She stood still for a moment, wondering if she should wake him or not, but then he blinked and waved to her.

"Oh, Sam, I was so worried about you." She moved closer and patted his arm that didn't have an IV in it. "I'm just glad Tex came and got me when he did. He's the one who saved you."

He pushed himself up higher, holding the mask away from his face. "Is Tex all right?"

"He's fine and he's hanging out at my house right now. Your garage and house are off limits while the crime scene investigators finish up. Do you remember what happened to you?" Kyra hesitated, not sure how much she should question Sam. "You don't have to talk about it if you don't want to. I'm sure the police have badgered you enough earlier. I saw Detective Andrews on my way in here."

Sam leaned back and then pointed to the chair next to the bed. At her frown as he pushed the mask aside again, he said, "It's okay. They said my oxygen is almost back to normal, thanks to you finding me so quickly. My memory has slowly returned, too."

He recounted how he'd heard Tex growling around nine last night at the kitchen door. When he opened the door to let him out, Tex had taken off into the backyard, barking. Suddenly, Tex yelped and stopped barking and Sam stepped out onto the patio. He heard a movement behind him and then he was hit on the back of the head. The next thing he knew, he'd woken up in an ambulance with a headache and feeling rather nauseated, with the oxygen mask on his face.

Kyra then told him her side of the story and said how thankful she was that Tex had come to her door. "Even Darren across the street played a role in helping to save you," she added. "Thank goodness for kids and their smartphones. He called 911 in record time, and he even told me the best way to break your car window."

"Break my car window!" Sam looked outraged for a moment and then frowned. "Oh, I forget that they said I was locked inside my car."

Placing the oxygen mask over his face again, he lay back against the pillows. He winced and then rubbed the back of his head.

"Is that where you were hit?" Kyra asked.

"Yep, got a big goose egg there, but no bleeding. The doc said I must have a hard head."

They laughed as the door opened and a middle-aged woman in a lab coat entered. Anita Foley, M.D. was stitched above the pocket.

"Good to see you smiling, Mr. Atkins. Feeling better now?"

Kyra slipped out the door, saying she needed a cup of coffee and she'd be right back. She stared up and down the hallways, wondering if Sam was safe, even here in the hospital. If someone had tried to kill him last night, what was to stop him now? Frowning, she realized Sam's room was right in the middle of the hall with the nurse's desk on one end and the door to the stairs on the other end. Not good. She'd seen plenty of television shows where the killer wore a doctor or nurse's uniform and walked into the victim's room without anyone noticing. Until it was too late.

Just like Sam's doctor right now. What if? Halfway to the nurse's station, she veered around and returned to Sam's room. Without knocking, she entered and saw the doctor checking Sam's eyes with a small flashlight.

"Forget something?" she asked, smiling, and Kyra felt like a fool.

"I . . . um . . . thought I dropped my keys." She looked around the floor briefly and then touched the outer pocket on her purse. "Oh, sorry, here they are."

The doctor clicked off the light and nodded to Sam. "Everything looks good, and we'll just keep that oxygen on for another hour or two. You were an extremely lucky man, and it sounds like your dog deserves some special doggy treats when you go home tomorrow."

After the doctor left, Kyra stayed for a while longer until she could see Sam was fighting to keep his eyes open. "Time for your nap," she said. "I'll stop on the way home and pick up some dog food for Tex. Just tell me what kind you buy." She leaned over to kiss his cheek, and he caught her arm and pulled her down for a hug.

"Promise me you'll be careful, Kyra. If Tex acts funny about anything, call that police detective and get help. Don't do any exploring on your own."

He wouldn't release her until she promised. Walking away, she felt fear crowding out all her other emotions. Danger surrounded her, and after all these incidents, she still didn't know where it was coming from. She made sure to check all around her on the way to the parking lot, and then she looked under her car before getting inside. Following the same procedure at the grocery store, she finally drove home.

Her spirits lifted when Tex greeted her enthusiastically at the door. He sniffed her hands when she petted him, and she thought he picked up Sam's scent because he whined a little and tried to crawl into her lap. Laughing, she pushed him away and filled up the dog bowl she'd bought at the store along with his favorite dog food. Distracted, he began to crunch noisily. When Kyra glanced at the calendar on the wall, she thought about Brad coming tomorrow and how he'd assume she'd be going home with him this weekend.

That's if he even wanted her to come home again. And if she ever wanted to go home with him again. She sighed, wondering what had happened to her marriage. She knew Mary hadn't cared for Brad, but she'd never told Kyra that. She insisted Kyra needed to make up her own mind, and at the time Brad was everything she wanted. He brought her flowers, complimented her looks, and took her dinner and plays and symphonies. He expected sex sooner than she wanted, but when she finally agreed, he usually made sure she found the experience enjoyable. Looking back, though, she realized he had asked odd questions about her early life and her unusual closeness to her "Aunt" Mary. She thought maybe he was jealous of their relationship, although he always acted respectful to Mary when they were all together. Or was it all an act?

Her thoughts were interrupted when the doorbell rang. She looked out the peephole and was surprised to see Lee standing at the door. He held a small case in one hand and flowers in the other. Despite the way they had parted, she found she was glad to see him.

She opened the door and he immediately said, "Kyra, I know you told me to wait for you to get in touch with me, but I think it's important for us to talk. May I come in?" Tex appeared at her feet and woofed to show he was guarding Kyra. "I'm sorry. Is this a bad time?"

"No, it's fine, Lee. Come in and I'll explain why Tex is here."

Lee handed her the colorful bouquet of pink and red carnations with yellow daisies.

"Thanks. They're beautiful and I love the scent of carnations. I certainly needed something to brighten my day." She gave him a quick peck on the cheek. "Come into the kitchen while I find a vase."

He followed her, taking a seat at the table and setting the case down on top of it. As Kyra snipped the stems of the flowers and filled the vase with water, she gave Lee a quick rundown of the events from the previous night.

"Sam's lucky his dog knew to get your attention," Lee murmured. "And fortunate that you went to see what was wrong. But, Kyra, it could have been dangerous for you if the person who tried to kill Sam was hanging around waiting to make sure Sam died."

Kyra carried the flowers over to the table and set them in the center.

"I guess I didn't have time to think about that because Tex was frantic, and I knew something was terribly wrong. But if it makes you feel any better, I'll try to be more careful from now on." Kyra studied Lee's worried face. "Would you like to tell me why you found it necessary to come and see me this evening?"

"Because I have another confession to make." He sighed heavily before continuing, "I stole my letters to Mary that night I stayed here. I found them in her little desk upstairs and didn't want you to read them." He frowned and shook his head. "I was embarrassed by some of the things I said over the years when Mary suggested we get together permanently. I thought our occasional visits were enough, and we were happy without making any commitment." He shifted uncomfortably on the kitchen chair and placed his hand on the case. "Rereading some of my letters, I realized I sounded like a selfish old fool." He looked up at her. "And I didn't want you to know me that way."

"I see." She hesitated before adding, "You missed something in the desk when you took the letters." She hurried to the den to get her purse, and then sat down across from him. Taking out the photo, she set it on the table without saying anything.

Lee leaned over to study it. Sucking in his breath, he touched Mary's face with one finger. "We were so young," he whispered. "So young and so very much in love. We thought nothing could come between us, and then Jasper Owens claimed Mary for his own and threatened to kill me." Kyra saw his eyes sheen over with tears. "Mary was the strong one, and she said I had to go away; that my life meant more to her than the brief happiness she'd have before I was lost to her forever." He reached for Kyra's hands. "Your mother was the strongest woman I ever knew. Do you believe she was on cloud nine when she found out she was pregnant at forty-eight? Even when she knew she'd let her brother adopt you, she felt honored to give you life."

Kyra felt the tears gather in her eyes, and she squeezed Lee's hands. "Thanks for telling me. You showed me a side of Mary I never knew; I only knew the happy woman who loved having me to visit every summer. She kept our days busy with projects to do and places for us to explore. She filled a part of my life that would have been so empty after my mother died. I only wish she'd told me a little sooner about being my real mother."

"Don't!" Lee shook his head. "For whatever reason, it was the right time when you learned after her death, and why you found that note from her when you did."

Kyra brushed the tears from her eyes and said, "And now where do we stand? Two people who have lost the person who was the vital link in our relationship?"

"Right here." Lee pointed to his bag and dumped it out. "I'm sorry that I only have the last letter Mary sent to me. I usually kept one until I received the next one before throwing them away." He shook his head. "Didn't want to be considered a sentimental old fool."

Kyra looked at the letters tumbled across the table, before glancing back up at Lee. "I don't know. Maybe I should allow you to keep your privacy. They were never meant for anyone to read but Mary."

Lee reached across the table and touched her hand. "Please consider it. The letters reveal my relationship with Mary, but also who I am. What things I enjoy, my home in Italy, the ideas for my books. I hope they will allow you to see me as Leonardo Napoli, the man who loved Mary Wyndham and fathered a daughter whom he would like to get to know better."

Kyra nodded slowly, not sure how she felt about his request.

"And I would never have bought this house and taken it away from you. I was told that you had every intention of moving back to Pittsburgh, and you'd be thrilled to make a quick sale at such a high price."

Kyra's head jerked up. "Who told you that?"

"It was Peter Craig, the young lawyer who worked for Simon Berchtold, the one who was murdered. I was quite angry with him when

I discovered he'd given me the wrong information about you, but I still can't imagine why that detective thought I wanted to kill him."

Kyra rolled her eyes. "Oh, that detective suspects everyone, so join the crowd." She rubbed her forehead as she tried to work out why Peter would have said such a thing. "It just doesn't make sense, though, since I never spoke to Peter on my visits to Mr. Berchtold." Frowning, she added, "I guess he could have known all about Mary's will because he worked in the office, but I don't see why he would think I wanted to sell the house quickly."

"From what I've been hearing from Trudy, the young man wasn't reliable. Even his grandfather left his fortune to the library and not to Peter." Lee leaned back and gazed thoughtfully at Kyra. "Now if I were writing a book about Peter, I'd say he talked the real estate lady into sharing her commission with him if he could guarantee a quick sale without any fuss."

Kyra nodded. "You could be right." She told Lee about how he showed up one night to say he had forms she needed to fill out, and then asked numerous questions about the skeleton in the basement. "He probably thought he'd get the scoop and then sell his story to the papers. He was looking for ways to get money quick."

"Hmm. That could be the reason he ended up dead, too." At Kyra's startled look, he continued, "If he was studying Simon's clients and finding their weaknesses, he might have tried some blackmail. Sooner or later, a blackmail victim decided to strike back."

Tex suddenly uncurled from his blanket in the corner and slunk over to the door. He growled low in his throat. Kyra jumped up and Lee reached over and turned off the lights. At the same time, Kyra heard the window shatter, a whistling sound, and then something thwacked into the wall behind her.

CHAPTER 24

"**G**et down!" Lee shouted and Kyra hit the floor.

More glass shattered and Kyra crawled under the table. Tex barked and hurled himself against the back door as Lee held onto Kyra's arm.

"Here, take my cell phone and dial 911! I'll open the door and let Tex out."

"No!" screamed Kyra. "He'll get shot. Or that maniac will get in. Wait till I call the police." She frantically dialed and shouted that she was being shot at, stumbling over her address when she almost gave her Pittsburgh street number. Assured help was on the way, Kyra agreed to stay on the line. Suddenly, she realized the shots had stopped, and Tex had reverted to low growls again.

"Maybe it's over," she whispered, but Lee shook his head.

"I'm afraid he's just regrouping. Let's move into the hallway away from the windows."

Kyra snagged her purse from the table as she called softly for Tex to come with them.

He hesitated and then reluctantly followed.

"You don't happen to have any guns in the house?" Lee asked, looking down at Kyra, but she shook her head. "Everyone in the neighborhood must have heard those shots and called the police, so we just have to stay safe for a few more minutes."

Although dusk had come, it wasn't yet fully dark. When Kyra thought she saw a shadow outside the kitchen door, she held the phone against her ear and whispered, "How long? Someone's near the back door."

"Two minutes, ma'am. If you can, lock yourself in a room and bar the door."

The glass in the door window shattered, and Lee grabbed Kyra and pulled her toward the front door. She held onto Tex's collar and yanked him along with her.

They stumbled into the living room, but Kyra couldn't hold Tex back. He sprinted back down the hall as Lee grasped her arm and wouldn't let her chase after him.

"It's too dangerous," he whispered in her ear. "Get behind the sofa and stay there. I'll see if it's safe to go out the front door." He moved away from her just as another shot rang out.

Tex immediately stopped barking. In the sudden silence, Kyra screamed, "No!" She dropped the phone and jumped up to run to the kitchen, but Lee reached out and pushed her back behind the sofa.

"Wait! We don't know where the shooter is."

Kyra tried to control her sobs, knowing they could be in terrible danger any second. That's when she realized the sound of sirens had increased in volume, and she heard several vehicles squeal to a stop in front of the house.

The thought of Tex being killed nearly drove her crazy, and all she could think of was how Brad swore he'd kill that dog the next time he found him in the house. She fumbled around on the floor until she found Lee's phone again. If he answered, she could be pretty sure Brad had nothing to do with tonight's shooting. However, the phone rang and rang and then went to voice mail.

Turning toward Lee, she mumbled, "I'm afraid it's Brad."

"What? Your husband? Why in the world would he want to shoot at us?"

"Because he hates Tex, and he said he'd kill him the next time he saw him in this house."

"But . . ."

Shaking her head, Kyra hurried into the hall as they heard pounding on the front door and the shout of "Police!"

"I know; it's crazy. But whoever it was, he's gone. I've got to see if Tex is still alive."

"Wait until we're sure it's safe," Lee said, heading toward the door, but Kyra heard a whimpering sound.

She raced to the kitchen and saw Tex lying next to the table with a trail of blood behind him. Dropping to her knees, she tried to turn him over, but he growled deep in his throat.

A policeman appeared at the back door and called through the broken window, "Are you folks all right?"

"We're fine," she said. "But the dog was shot. He needs help."

Kyra crouched beside Tex, petting him, even when Lee joined her with another policeman behind him. She was glad Tex kept looking at her as if understanding she'd make sure he was okay. She prayed his faith in her would be rewarded.

Many hours later, Kyra found herself standing in the hotel room next to Lee's. The police had made her home a crime scene and only allowed her to gather her belongings for the next couple days, including her laptop and Lee's letters. Tex had been transported to the local veterinary office, and the doctor had extracted a bullet from his back leg, giving Kyra a positive report for his recovery. After giving their separate statements about the incident to the police, Lee had taken her back to the hotel, and luckily he'd been able to secure this room.

Kyra thought about calling Sam, but decided it was too late to phone a patient's room at the hospital. Then she looked longingly at the bed, but she needed to do one thing first. After setting the case of letters down on the table, she searched through all the envelopes until she found Mary's last letter to Lee. It was dated May 15. She looked away for a moment before she slowly opened it and took the letter out. Taking a deep breath, she read:

Dearest Lee,

I can't believe you've made the decision to return home after all these years. I know it wasn't easy for you because Italy had cast a spell on you for so long. Will you still continue to write your Italian detective stories? Or have you decided on a new character from somewhere in the States?

I can't wait to see you and I hope you still agree with me that it's time for us to talk to Kyra and let her know that you and I are her biological parents. Occasionally, I think she suspects something, but she's never said anything to me. We also need to tell her our history and why we made the choices we did, for right or wrong. I just hope the bond of love between me and Kyra isn't destroyed because of the truth. And I hesitate to say this, but I'm also worried about the bond of love between me and you. I can't believe that at my age I still long to hold you in my arms just like I did all those years ago when we were in the first flush of love.

Kyra looked up and wiped the tears from her eyes. Knowing that Mary never had the chance to hold Lee again almost made her shove the letter back in the case. Mary had gone on with her life for many years without living with her lover, and yet she always showed a contented face to the world. Looking back, Kyra realized Mary had treated her like a beloved daughter and Kyra had taken her for granted. Sighing, she steeled herself to finish reading the letter.

Sometimes I worry that we've waited until too late to have this reunion. I've noticed a few heart palpitations lately, but it's probably all my excitement about you coming home for good. I guess it's the worries of an old woman, but just in case, please know that my love for you and Kyra has filled my soul for years. It sustained me and brought joy to my every waking moment.

With all my love,
Mary

For a long time, Kyra sat holding the letter tightly in her hand as she let the tears fall. The sadness competed with her own joy in knowing that Mary hadn't just acted happy, but she truly was happy. That knowledge filled her with a strength of purpose, and she determined that it was time for her to find her own happiness. But first, she had to solve the mystery of why Mary's death had started the domino effect of criminal activities and murders.

Exhausted, she looked at the double bed with the blankets turned back invitingly and realized how tired she was. After setting the letter on the bedside stand, she reached over to turn off the light, and then hesitated. She didn't think she could lie in the dark as thoughts of a gunman haunted her thoughts. With the bedside lamp on, she slid into the bed and stared around the room. Forcing her eyes closed, she finally drifted into a restless sleep. When she awoke to bright sunlight, she stared in puzzlement at her surroundings. Then memory returned, and she sat upright. The letter still sat next to the bed, and she reached out and touched it before swinging her legs over the side of the bed.

Glad to be awake after a night of frightening dreams, she knew she had a list of things to do, but first she needed a shower and several cups of coffee. When her cell phone rang, she saw the call was from Lee. After she assured him he hadn't woken her up, she agreed to have breakfast in his room in twenty minutes. She inhaled the scent of fresh coffee the minute Lee opened the door, and it magnetically pulled her toward the breakfast laid out on the table.

After eating bagels and cream cheese with several cups of coffee, Kyra and Lee were ready to get down to business. First, Kyra told Lee she'd read Mary's last letter to him and how much it had affected her. Mary had found ways to be happy with limited access to her lover and daughter and enjoyed her life. When Lee tried to say how sorry he was, Kyra stopped him.

"No, Mary made her choices, moved on, and still found joy. We must honor her and do the same things." Kyra sighed. "That brings me to my second point: my husband. I don't want to go into details, but we've been having problems. Last night when Tex was shot, I thought it had to be Brad because he hates dogs. When we talked on the phone the night before, he heard Tex bark and got so angry. He wanted me to get rid of Tex, just because he was bitten as a child. But I must be crazy. Even if we're not getting along, I can't imagine he'd actually shoot at us. I just kept remembering how he hated dogs." She stared out the window blankly. "But I will have to call him today and explain that the police won't let me come home this weekend. He's not going to be happy."

Lee cleared his throat. "It seems to me if your husband cared about you at all, he'd hurry to your side right now. He wouldn't leave until this mystery was solved and he knew you were safe."

Kyra shifted her gaze back to Lee. "I know," she murmured. "So that means something is terribly wrong with our relationship. Brad was so caring and couldn't wait until we got married, but when we did, he seemed more interested in my family history and Mary's relationship to me. I never understood what was so important about Mary being my aunt. And he hated the idea that I wanted to be a writer."

"That's odd." Lee hesitated. "Did it ever occur to you that he found out somehow that Mary was your mother and I was your father?"

Before Kyra could reply, her cell phone rang. Glancing down, she saw that it was Stonecliff Community Hospital. She quickly answered. "Hello?"

"Hi Kyra, it's Sam. I don't seem to have my cell phone with me so I'm using the hospital's phone. I hate to bother you, but the doctor said I could go home today. Is there any chance you could come and pick me up?"

"Oh, Sam, of course. I'll be there in half an hour."

"Don't hurry. Just come when you can."

"Look, Sam, I'm not sure you can get into your house yet. And there's a problem with my home, too. It's possible you might have to stay in the hotel tonight."

Kyra tried to stem Sam's questions by saying, "Wait until I get there to explain. I'll see you shortly."

"He can stay with me," Lee said. "So maybe I should go with you."

After Kyra passed on Lee's offer to Sam, her phone rang again. It was Detective Andrews asking if she could stop at the police station. Sighing, she replied that she needed to pick up Sam at the hospital and take him to the hotel first.

"Hmm." Kyra could picture the detective's frown just from that one word. "All right. But I'll expect you at my office as soon as possible."

Shaking her head, Kyra said, "That detective is going to drive me crazy." She reached for her purse and motioned to Lee. "In the meantime, let's go get Sam, and then you can set him up in your room for the night. With any luck, we'll both be able to return home tomorrow."

On the way to the hospital, Lee tried to convince Kyra to stay in the hotel for safety until that maniac was caught.

"Brad should be here tonight," she said. "So I'll need to fill him in on everything that's happening. I'm sure he'll want to prove he can take care of me."

Lee gave her a look of disbelief, but he didn't say anything more. Kyra kept thinking about how Brad would hate staying in a hotel room right next to Lee and Sam. He'd probably want to move back to the house tonight, broken windows and all. With any luck, the police would keep the house off-limits for the entire weekend.

By the time they collected Sam, got him installed in Lee's room, and explained the latest happenings, he was ready for a nap again. Kyra left, saying she had to drive to the police station. Once she got back in the car, though, she thought about Sam's worrying over Tex's health. She decided she'd stop at the vet's and get a firsthand report for Sam, and on her way she'd check and see if the police had finished collecting evidence from her house.

The police tape was still up, but Sam's house and garage were clear. Since Sam was exhausted, he had planned on staying at the hotel tonight. Maybe she could run in and pick up a change of clothes for him. He'd told her before about the key hidden under the oblong rock in the back corner of his patio, and there it was. Still, she felt like a housebreaker as she fitted the key into the lock and slipped into the kitchen. Sam's bedroom was the first room on the right upstairs, and she opened several drawers before finding a brown t-shirt, jeans, and pajamas. Feeling awkward, she snatched up underwear and clean socks. She hoped Sam didn't mind. Biting her lip, she wondered about a carryall of some kind, and finally spotted a gym bag on the top shelf of the closet. She stopped at the small bathroom and added a toothbrush, comb, and shaver.

Downstairs again, she peeked into the living room before leaving. She hadn't been in there for several years, and she was surprised to see the variety of knick-knacks on his mantel. Moving into the room, she sucked in her breath. Sitting in the back row behind several colorful bowls were two of Aunt Mary's favorite statues she'd brought home from Rome. One was the Tivoli Fountain and the other Romulus and Remus, the founders of Rome. They weren't worth much money, just sentimental value. She couldn't remember when she'd last seen them, but she supposed Mary could have given them to him. A little puzzled, she let herself out of the house and replaced the key.

Back in the car, she decided to call Brad before stopping at the veterinary clinic. He'd be leaving work soon, and she didn't want him driving straight to Mary's house. When he didn't answer his cell phone, she called his direct line at work. He didn't pick up there, either. Frowning, she dropped her phone back in her purse and backed out of the driveway. She'd try him again shortly, and if he didn't answer then, she'd leave a message.

At the vet's office, the young girl at the desk offered to take Kyra to the back to visit Tex. He thumped his tail upon seeing Kyra and tried to stand up. She hurried over to pet him while the doctor gave her a quick rundown on his care. When she explained his owner had been released from the hospital, Dr. Sturgess said Tex would be ready to go home in about two days.

"Sam will be so glad to hear that news," she said.

When she finally made it to the police station, she ran into Detective Andrews in the lobby.

"Well, it's about time!" he said. "Follow me." He reached his office and gestured for her to precede him.

She ignored his brusque manner and moved to the first chair and sat down. "Hello to you, too."

"Forgive me for being worried, but I expected you here quite a while ago."

Calmly, she set her purse on floor and sat back with her hands folded in front of her before looking toward him.

He settled behind the desk and asked, "How much do you trust Simon Berchtold?"

That got her attention. "What do you mean? He was Mary's lawyer and took care of her will. I assume he did a good job, but I don't know anything about law offices."

"But you didn't feel anything off about the will or that he might be lying to you in any way?"

Kyra took a moment to think back over the times she had met with Mr. Berchtold, but couldn't put her finger on anything specific. "No, I don't think so, but I didn't like Peter Craig, and I thought he had some agenda of his own."

"Yes, you mentioned how Peter came to your house trying to find out more about the skeleton in the basement. Were you frightened?"

"No, I don't think so. More like annoyed. I did call Mr. Berchtold to complain about Peter being unprofessional."

"I'm sure Peter didn't appreciate that. Did you ever see him afterwards?" When she shook her head, he asked, "When was the last time you spoke to Mr. Berchtold?"

"I'm not sure. I know I called his home after you picked up Lee because I thought he might need a lawyer. So I guess that was last Sunday, but a woman answered and said he couldn't come to the phone. Of course, at that point, I didn't know Peter was dead."

"And no contact since then?"

"No. Why does it matter?"

"Because the coroner is releasing Peter's body to his family, and we haven't been able to contact Simon Berchtold at his home or office."

"Oh, that is odd," she said. "I think Peter has family elsewhere, though. His complete name is Peter Craig Cartwright, you know. He must have other relatives in the Cartwright family."

"That's the information we had. We finally tracked down his father, Gerald Cartwright, who lives in upstate New York in a nursing home. He said Mr. Berchtold, his brother-in-law, had informed him of his son's death, but he had no money for Peter's burial. What money he has from his father pays for the nursing home and a few other small items, but he lost all his money gambling years ago."

"How terrible. It sounds like Peter's background made him easy prey to someone with get-rich-quick schemes."

"It also means Mr. Berchtold might have discovered Peter's misuse of clients' money or information after his death. He could be frantically trying to review the damage and protect himself before it becomes common knowledge." Detective Andrews shuffled some papers on his desk, tamped them straight, and lay them back down again. "I've sent detectives to Mr. Berchtold's home and office because we need to interview him."

Kyra shifted in her seat and then asked if Mr. Berchtold had suddenly become the prime suspect in Peter's murder.

"All we want to do is talk to him right now, so don't go spreading rumors." He assumed a bland expression, and Kyra knew it was his professional policeman look.

"Of course not!" She hesitated before adding, "But even if he did fight with Peter, I can't picture him as the man who shot into my kitchen windows last night and tried to kill Tex. Why would he do that?"

Instead of answering, Detective Andrews just stood up and said, "I want to thank you for coming in today and giving me the information I requested. I hope you'll stay in the hotel for now until we can clear up this matter." He walked over and opened his door.

Kyra had a million other questions, but understood she wouldn't be getting any more answers at this time.

"My husband will be joining me this evening, so we may decide to move back to the house tomorrow; that is, if the forensic team is finished."

"I'll let you know," he said, frowning. "It might still be safer—"

"Thanks." She quickly walked away from him down the hallway, thinking it was good to get in the last word. She knew he was right, but she hated to allow herself to be frightened by some unknown crazy person.

As she drove back to the hotel through what passed for Stonecliff's afternoon rush hour, she realized she didn't believe any of these attacks came from a deranged individual. There had to be a definite plan, if she could only unravel the logical reasons, or at least logical to the perpetrator. If Peter had been working with someone else, Kyra found it hard to believe it was Mr. Berchtold. She decided to use the internet and see if she could find out more about Peter's background when she got back to the hotel.

Hearing only silence when she knocked on Lee's door, she slipped into her room and booted up her laptop. In minutes she was scrolling down the information on Peter's mother, Donna Larson Cartwright, who sometimes worked for the Cartwright Foundation fundraising activities, and his father, Gerald Cartwright, the former CEO of Cartwright Investments, and then Peter's birth records. Peter had been a star soccer player at his prep school. After his high school graduation, he had moved around to several colleges, finally getting a business degree from Jackson University. He managed to squeak by and get into law school, but never passed the bar.

Frowning, Kyra felt like the name Jackson University sounded familiar, but she couldn't remember why. Then it came to her; Brad had gone to Jackson before moving to New York and graduating from NYU a year later. She'd have to ask Brad if he'd ever met Peter, although she would imagine the school was so large that it wasn't likely. Thinking of Brad, she tried to call his cell again, and this time he answered.

"Why didn't you answer when I called earlier?" she asked.

"Sorry," he replied. "It's been crazy at the office today."

"So crazy you couldn't even pick up the phone on your desk?"

"What are you talking about, Kyra? Why the third degree? I happen to work every day and can't just have a friendly chat whenever I feel like it."

Kyra took a deep breath and decided to drop it. "Okay, forget it. Do you know what time you'll get into Stonecliff? There was a problem at the house yesterday and I'm at the Four Seasons Hotel in town."

The other end of the line went quiet, and Kyra wondered if Brad had moved into a dead zone. Finally, he said, "*Another* problem? And is that the hotel where your famous writer father is staying?"

Kyra sighed and responded, "Yes to both questions. Anything else?"

"What kind of problem?"

"I thought I'd order a dinner for us when you get here, and I'd explain everything while we're eating."

"Forget it. Why don't I just wait and come tomorrow if we can get into the house then. That way we can pack up your things and leave early Sunday morning."

By the time Kyra explained she was under police orders to stay in town until the attack at her house reached some resolution, Brad was furious again. Somehow, though, she felt as if he already knew about the problem and was acting the role of the exasperated husband.

"Who called you with the news?" she demanded.

"What? I don't know what you're talking about." He took a deep breath. "You need to come home, Kyra, or you're going to lose your job. Or don't you care?" When she didn't respond right away, he murmured, "Oh, I see. You never had any intention of coming back home."

"Brad," she began, but he cut her off.

"Well, I'll never agree to a divorce. Not now, not when everything is so close I can almost taste it. You're stuck with me, babe." And with that surprising statement, Brad disconnected.

CHAPTER 25

Kyra set her cell phone down on the table, puzzled and rather annoyed. As usual, Brad didn't actually listen to what she was telling him, and instead put his own spin on her words. Why did he claim he'd never leave her? Was it because he truly loved her or was it because he didn't want to be shown as a man who couldn't keep a woman?

To avoid further thoughts about Brad, Kyra scanned through her documents on her laptop and opened her book. Rereading the last chapter, she found she had left Jennie's lover, Dan, at the point where he discovers messages from his father on her email account. Assuming Jennie is two-timing him with his estranged father, he plans to murder the man. Jennie had met Colin at the library where she worked and accidentally found out he was Dan's father. Colin convinced her to act as a go-between to reunite him with his son he hadn't seen in twenty years. To her horror, she discovered that Colin just wanted Dan's property to sell to developers to make millions, and he was willing to do anything to get it.

With her fingers tapping away, Kyra found herself engrossed in Jennie's desperate attempts to stop Dan and Colin from killing each other. Two hours later, she realized she was starving and she'd never heard from Lee or Sam. Worried, she shut down her laptop and called

Lee's cell. When he didn't answer, she hurried over and knocked on the door again. *Now where did they go?* She didn't know if she should panic or not. Deciding they would probably be safe if they were together, she took the elevator down to the lobby to check if anyone at the front desk had seen Mr. Napoli leave the hotel.

She lucked out because the young man clicking away at the computer at the desk nodded immediately when she asked.

"Mr. Napoli and another man left the hotel a couple hours ago. I only noticed because the lady checking in asked if that was the man who wrote those detective novels. She was excited to hear he was staying here and wondered if she'd be able to get his autograph." When he saw Kyra's worried look, he hastened to add, "I didn't give out any personal information on Mr. Napoli."

"No, of course not. Thanks for your help." Kyra smiled at him before walking outside and looking toward the parking lot. Frustrated, she pulled out her phone and called Trudy, who answered on the first ring.

"Kyra, I'm so glad you called. I heard about Sam and the attack at your house. How are you?"

"Trudy, I'm so sorry I didn't call sooner. Right now I need some company. Could you meet me at the Four Seasons Hotel for dinner?"

"Yes, that sounds great. In about forty-five minutes?"

Later, when they were settled in their booth and their dinners were ordered, Kyra said, "I'll explain everything in a minute, but you haven't heard from Lee today, have you?"

Trudy tilted her head in puzzlement. "I assume you've already tried his room?"

"I did, but he and Sam seemed to have run off on some adventure of their own without telling me. All I get is Lee's voicemail."

"Do you have a reason to worry about them?"

She sighed. "I'm afraid they're out there playing detective and might get in trouble."

"Maybe you should give me all the details of Sam's attack and what happened to you and Lee. I only saw the news reports."

Kyra filled her in and then studied the embossing in the white table-cloth so she wouldn't have to look up at Trudy. "I'm worried that something really sinister is going on," she whispered. "I don't think Detective Andrews believes it, but he did hint that Sam was so sure Tex would get help in time that he took the chance to look like a victim."

Trudy reached across the table to hold Kyra's hand. "But that doesn't make sense at all. It's your writer's mind creating a series of plots to fit the facts. Why don't you let the police figure it out so you don't drive yourself crazy?" When Kyra finally looked up, Trudy said, "You know men. They claim to be the ones who solve problems with their logical brains, when all along we women follow our intuition and our insights into character to figure it out."

"Hmm," Kyra said, thinking of Mary's statues in Sam's house, but admitting to herself that Trudy had a point. Just then the waitress brought their salads and Kyra decided her worries could wait until after they enjoyed dinner. "I guess I won't panic until after we eat. I just hope we hear from them soon."

It turned out she didn't have to wait that long because just as the main entree reached their table, Kyra spotted Lee and Sam entering the restaurant.

"Here you are!" Lee exclaimed as they joined them. "We wondered where you went, Kyra, when you weren't in your room."

"We were worried you were stuck at the police station," Sam added, a little out of breath.

Kyra frowned, thinking that Sam wasn't completely recovered from the carbon monoxide poisoning, but her anger overrode that thought. "And where were you?" she demanded. "And why didn't you answer your phone, Lee?"

"What? Oh, my phone." He pulled it out of his pocket and frowned. "I guess I forgot to charge it." He smiled at both of them. "If I apologize for worrying you, will you invite us to join you for dinner?"

"Only if you tell us what you were up to." Kyra tried to sound cross, but she was so relieved to see them that it didn't quite work.

"We're sorry," Sam said, leaning heavily on the table. Trudy quickly slid across the booth seat, saying, "Sit down before you fall down."

Lee sat next to Kyra and studied her plate filled with veal parmesan and pasta. She pulled her plate closer and told him to order his own dinner. By common consent, they avoided any important talk until the dinners were consumed and everyone had their after-dinner coffees.

"Okay, we went to search Sam's yard and yours," Lee said. "We figured if Tex chased after whoever tried to kill Sam, he might have managed to pick up some evidence."

"What in the world are you talking about?" Trudy demanded.

"You know—like something the would-be killer dropped when Tex chased him." Sam's grin gave him away.

Kyra squinted at Sam as she tapped her fingers on the table. "Uh-huh. And it looks like Tex did find something. Care to enlighten us?"

Sam dropped a plastic baggie on the table with a dark blue scrap of torn material inside. "Looks like Tex bit off a chunk of the guy's pant leg."

"And maybe took a chunk out of his leg. If we can find those slacks and test for DNA, they could help identify our perp." Lee announced with satisfaction.

Kyra and Trudy looked at each other and shook their heads.

"What?" Sam's grin had disappeared.

"What if the guy threw his pants out when he found they were torn?" Trudy asked. "And why didn't the crime scene investigators find it before you got there?"

"We'd have to prove that scrap has something to do with the attack, and also we'd need a specific suspect in mind. We can't just check everyone's DNA in the city, or ask to check their legs for dog bites without a legal reason." Kyra turned to Lee. "You should know that after writing all those mystery books."

"What about Simon Berchtold?" Lee lifted one eyebrow. "Peter Craig was his nephew. Maybe they were in this together and Peter did something that made Simon angry."

Kyra shook her head. "I don't know. I really can't imagine Mr. Berchtold hitting Peter, especially hard enough to knock him down and kill him."

"But it didn't have to be deliberate." Trudy took a sip of coffee, before continuing, "Even if it's ruled accidental, it still could be involuntary manslaughter."

"Aren't we jumping to conclusions? For all we know Mr. Berchtold has an ironclad alibi for the night Peter died." Kyra felt like she was playing devil's advocate, even though she had wondered why Mr. Berchtold had taken his nephew's death so hard. She didn't think he got along that well with Peter the few times she had seen them together. "But what reason would they have to hire that man to act as Ethan Owens and try to frighten me?"

"What about the attack on me?" Sam asked. "Peter was dead by then, so that only leaves Simon Berchtold."

"I know the police are looking into your attack, and the one on me and Lee. It probably won't be long before they come up with the killer."

"Yeah, well, I'll bet that detective will just decide I tried to commit suicide so he can close the case. He won't even bother looking for my killer." He frowned. "But don't you worry. I'm sure he believes someone shot at you the other night. Lee was with you when that happened, so you have proof."

"I believe he'll look into finding your attacker, Sam. If he wants to keep his reputation as a good detective, he'll follow all the evidence until he finds the guilty party."

Sam remained silent for a moment before nodding. "Yeah, I guess you're right."

Kyra hesitated because she didn't know if she should try to convince Sam she was right or just let it go. Finally, she decided to move on.

"We need to find out exactly how Peter died now that his body has been released for burial." Tapping her fingers on the table, she murmured, "Detective Andrews didn't give me that information this afternoon."

Trudy held up her hand. "I know just the person to call—Mr. Berchtold's secretary. We've known each other for years." She moved out into the relative quiet of the hallway to make her call, and Lee turned to Kyra.

"I thought you said your husband would be joining you for dinner tonight. Was he delayed? I've been looking forward to meeting him."

Kyra sighed. "Yes, in a sense he was delayed. He's unhappy about the turn of events, and he can't wait until I return home again and forget all this nonsense."

"What nonsense?" Lee demanded. "Doesn't he understand you almost got killed?"

"I'm afraid he thinks I've overstated the attack so that the police will insist I stay here until the problem is solved. It's all a plot to make his life miserable."

Lee studied Kyra's face while Sam stared down at his empty plate. When Lee started to say something, Kyra shook her head. "No, don't. It will be all right; he's just not used to me living on my own. I'm sure we'll work it all out when our lives settle back into our normal routine."

"I'm not the best person to consult about marriage, but I sense a deep underlying problem there." Lee reached for her hand just as Trudy returned to their table.

"My contact said that Peter's death was ruled accidental. Sadly, he died of a head injury, but he possibly could have been saved if he'd been found sooner. They believe he slipped and fell backward against his granite counter top, and then he crashed forward onto the floor."

"And there was no evidence of foul play?" Lee asked. "It sounds shaky to me."

Trudy shrugged. "I guess not. I'm sure they'd check for that before making a ruling."

"I didn't like him, but I didn't wish him dead." Kyra sighed before asking Trudy about the funeral home.

"The visitation is at Morrow's Funeral Home tomorrow. Peggy said the hours are from 2 to 4 in the afternoon and then 6 to 8 in the evening. The church service is Monday morning at 10 at the United Methodist Church."

"I guess we should all go," Kyra said, even though she hated the thought of visiting a funeral home so soon after Mary's death.

Trudy frowned. "No, I think Lee and I should go. You don't need to visit, and Sam looks worn to a frazzle. He needs time to recuperate. Since it's late already, it's time we all get some rest."

"How can I rest when so much is unresolved?" Kyra demanded. She hesitated and then added, "Brad will be coming tomorrow and he can take me to the funeral home." She felt like crossing her fingers as she made that comment, not sure if Brad would support her in anything the way he'd been acting. Still, he had to understand how upsetting it would be for her. "That way I won't be alone."

Lee walked Trudy to her car after giving Sam the keys to his room, and Kyra and Sam rode the elevator upstairs.

"Are you okay, Sam?" Kyra asked.

"I'm fine. Just need a good night's sleep. You know how it is in hospitals. Just when you fall asleep, they wake you up to take your temp or some other silly thing." He laughed, shaking his head. "See you in the morning. I'll be glad to get back home tomorrow."

After Kyra leaned over to kiss his cheek and wish him pleasant dreams, she entered her room and stood with her back against the door. Her head buzzed with endless questions about all the frightening incidents of the last couple weeks. She knew that a common thread tied them all together, if only she could find it. She forced herself away from the door and went to the window.

Staring out at the starless night, she remembered Mary's calm voice talking to her that summer after her mother's death. Kyra's world had fallen apart that year as her mother received the cancer diagnosis and then went through months of chemotherapy. When Beth Wyndham had died despite all that medicine could do, Kyra couldn't eat or sleep. Mary brought her back from the precipice and helped her find joy and laughter again, along with ways to remember her mother without pain. As she continued staring into the dark sky, the clouds shifted and a bright star appeared. Wiping the tears from her eyes, Kyra nodded and got ready for bed.

CHAPTER 26

After checking out of the hotel the next morning, Kyra drove Sam home with her. She hoped she'd have a little bit of time to walk through the house before Brad showed up, but no such luck. His car was parked in the driveway. She hurried to drop Sam off at his house, and he waved her away when she offered to come in with him.

As she pulled into her driveway, she saw Brad sitting and reading the newspaper on the chair next to the front door, and she suddenly remembered he didn't have the keys to the double lock.

"I wondered when you'd get here," he said, tearing his gaze away from the sports section of the paper. "I no sooner got here than a policeman showed up. Wanted to see my identification." He shook his head. "This town is turning into a police state."

Kyra dropped her bag and leaned over to kiss him. "I missed you, too," she said. To her surprise, he kissed her back and pulled her onto his lap.

"That's better," he said. "Sorry for sounding so crabby but I wasn't expecting the third degree." He kissed her again, and Kyra allowed herself to relax in his embrace. Maybe she'd been overdramatizing the divide between her and Brad for the past month. It felt so soothing to have his arms around her and hear his loving words. Just when she thought he'd suggest they go inside for some privacy, he sighed.

"Is it true that you can't come home tomorrow?"

She nodded. "Unfortunately, that's what the detective told me. It's frustrating, but they still need to pursue some of the leads relating to the man who shot at me and Lee, and find out if it's the same person who tried to kill Sam."

Brad sat up straighter and nudged Kyra off his lap. "I guess we'll just have to manage apart a little longer then," he murmured. As she stood up, Kyra saw his eyes go opaque and his face harden. In a split second, he changed his demeanor and smiled up at her. "How about having a late breakfast?"

Kyra hesitated before she put her key in the lock, suddenly remembering the sounds of the shots hitting the house, and Tex's whimpering after being hit.

"Now what's the matter?" Brad asked. He took the key from her shaking hand and unlocked the door. "Don't worry; nothing's going to happen today. I'm here to keep you safe, aren't I?"

Taking a deep breath, she allowed him to usher her into the house. After they finished their scrambled eggs and toast, Kyra poured them each another cup of coffee. She hated to bring up a subject that might ruin their temporary accord, but she couldn't wait much longer.

"Today's the funeral visitation for Peter Craig, so I was hoping you'd go with me." She sat down and reached for Brad's hand where it rested on his coffee cup, but he pulled it back as if the cup had scalded him.

"Peter Craig? Why in the world would you go to his funeral?" Frown lines had formed on Brad's face as he stared at Kyra.

"He worked for Mr. Berchtold, and Simon was Mary's lawyer. I've talked to both of them at the office. I thought it was the least I could do." When she saw Brad's irritated look, she added, "We wouldn't have to stay very long."

"It would be better yet if we didn't go at all. I hardly think it's necessary to visit some relative of your aunt's lawyer."

"Just because something isn't necessary doesn't mean it's not the kind or polite thing to do." Kyra could feel the recent animosity building between them. Sighing, she said, "If you don't want to go, I'll ask Sam or Lee."

"Whatever. Just don't be too long. We finally get a chance to spend time together, and you're already going out somewhere." He looked away from her and studied the plywood on the back door. "Have you arranged for the window to be replaced yet?"

When she explained she hadn't had time since the crime scene investigators had only finished their work, he said, "Then maybe I'll head to the hardware store and see if I can pick up some window trim and spackling for those bullet holes in the wall."

Surprised, Kyra wondered what had brought on Brad's sudden need to become a handyman. Normally, she'd always had to call a repairman for even simple things, like a leaky faucet. She shrugged, though, since it might keep him busy and stop him from concentrating on the fact that she wasn't doing what he wanted.

"Wait and I'll give you the extra key to the front door," she murmured. "Then I guess I'll give Sam a call and see if he wants to ride with me since he's still recuperating from his ordeal the other night."

"I saw in the paper that it was called a possible suicide. Do you think he was in love with your aunt and felt he couldn't live without her?"

Kyra stared at Brad for a few seconds before blurting out, "You can't be serious!"

He laughed at her look of utter disbelief. "For someone who claims to be a writer, you have no understanding of human nature. Anyone seeing them together would know he was madly in love with her. He was mooning around here all the time trying to help your aunt do something, anything, so he could be near her."

"Yes, he was helpful, but I hardly think he was 'madly in love,' as you say. He was a good neighbor and he enjoyed her company," Kyra said, trying to keep her cool.

"I'll say this for the old lady; she knew how to keep the men dangling after her. Not only Sam, but Leonardo Napoli couldn't stop coming back for more. The funny thing is that you're just as obsessed: you even want to claim the woman as your mother!" Brad's eyes glinted with devilish satisfaction.

"Brad! Stop it! Mary *is* my mother. Simon Berchtold, her lawyer, had her will and all her papers to prove it. Lee has letters from her telling of my birth and the adoption by the parents who raised me. It's not just a wish of mine." Kyra drew a deep breath and tried to stop arguing with him. She realized he was enjoying himself at her expense, and she regretted allowing herself to believe in his loving gestures only minutes ago.

Brad walked over to look out the window and asked, "So if you are the daughter of Mary and Lee, has Lee put you in his will?"

Kyra froze suddenly as she stared at his rigid back. Something about the question and his listening pose made her realize they had reached the crux of the matter. This was the question Brad had wanted to ask through this whole charade of a conversation. He had turned away from her because he didn't want her to read his expression when he asked about Lee's will. She shrugged, told him she had no idea, and walked upstairs to change for the funeral visitation. Although she expected him to come stomping into the bedroom, the next thing she heard was the front door closing and then his car starting up.

When her cell phone rang, it was Lee asking if he should pick her up in his rental car or if she and her husband would meet him at the funeral home. She accepted his ride without going into detail about the problem with Brad, and he didn't ask any questions. He suggested she call Sam and tell him to meet at her house.

An hour later they also picked up Trudy and drove to Morrow's Funeral Home. Kyra was surprised to see the parking lot quite full, and said, "I guess the visitors are here for Mr. Berchtold and not Peter Craig. He didn't seem to be a person who befriended many people."

Lee surveyed a group of men dressed in suits as they returned to their cars. "Don't forget that Mr. Berchtold is a lawyer and has many clients, too, so these may not actually be friends or family."

Sam opened his door, saying, "Let's get in there and start snooping. I'm sorry the guy's dead, but we have a crime to solve."

Trudy frowned. "Just remember there will be people who are mourning his passing, so be polite. We're not here in any official capacity."

Sam frowned but reluctantly nodded.

Kyra felt grateful when Lee reached for her arm as they entered Morrow's Funeral Home. With his comforting presence by her side, she studied the roomful of people before finding Mr. Berchtold next to a middle-aged woman near the closed coffin. She breathed another sigh of relief when she realized she wouldn't have to look down on Peter Craig's face. Glancing back at Sam, she almost laughed when she saw Trudy leaning heavily on his arm, keeping him into place beside her.

"Ready?" Lee whispered and Kyra nodded.

As they approached to offer their condolences, Mr. Berchtold broke off a low-voiced conversation with the woman beside him and reached for Kyra's hand.

"Ms. Martin, thank you for coming."

"I'm so sorry for your loss," she managed to say, trying not to stare at the elegant mahogany coffin and thinking of Mary's death only weeks ago. She continued, "This is Leonardo Napoli—"

"Yes, of course, Mr. Napoli, how good of you to come," gushed the woman, and Mr. Berchtold hastened to introduce her as Peter's mother, Donna Cartwright, his sister-in-law.

When Kyra leaned closer to offer her sympathy, Mrs. Cartwright waved her hand as if it didn't matter. "We were never close," she said, almost falling into Lee's arms. "I've read all your books," she gushed. "I hear you're quite the celeb. . . celebrate. . . uh. . . you know, famous in It. . . tall. . . ee." After dragging out the word, she began to laugh.

Kyra looked with alarm at Mr. Berchtold and saw his face had turned red. "Come along, Donna, I think you need a little rest in the other room."

She shook her head and pulled away from him. "I need a little drinkee! I've just lost my son, my baby!" and then she burst into tears.

When the funeral director hurried over, he helped Mr. Berchtold lead Mrs. Cartwright from the room, murmuring soothing words the whole time. The silence that had come over the room suddenly filled with the babble of conversation as people tried to sympathize with the woman's meltdown.

"Poor thing," "Her only child," and "It's all too much for her" drifted around the room as Kyra and her friends found a quiet corner to stand in.

"That was interesting," Trudy said. "Poor Mr. Berchtold."

"Maybe, maybe not." Sam frowned. He lowered his voice as he said, "He could be the reason she's so upset and found comfort in the bottle."

Lee studied the room to make sure no one was paying attention to their conversation before saying, "I doubt if her drinking is a new problem brought on by her son's death. I suspect she's been doing it for years. Where's Mr. Cartwright?"

"The last I heard he was still in a nursing home," Trudy said. "Gerald Cartwright was a gambler; he'd bet on the lottery, horses, poker games, whatever. One day he attacked the owner of the bar after getting kicked out, and the guy hit him on the head with a whiskey bottle. Gerald was never the same afterwards, and his father, Thomas Cartwright, placed him in the home where the Cartwright money will take care of him for the rest of his life."

"Hmm. That's a little more information than Detective Andrews gave me," Kyra said. "I guess he wasn't much of a role model for the young Peter."

Shrugging, Sam observed, "Isn't it funny how Peter got hit over the head, too, only he died."

"Meaning what?" Trudy asked. "That Mr. Berchtold decided bashing someone on the head was a good way to get rid of him?"

"We're not getting anywhere making guesses like this," Lee said. "Maybe we should just politely take our leave."

Kyra looked down the hallway where Mrs. Cartwright had been hustled away. "I'll be right back. I have a sudden urge to find the bathroom." When Trudy suggested she join her, Kyra shook her head. "I think I'll be less conspicuous by myself."

As she suspected, the hallway led to the restrooms, but also a large empty room on the left and another room on the right. She could hear the murmur of voices from that room. After making sure no one was paying any attention to her and giving thanks for the thick carpet underfoot, she moved closer until she could distinguish words.

"Peter was in some kind'a trouble." Donna Cartwright hiccupped before adding, "Maybe we weren't close, but he had that same funny look in his eyes the last time I saw'm. Like he had when he was a kid and I knew he was lyin'."

"Donna, what are you talking about?" Mr. Berchtold sounded aggravated. "Your son just wanted to find easy ways to make money. That's why he wasn't happy working for me. What kind of trouble would he be in?"

"I . . . uh. . . need a drinkee, Simon. Please."

"Oh, forget it! You're hopeless! Just hang in there until 8 o'clock tonight. Then you can have a drink."

Worried that someone would catch her listening, Kyra decided to search the floor as if she'd lost something.

"Simon, don' go. It had t' be that other boy, ya know, that one that got'm into trouble in college. They charged kids t' write their Eng . . . English papers, only they started using th' same papers with a coupla words changed. The dam' teachers caught on. Wha'was that boy's name?"

"I have no idea," Mr. Berchtold said just as Mrs. Cartwright exclaimed, "It was Ford . . . uh . . . something. Um . . . it's on the tip of my . . ."

"You're imagining things," he interrupted her.

Kyra jumped to her feet when a door opened down the hall and Mr. Morrow appeared.

"Are you all right, miss?" he asked as he walked toward her.

"I'm fine," she said. Trying to keep her voice steady, she added, "Just thought my key fell out of my purse, but here it is on the bottom. I usually have it in this side pocket." She smiled and crossed the hall to the restroom. As she closed the door, she glimpsed Mr. Berchtold standing in the hall and studying her.

CHAPTER 27

After returning to Lee's car, Kyra relayed the conversation she had heard between Mr. Berchtold and Mrs. Cartwright.

"So Peter and someone called Ford worked together in college on a scam where they wrote English papers for other kids for money," she said, turning sideways in the front seat so she could see Sam and Trudy. "Only it sounds like they got caught."

"If they were in trouble then, it makes sense they could have been working together now." Trudy hesitated before saying, "But Peter is dead and so is Max Keller . . ."

"So who is Ford?" Sam asked. "If Peter's mother even knows what she was talking about." He shook his head in frustration. "That lady was pretty tipsy."

"I almost got caught eavesdropping when Mr. Morrow came out of his office. Then Mr. Berchtold saw me in the hall, and he gave me an angry stare."

Lee groaned. "Oh, great, if he's the mastermind behind all this, he now suspects you of knowing too much."

"I just can't believe he would be the kind of man who attacks people and runs around with a gun." Kyra tried to picture Mr. Berchtold dragging Sam into his garage and shooting at her house, and it just didn't seem possible.

Trudy patted Kyra on the shoulder from the back seat. "I know it's unbelievable, but that's exactly the kind of man who gets away with crimes. No one would ever suspect him."

They discussed the matter for a few more minutes before dropping Trudy off at her house. Kyra worried about her safety, but Trudy laughed it off, insisting her neighbors were such snoops that no one could get within ten feet of her house without being recorded and talked about.

When they pulled into Kyra's driveway, she noticed with a sinking heart that Brad's car was still gone. Sam had begun to doze in the car and he mumbled that he was going home to take a nap. Lee joined Kyra beside the car as they continued to talk, and she thought he wanted an invitation to come inside. Dusk was settling and Kyra realized she was hungry. When she first heard the crack, it didn't mean anything to her until Lee yelled, "Down, get down!" She ducked just as the next crack shattered the window on the driver's side and Lee fell to the ground.

"No!" she screamed, crawling toward Lee, but he whispered, "Hide!" When she glanced up, she saw the shadowy figure advancing across the lawn, gun upraised. Another shot pinged across the hood of the car as she tried to pull Lee to safety around the back.

"Go!" mumbled Lee, but she reached up to whip open the car door instead to give Lee some cover. A moment later, she leaned on the car horn and didn't let go. The blare rang through the neighborhood as she screamed and screamed. The figure halted and then took one more shot that went wild as he ran away. Sam darted across the yard, brandishing a bat and what looked like a kitchen knife.

"Where'd he go?" he huffed, and Kyra let go of the horn and pointed. She slid to the ground and crouched beside Lee, touching his face and then his arm. Her hand came back sticky with blood.

"Lee, Lee, can you hear me?"

He moved slightly, but didn't respond to her. Afraid to move him, she continued feeling along his body, but she didn't find any more blood.

Just as she heard the sirens approaching, she sensed a movement behind her and she spun around, expecting to find the gunman. Instead, it was Darren, the teenager from across the street, and she started breathing again. Next to him stood a tall man who looked like an older version of Darren.

"Is there anything we can do?" the man asked, careful to keep his distance. Darren hovered beside him, his eyes wide with shock, and whispered, "I hope he's okay."

"I don't know." Reaching for Lee's hand, she held it tightly, and then relief flooded through her as she felt a slight pressure from his fingers in response. Maybe he wasn't too injured. Sam returned just as the police car and ambulance pulled into the driveway. He shook his head, murmuring, "He got away."

Two policemen jumped out of the car and ordered Sam to drop his weapons. Indignantly, he explained that he wasn't the bad guy and the shooter was getting away.

"Sir, just put down your weapons," the tall, thin officer repeated and rested his hand on his gun.

"Sam, don't argue. We need to get help for Lee right now. He's bleeding."

Sam dropped the bat and knife, and the other cop quickly handcuffed his hands behind his back. A medic hurried over to check Lee, and Darren and his father moved back to give her room. The dusk to dawn light flashed on and suddenly the area was flooded with light. The shorter policeman suggested Kyra tell him what had happened.

"I will," she said, distracted. "But first I need to make sure my father is all right, and then ask you to take the handcuffs off my friend, Sam."

It took a few frustrating minutes, but finally the medic discovered that Lee had a bullet wound in his shoulder while Sam pointed out several shell casings on the driveway. Officer Rogers released Sam, but kept a close eye on him. Kyra followed the stretcher to the ambulance, holding onto Lee's hand until they explained she'd have to follow them to the hospital.

"But he's going to be all right, isn't he?"

"Looks like the bullet went straight through, so he should be okay. He may have a concussion from falling to the pavement after getting shot. At his age, recovery could take a while. But don't worry, miss, Stonecliff Community Hospital will take care of him."

As additional police cars pulled into the street, policemen fanned out and spoke briefly to Darren and his father and several other neighbors who lined the streets. Since no one had seen what happened, they sent everyone home.

When Officer Rogers wanted to take statements from Kyra and Sam before they left for the hospital, Kyra asked that they contact Detective Andrews to see if he could meet them there. She explained that it wasn't the first time they'd been attacked, and she was sure the detective would want to hear their stories. It took a few minutes, but finally he was instructed to drive them directly to the hospital. By then the crime scene investigators had reached the house, and suddenly Kyra wondered where Brad had gone.

"My husband may show up soon, and his name is Brad Martin. He owns a gray Toyota Camry," she explained. With her luck, he'd pull up to the house as soon as she left, and then he'd be upset when he saw the police at Mary's house again.

"Why don't you give him a call?" Officer Rogers asked. "That way he can meet you at the hospital."

Kyra exchanged a look with Sam before nodding and walking a few steps away to call. When the phone rang and rang, Kyra breathed a sigh of relief, at the same time wondering why she often had trouble getting in touch with Brad. Did he deliberately turn off his phone for some reason? Deciding she didn't have time to worry about it now, she walked back to the police car, saying, "He must be out of range because he's not answering."

The policeman's eyebrows rose in a questioning manner, but he murmured something about trying again after they reached the hospital. Sitting in the back seat of the car, Kyra stared out the window, trying to calm the butterflies in her stomach. Lee had to be all right; she couldn't accept that she would lose him not long after finding him and starting their father-daughter relationship. Sam touched her arm, saying, "He's going to be fine, Kyra. Don't think anything else." When she turned to him and saw his eyes full of certainty, she took a deep breath and nodded. "Thanks, Sam."

After Officer Rogers dropped them off at the emergency entrance, she marched into the waiting room. The first thing she saw was Detective Andrews standing by the check-in counter. When he turned and saw them, he said, "Good, you're here. The hospital staff has graciously made a private room available for us."

As she followed the detective down the hallway past several cubicles with patients lying in beds, Kyra wondered where Lee had been taken.

"Please, I'd like to see Lee before we talk about what happened tonight," she said, glancing at Sam for back up.

Before he could say anything, though, Detective Andrews held up his hand. "I'm afraid you can't do that right now."

Kyra's heart clenched and the blood drained from her face.

"No, no, it's not that." He hastened to add, "As far as I know, he's still alive and isn't in imminent danger of dying. It's because he's being prepped for surgery."

As Kyra began breathing normally again, the detective opened the door to the room at his disposal and ushered them inside. After the door was closed, he told them that although the bullet had passed through Lee's shoulder, it needed cleaned and bandaged up.

"The other problem is that he has a mild concussion and will have to be hospitalized until the doctor is sure he hasn't sustained any long-term injury from falling to the concrete driveway." His gaze moved from Kyra to Sam and back again. "Have a seat," he said, pointing to several plastic chairs arranged in a semi-circle in front of a small desk. He hesitated before saying, "There's one other complication that I want to discuss with you."

Kyra glanced at Sam again and then carefully seated herself in the middle chair with Sam settling next to her.

"What kind of complication do you mean?" Sam demanded. "What's the big secret?"

"Since Mr. Napoli might be the target of this criminal, we think it would be better not to let anyone know that he's survived the attack." He studied Kyra's face before asking, "Did you see anything that would help us identify the attacker?"

She stared at the floor and rubbed her forehead, desperately trying to focus on that shadowy shape hiding among the bushes. His features were too indistinct in the semi-dark, but she thought the form was thin and maybe about average height. When she told the detective as much as she could remember, he asked, "But it was definitely a man?"

Kyra started to nod, but then hesitated. "I think so. But I guess it could have been a woman. Oh!"

"What?" Detective Andrews and Sam both asked.

"He, or she, wore a baseball cap. When he turned sideways slightly, I could definitely see the shape of it."

Both men sighed and Kyra frowned.

"It doesn't matter." Sam patted her arm. "We're pretty sure it's Mr. Berchtold, anyway. Tell him what happened at the funeral home."

"I don't think . . ." Kyra began, but Detective Andrews quirked an eyebrow.

"Please continue," he said. "I'd like to know what kind of snooping you were doing at the funeral home."

Feeling her face turn pink, Kyra hurried through an explanation of the words she overheard by "accident" in the hallway. "Mr. Berchtold did not seem happy when I turned back to look before going into the restroom." Somehow their suspicions of Mr. Berchtold being the killer sounded sillier when she repeated the words to the detective.

"I see," were his only words before he changed the subject. "For now, I want both of you to swear that you won't let anyone know that Mr. Napoli has survived his injuries."

"Not even my husband?" The words popped out before Kyra could stop herself.

"Will that be a problem?" he asked. "If so, I can keep you here for questioning overnight."

"Oh!" Kyra again glanced at Sam who gave her an encouraging look. "No, it won't be a problem. He'll be going back home tomorrow, so I can manage for tonight." Thinking of the many questions he might ask, she said, "He can be really inquisitive, though, so what exactly should I say?"

"Why don't you just tell him that the police aren't releasing any details at this time? If he has any questions, he can come to me directly." When Sam started to say something, the detective held up his hand. "We'll check into Berchtold, Mr. Atkins, but we're pursuing another line of inquiry at this time, too."

Before the policeman came to usher them downstairs, Detective Andrews asked Sam how Tex was doing. Kyra suspected the detective knew that was a positive note to the end of their discussion and would distract Sam. She almost smiled before remembering the seriousness of Lee's condition.

"Tex is coming home tomorrow if the vet gives the okay," Sam replied. "Too bad he wasn't home today or maybe he could've warned us of this shooter."

"Or he could have been hurt again," Kyra said. She placed her hand on Sam's arm to urge him to leave, but then turned back. "Are you sure I can't see Lee before leaving?"

"I'd rather you didn't." He walked with them to the door where their police escort waited. "I'll be in touch tomorrow evening and we can set up a visitation time then. How about that?" He studied her face. "And in the meantime, Lee couldn't be saved and that's all you know."

Kyra drew a deep breath and nodded. Tears stung her eyes just hearing those words and she turned away to blindly follow Officer Rogers back to the emergency department entrance.

She managed to calm herself down on the drive home, where she found the driveway encircled by crime scene tape. The officer explained that Lee's rental car had been towed away to be inspected by the forensic team. He offered to come in and check the house, but his cell phone rang and he was needed to check out a break-in several blocks away.

When Sam assured the policeman he'd go inside with Kyra, the officer nodded his thanks and took off. Since the lights weren't on in the house, it was obvious that Brad still wasn't home. Kyra wondered where he could possibly be, and then worried that he'd driven to the hospital to pick her up. If so, he'd be angry he missed her. She sighed, thinking of all the things that seemed to upset Brad recently. Was it only two years ago they were so happily in love that they couldn't stop touching each other, even if was only to hold hands in the grocery store?

"Don't worry, young lady, Uncle Sam will take care of you." Sam patted her back and Kyra tried to smile at his deliberate use of "Uncle Sam." "You know, I was in the Army a long time ago. I was pretty handy with the rifle, too." He entered the front door first and murmured, "It's too bad I didn't have one earlier or that bast—I mean, bad guy, wouldn't have gotten away."

They moved from room to room, turning on lights as they went, until they ended up in the kitchen. "Would you like some iced tea before going home?" Kyra asked.

"Listen, Kyra, I'm not leaving until your husband gets back." When she started to object, he raised his hand. "It's not negotiable. Too many things have happened here, and it might even be safer if you come to my house."

Although she worried about what Brad would say when he got back and saw Sam at the house, Kyra was relieved she wouldn't be alone. She nodded and said, "Let's just wait here a little while longer and see if Brad shows up. Thanks, Sam."

"Let me check upstairs first and then I'll have some of that iced tea."

Kyra filled two glasses with ice and reached into the refrigerator for a lemon. Suddenly, Sam cursed, grunted, and she heard a loud crash directly above her. She dropped the lemon and ran to the stairs.

"Sam! Sam!" she screamed.

CHAPTER 28

Terrified, Kyra started up the steps when a hoarse voiced shouted, "You little liar! I just caught your boyfriend Sam in your bedroom!" For a few seconds, Kyra couldn't comprehend what she'd just heard. As reality hit, the voice continued, "Don't worry. I only did what any other red-blooded man would do."

Self-satisfied laughter followed and Kyra balled her fists against her chest. Brad!

"No, no! Brad, what are you doing here?"

The hallway light came on and Brad appeared at the top of the stairs. "I've been waiting for you, *sweetie*. I didn't expect you'd bring your boyfriend home."

"Oh, Brad, Sam's not my boyfriend. The house was all dark and someone shot at me and Lee earlier. He was just making sure it was safe." Kyra took a few more steps up, but Brad waved his hands.

"Stay where you are; I'm coming down."

"I need to check on Sam and make sure he's all right." Kyra stared at her husband approaching her and she wanted to run away.

"Don't worry about Sam. What about Lee, your father? When I drove back to the house earlier, I saw a police car and all that crime scene tape.

I didn't stop, but I heard a policeman say the old guy probably wouldn't make it. Is he dead?"

Kyra heard the hopeful note in Brad's question and knew he didn't want Lee to survive for some reason of his own. Without planning it, she covered her face and broke into tears.

"There, there, my dear, he was an old man." Brad reached the bottom step and placed his arm around her shoulders. She flinched and pulled away, even as he said, "It was probably a blessing. The old have so many health problems."

Kyra shivered as he called Lee's "death" a blessing and raised her head to study his face. Why hadn't she noticed the emptiness behind his eyes before? The rest of his face was arranged to show sadness, but his dark eyes were blank. Worried about Sam, she turned away from Brad and darted up the stairs.

"Kyra, get back here!"

He pounded after her, but she made it all the way to the top step before he managed to grab her leg. As she fell, Brad flung himself on top of her, driving all the breath from her body. Gasping, she tried to reach back and claw his face. He just laughed.

"Kyra, Kyra, you had me so fooled. But it doesn't matter. You're my wife for as long as you live, so forget Sam."

Kyra stopped struggling and went limp so Brad would relax his body and allow her some wiggle room. "Sam is a friend and nothing more," she said, her voice icy. "He was only trying to protect me."

"So why did he walk into your bedroom and go straight toward your bed? In the dark, like he knew exactly where it was."

"What? You made that up." She froze then when she heard a groan from her bedroom. Sam! "Get off me, Brad." She softened her voice and said, "Please."

Brad eased up enough to roll her over and then he leaned forward with his elbows on either side of her. "There," he said. "This is much cozier." He shifted his body so his torso lay on top of her and shoved his legs between hers.

"Brad, don't." Kyra couldn't believe his disregard for her comfort and the fact that Sam lay hurt only feet from them.

"Brad, don't," he mimicked, grinning at her. "You liked it well enough before, my dear."

She wrapped her arms around him, hoping she had enough strength to push him to the side until her fingers touched cold metal. She gasped when she realized Brad had a gun shoved into the back of his pants. Brad nuzzled her ear and whispered, "Don't worry. I'm not planning on using it now."

In a panic, she tried to pull the gun out and throw it down the stairs, but Brad was too quick for her. "Stop wriggling around like that unless you want to finish what we started right here in the hallway."

Kyra immediately stopped moving and stared at the face inches from hers. Trying to sound reasonable, she asked, "Brad, what happened to you? You can't be acting this way just because I stayed in Mary's house to write my book. What's going on?"

He sighed and shook his head. "See, it always comes back to that stupid book. It's not the book; it's because you keep drifting away from me and I want you back. I think it's time we started a family."

Kyra couldn't have been more surprised than if he said he wanted to fly on the next space mission to Mars. Her back hurt and her one leg was bent in an awkward position, but she hated to show any weakness by begging him to move. "A family? But why now? I don't understand."

"Because it's the right time."

To Kyra's surprise, he shifted away from her and sat up. She hurried to do the same and scrambled back to put some distance between them. "I'm going to check on Sam," she said, but Brad lunged for her leg and wouldn't let go.

"First, we're going into your aunt's room and make love. I want to start making that baby right now."

"Make love?" Confusion mixed with the panic she was feeling. Why had he sat in total darkness waiting for her to come home? Love didn't seem to have anything to do with his sudden urge to force her to have sex with him. Why was he intent on having a family right now? Maybe he believed a child would bind her to him forever. Desperate to distract him, she remembered the gun. Without considering the possible consequences, she asked, "Where did you get that pistol?"

"It doesn't matter where I got it, but if you're so interested in it, I'll show it to you!" He pulled out the gun and pointed it toward her. She sucked in her breath as he leered at her. "Hey, we could play a little game. I'll pretend I'm a rapist and I'll force you to do whatever I want."

In the glare of the overhead hall light, Kyra stared into Brad's eyes, trying to find the man she'd fallen in love with. He kept smiling, but his eyes looked back with clever calculation. He was trying to see how far he could push her before she screamed or begged him to stop. With a suddenness he didn't expect, she lunged across the short space and shoved him hard, throwing him off-balance. The gun flew over the railing, discharging as it hit the lower floor and Brad tumbled down the stairs.

Kyra didn't wait to see what happened to him. She flew across the hall and into her bedroom, slamming the door. Frantic to keep Brad out, she knew the chair-under-the-knob trick wouldn't work. Her gaze settled on the dresser behind her, and she started shoving it across the doorway. Out of the corner of her eye, she saw Sam struggling to his feet, and a moment later he added his strength to hers. With the dresser in place, she turned to look at Sam and saw the blood dripping down the side of face from a head wound.

"Oh, Sam, I'm sorry," she murmured. "We need to stop that blood."

"Don't worry about it now," he said hoarsely. "We got to save our lives. I heard the last bit as I regained consciousness." He waved to the phone on the end table. "Call 911!"

Even before Kyra reached the phone, she could hear Brad cursing downstairs. Hoping he'd broken both legs, she picked up the phone, only to realize it was dead. She couldn't believe he'd cut the lines. What was wrong with him?

"You ruined everything, Kyra!" he screamed. "I said I wouldn't hurt you and look what you've done." He cried out in pain and Kyra hoped it meant he couldn't get back up the stairs.

"My cell's downstairs in my purse," she said, turning frightened eyes to Sam. "Please say you have yours."

Still woozy from the hit on the head, Sam clumsily patted his pockets. "I should have it right here," he said, pointing to his shirt pocket, "but it's empty." He stared around the floor and Kyra dropped to her knees to check under the furniture. Just as she was about to give up in despair, she caught sight of something under the bed in the far corner. Running around the bed, she lay flat and reached in. Her fingers clasped the cold plastic of the phone and she held it up in triumph.

The sound of thumping riveted their attention toward the door and Kyra's fingers flew over the numbers 911. She rattled off their immediate danger about her husband's attack and the house address and promised to stay on the line. As Brad's heavy breathing and grunts of pain got closer, Kyra begged the 911 operator to send help quicker. A shot rang out and splintered the door. Sam shoved Kyra down behind the relative safety of the bed and they cowered there.

"Kyra, if you come out now, I'll forgive you and save Sam's life. Otherwise, I'll have to kill Sam." Brad's voice held menace, even as he gasped for breath.

"Brad, I'm sorry. I just wanted you to stop holding that gun in my face," Kyra called, hoping to keep him preoccupied until the police showed up. "I was afraid."

"I told you I wouldn't hurt you!" he screamed. "I need you."

Terrified, Kyra looked at Sam, who rolled his eyes. "He makes no sense," he whispered. "Just talk some more."

Before she could continue, another shot shattered the door. "I mean it, Kyra. Get out here now!" He laughed in derision. "I have a lighter in my hand." She heard the distinctive click as he flicked it on and off. "I'll burn the whole damn house down if I have to. I never liked the place anyway."

"He's crazy!" Sam reached for the bat Kyra kept beside the bed and headed toward the door. Kyra grabbed his arm and pulled him back.

"No, he wants me. I'll go and try to calm him down." She shoved the phone into his hand and ran across the room to the dresser. "I'm coming out now!"

Sam followed and hissed, "Don't do it! He'll kill you."

She grabbed him again and said, "He won't. He wants me alive and I need to take this chance. Stay here, at least until I can distract him."

Sam groaned but she insisted, so he finally nodded and helped her push the dresser aside. Giving her shoulder a quick squeeze, he let her start opening the door.

"It's me, Brad. I'm coming out alone." Kyra peeked around the open door and saw Brad sitting awkwardly in the hallway directly across from her, and she suspected one of his legs was broken. He held the pistol again and pointed it at her. "Could you please set the gun on the floor?"

"Not until you come out here and Sam stays farther back in the room where I can see him." His eyes glinted and his mouth curved in the travesty of a smile. "You didn't have to attack me like that. I told you I wouldn't hurt you; I need you alive."

Kyra couldn't understand why he kept saying that and wondered how many bullets were left in his gun. When she hesitated, he continued, "I promise I'll forgive you for this mistake. Just come out so we talk a little."

Confused, Kyra glanced back at Sam, but Brad screamed, "Don't look at him! He's our enemy. Get out here and close the door behind you."

"Okay," she said, trying to placate him, but she had no intention of closing the door. As she slowly stepped into the hall, the wail of police sirens shattered the night.

"You bitch!" Brad raised the gun just as Kyra flung herself to the floor.

CHAPTER 29

The bullet splintered the doorway where Kyra had been standing and she scrambled to her knees. Gulping air, she knew she wouldn't be able to run before the next one slammed into her body. Suddenly, the bat flew through the air and knocked the gun out of Brad's hand. It skittered toward the stairs. As he leaned toward it, Kyra pushed against his wounded leg. He gasped as his broken bones ground together, and Kyra stretched until she touched cold metal. Brad grabbed her shirt and yanked backwards, but Sam charged into the hall and punched him in the side of his head. Brad fell over, moaning.

Panting, Kyra stood up with the gun held tightly with both her hands. "Don't move, Brad, or I swear I'll shoot you." Her voice quivered and her whole body shook, but she meant every word.

Sam stood over Brad, the bat ready to swing if he made another move. Police cars screeched to a stop and seconds later, the police were pounding on the door.

"Go!" Sam shouted and she gladly handed Sam the gun and hurried down the stairs, clinging to the handrail to keep from falling. She reached the door and scrabbled to unlock it with her shaking fingers. When she pulled it open, she was almost knocked down by Detective Andrews and several policemen.

The detective grabbed her by her elbows to hold her upright and demanded, "Are you all right?" As she nodded, he asked, "Brad?"

"Upstairs. Sam and I stopped him." She started to laugh. "Brad looks like the victim; he's a mess." She laughed harder and Detective Andrews motioned his officers toward the stairs. Then he walked Kyra to the sofa and sat down beside her. That's when she started crying and couldn't stop. "I'm sorry," she gulped. "I don't know what's wrong."

"Shh! Shh! It's okay," he said. "It's shock."

She pulled herself into a tight ball and rocked back and forth. "He didn't make sense. He kept saying he wouldn't hurt me because he needed me alive. And then he shot at me when he heard the police cars. Sam threw my bat at him to save me."

When the detective placed an arm around her shoulders, his calm voice and steadiness helped her to relax and sit up a little straighter. "I even grabbed his gun and pointed it directly at him. I never held a gun before in my life!"

"Detective!" the blond-haired policeman stood in the hallway. "I'm not sure how to handle those guys upstairs. The old guy is holding the gun on the other one who looks like he's beat up pretty bad."

"I pushed him downstairs," Kyra said, and she noticed with surprise that the quiver in her voice had disappeared. The policeman stared at her in disbelief. Briefly, she described the events that showed Brad had tried to hurt them.

"You heard her," Detective Andrews said. "Call an ambulance, but stay with Mr. Martin. He's the criminal. Send Mr. Atkins down to me."

Kyra insisted Sam needed to be checked out by the EMT's, too, since Brad had knocked him out earlier in the evening. Of course, Sam tried to argue, but Detective Andrews backed her up.

"You could have a concussion and you're just recuperating from carbon monoxide poisoning. No argument. I'll get your statement in the morning."

Sam sighed in aggravation, but followed the EMT out to the ambulance. Other EMT's finished stabilizing Brad and then carried him downstairs on a litter. As they pushed him by the living room, he shouted, "Wait!"

Detective Andrews ordered them to continue, but Brad begged to speak to Kyra. The detective turned to her and she sucked in her breath, but stepped forward.

"What is it?" She stared into his bruised face but didn't feel any sympathy at all.

"You know I was only shooting to scare you. I still need you. With Lee gone, I'll never agree to sign any divorce papers. Just remember that," he hissed.

Kyra rubbed her forehead. "What are you talking about? Lee's in the hospital."

He laughed. "Good try, Kyra, but you don't fool me. I shot him and I watched him fall down. I know he's dead."

Detective Andrews leaned over Brad. "It turns out you're not such a great shot, after all. But I'll still make sure you sit behind bars for the rest of your life."

"You're lying! You're all lying!" Brad tried to move, but he was strapped down on the gurney. Detective Andrews motioned for the EMT's to take him away.

Kyra felt herself shaking again after Brad's outburst, and the detective asked if she had someone she could stay with. She nodded, saying, "I'll call Trudy Dawson."

"Good. The crime scene investigators are on their way, so your house is off-limits again. If you want to pack a bag, I'll come up with you. Then I'll drive you to Trudy's house."

Kyra shook her head. "I don't think I can face that right now. I'll just take my purse, and that's in the kitchen."

She sat in the car, staring out the front windshield. She was afraid if she tried to talk she'd just dissolve into tears again and she wouldn't be able to stop. Remembering the detective's comforting presence as they sat on the sofa earlier, she almost jumped out of the car when they reached Trudy's house. Otherwise, she would have flung herself into his arms and really embarrassed both of them.

"I'm fine now," Kyra said, trying to keep her voice steady. "Thanks for all your help tonight."

He got out and walked around the car. "I'll make sure a squad car does an hourly check of Trudy's house all night." He handed her a card with his private number. "Call me night or day if you need anything. You've been through a rough couple days."

She nodded because her throat had tightened up again. Knowing he was watching as she walked up the sidewalk, Kyra turned and waved when Trudy opened the door. Despite all her best efforts, the minute Trudy reached out to hug her, Kyra fell apart. They talked long into the night and Trudy plied her with several cups of sweet tea to calm her nerves. Finally, near dawn, Kyra fell into a deep sleep for several hours in Trudy's guest bedroom.

She awoke suddenly, drenched in sweat, and sat bolt upright in fear. She stared around the room where fingers of sunlight slipped through the closed curtains. Slowly she remembered she was sleeping in Trudy's house and her heartbeats returned to normal. With memory returning, though, she also saw the horrible moments when Brad aimed his gun at her and shot. Her whole life had turned upside down last night and she wasn't sure she would ever be the same.

There was a knock on the door before it opened and Trudy peeked inside.

"Oh, good, you're awake," she said. "I'd ask how you're doing, but I can see the haunted look in your eyes. If it's any help, Lee is awake and asking for you."

Kyra forced herself to smile. "That's wonderful news." She swung her legs over the side of the bed and stood up. The nightgown Trudy lent her nearly slipped off her shoulders.

"I'll start breakfast while you shower and get dressed. I'd offer you slacks and a shirt but I'm afraid you'd get lost in them." Trudy looked down at her more ample figure. "But there's a new toothbrush and comb on the bathroom sink."

"Thanks. You're a lifesaver."

By the time Kyra entered the kitchen, her stomach was growling. She couldn't believe she would ever do normal things again, but here she was, craving coffee and starving. Trudy ordered her to sit, poured her coffee, and placed a plate of blueberry pancakes in front of her.

"I know it feels weird, but our bodies betray us every time. We need sustenance even when it feels like our lives have changed forever." When Kyra started to tear up, Trudy shook her head. "Not now. I went to all this trouble to make breakfast, and I expect you to do the polite thing and eat it."

Kyra nodded and relaxed. "You're a good friend, Trudy. First to Mary and now to me."

An hour later when they reached the hospital, Trudy insisted on sitting in the waiting room while Kyra visited Lee. "You need time alone together. I'll join you in a little bit." She picked up an issue of WebMD and started reading.

Kyra drew a deep breath and stepped into Lee's room. He lay on the bed, his head and left shoulder wrapped in bandages and his eyes closed. He looked smaller and paler than she remembered and her heart clenched. She couldn't lose him now, not when they'd finally begun to feel like family. Then he opened his eyes. "Kyra!" His voice was a mere whisper, but his blue eyes danced with joy.

She leaned down and hugged him carefully, mindful of his injuries. He patted her back with his good arm, despite the IV line connected to it.

"I was so worried about you," Kyra said, her voice muffled. He held her awkwardly with one arm as she cried, memories of the terrifying night blending into the relief that they were both all right. Finally, she shifted back a little to see his face and scrubbed at her tears.

"You think you were worried!" Lee shook his head and then winced at the movement. "I keep forgetting about my stupid head!" He closed his eyes for a moment and then continued, "That detective came in awhile ago and told me what happened after I collapsed. That almost made me have that heart attack they were afraid I had when the EMT's brought me in last night."

He motioned to the chair beside his bed. "Have a seat and tell me how you're doing." When Kyra settled next to the bed, he reached for her hand. For several minutes, they didn't speak, just held on tightly, drawing comfort from each other. Finally, Kyra gathered the strength to tell Lee the events of last night.

"Brad thought he'd killed you last night, and he didn't believe me when I said you were still alive." Kyra frowned. "He kept talking about how he needed me so much and he never wanted a divorce. It didn't make sense when he obviously didn't really love me at all."

"Brad's going to jail for a long time, so I don't think you'll have any trouble getting a divorce, whether he likes it or not." Lee sighed and looked toward the ceiling. "I know why he needs you so much, and I guess you could say it's all my fault."

Kyra shook her head. "No, it obviously started when Mary died."

"And that's because Mary was my heir," Lee said, tightening his hold on her hand. "Now that she has passed away, you're in my will to inherit."

"Oh, of course!" She closed her eyes as everything of the past few weeks suddenly made sense. "So if you were out of the way, I'd become heir to everything you own. That's the reason why Brad needed me so much!"

"I tried to tell you about the will several times, but somehow the right moment passed. I'm sorry we didn't talk about it until now. I never dreamed your husband would put you through such a horrible experience."

"I can't believe I ever cared for Brad." After gathering her thoughts, she asked, "But how did he know anything about your will?"

"Peter Craig, of course," he said. "My lawyer in Italy had contacted Simon Berchtold about two years ago to coordinate my will to have Mary inherit everything. If she passed away before I did, then you would inherit." He studied her face. "It took me a long time, but I finally realized I needed to take care of my daughter, even if I hadn't yet met you. Mary told me stories of you over the years, and I knew how much she loved you. I trusted her judgment when I included you in my will."

"Oh, Lee, I don't know what to say. So much has shifted in my life in such a short time; it's hard for me to process." She rubbed her forehead as she contemplated all the issues. "It sounds like Brad and Peter made a plan to use me as their path to riches, but first you had to die."

She stared at Lee. "Wait a minute! I think it's possible Brad and Peter met in college."

"How did you meet Brad?" he asked. "At work? Through friends?"

"No, it was kind of odd. I was in one of the libraries in Pittsburgh, looking through the shelves for a book by Louise Penny. He literally came around the corner and bumped right into me. We started talking, and the next thing I knew, he asked me if I'd like to go for a cup of coffee."

"So, an accidental meeting," murmured Lee, a thoughtful expression on his face.

"Or a planned meeting." Kyra frowned. "I wonder if he got my address from Peter and followed me from home." She rubbed her forehead. "I'll bet our whole relationship was set up ahead of time, and now he was getting tired of playing the part." She looked down at her lap as Lee tightened his grip on her hand.

"Don't do that to yourself," he said. "You're a trusting and honest person, and you had no reason to suspect he was anything other than what he seemed. If he and Peter had hatched a plan to eventually get rid of me so you could have my money, they're responsible for their actions, not you."

"Then Mary's death was the inciting incident. At that point, Brad must have decided he couldn't wait any longer. He wanted to speed up his access to all your money, so he and Peter launched their plan to scare me into leaving Mary's house. The fact that you had returned to Stonecliff gave them the chance to try and eliminate you at the same time." She shook her head, thinking about how she didn't really know Brad at all. Then she frowned. "But then why did Peter die? And that false Ethan Owens? Were their deaths really just accidents?"

They were interrupted by a knock on the door, and Mr. Berchtold walked in, followed by Trudy and Sam. Kyra smiled at Sam, but didn't have a chance to ask how he was feeling.

"I heard you talking, and I'm pretty sure their deaths weren't accidents," Mr. Berchtold said. He looked pale, and dark half-moon smudges lay under his eyes. "Your husband had the nerve to call me to represent him at the police station today. I refused to go, explaining that I wasn't a trial attorney, and I suggested other lawyers. He became extremely angry, screaming that he'd take care of me just like he got rid of Peter." He closed his eyes for a moment and then looked out the window. "I called Detective Andrews to complain about your husband's behavior and to tell them he confessed to killing Peter. Now I'm worried he'll try to get back at me in some way."

Trudy reached for his arm and led him over to the only other chair in the room. "Please, sit down. You look exhausted."

He sat and then looked toward the bed. "I'm sorry, Ms. Martin and Mr. Napoli, that I didn't understand sooner that Peter and Mr. Martin were working together to cash in when Ms. Martin inherited your money. I should have realized Peter was asking too many questions about things that were none of his business." He sighed. "At the time I felt glad he was showing some kind of interest, and so I ignored any reservations I had. Big mistake!"

"I'll tell you the same thing I told Kyra," Lee said. "Don't beat yourself up over what Brad or Peter did. They're responsible for their actions, not you."

Mr. Berchtold shook his head. "It gets worse, though. Detective Andrews talked to me privately to let me know Peter had multiple phone calls to Max Keller, the man who impersonated Ethan Owens. Even worse, the angle of trajectory shows that Max Keller didn't fall on his knife. Someone deliberately stabbed him, and a partial thumbprint was found on the knife. It matches Peter's fingerprints taken from his apartment."

He raised a trembling hand to his eyeglasses and pulled them off. "I should have known there was a reason why Peter's grandfather, Thomas Cartwright, chose not to leave his fortune to Peter, but at the time I thought he was being cruel to him. Obviously, he understood Peter was a bad apple through and through." He used his handkerchief to clean the glasses and placed them back on his face. "Funny thing, I remember now that Peter was friends with a Brad in college, and maybe it was your husband. Maybe he was responsible for leading Peter astray."

He stood up abruptly and nearly pitched forward onto the bed. "Sorry, I need to go now," he said as Sam helped him regain his balance. "You have my sincerest apologies." He shrugged Sam off, insisting he was fine.

Kyra looked at Lee and her friends. "There's so much I didn't know about Brad. I feel so stupid because I believed he loved me, especially in the beginning. He was so caring." She drew a deep breath, turning to Sam. "Last night Brad was convinced we were lovers and that was why he tried to kill you. And we know why he wanted Lee out of the way. I feel so awful." She tried to pull her hand away from Lee, but he held tighter.

"Let me be your strength now, Kyra," he said. "I was devastated that I didn't get back here in time to make more of a life with Mary, but now I'm here for you. Don't forget that."

Trudy stepped over and rubbed Kyra's back. "You have friends and family who care for you, so listen to Lee and let us give you strength. I know you're hurt but we'll be here for you."

Sam studied her distraught face and said, "You know you can count me in, too."

His simple words touched her and made her smile. Despite all the hurt, disappointment, and terror of the last month, she finally felt that she had made a home at Mary's house in Stonecliff.

A knock sounded on the door and Detective Andrews walked into the room, his face tight and drawn. "I have news and I thought it best that you hear it from me."

CHAPTER 30

The detective looked around the room and then his gaze settled on Kyra. "I'm afraid we've discovered some surprising news about your husband. His full name is Bradford Martin Owens, and he's Ethan Owens' son."

"What?" Kyra stared at him in confusion. "That doesn't make sense." She thought of those intimate moments when Brad held her close, whispered words of love, even made love to her, and all the time he was someone else. Her stomach tightened and queasiness threatened to overwhelm her. "I guess I hoped maybe some of our life together had been real, but it was all a charade from the beginning."

"I'm sorry," he said, and Kyra studied his eyes, seeing true sorrow there.

"Kyra, take it easy." Lee tried to sit up so he could give her a hug. Alarmed, she pushed him back down gently and leaned over to let him hold her. For a few seconds, she gathered strength from his closeness and then she edged away from him.

She looked around the room and said, "I should have trusted Mary's instinct. I knew she didn't care for Brad, but she always insisted I should make my own decisions. I could tell she'd been forced to do things when she was young, and she never wanted that to happen to me."

"I'm sure she'd have a different opinion if she knew Brad was Jasper Owens' grandson," Trudy said, frowning. Then she turned to Kyra. "Remember when Marian told us Ethan's story and how he returned home when his son was fifteen?"

"Oh!" Kyra stared up at the detective. "His son's name was Ford! A shortened form of Bradford?"

Detective Andrews raised his eyebrow and nodded thoughtfully. "That makes sense."

"I wish I'da hit him a couple more times with that bat," Sam rumbled, his hands clenching.

The detective cleared his throat and said, "Since you're all here, let me give you the rest of the news. Sadly, it looks like Brad Martin, or actually Bradford Martin Owens, also killed his own father, Ethan Owens, because Ethan tried to stop him from spying on Mary. Brad held a grudge against her because he was sure she had killed his grandfather and gotten away with murder. After convincing his old college friend, Peter Craig, to help him, they buried Ethan's body in Mary's basement. His original idea was to call the press with an anonymous tip so Mary would be accused of murder again."

"But how did he get access to Mary's home?" Kyra asked, her mind trying to understand how Brad hid his real character behind a mask of decency for so long. When the detective hesitated, she murmured, "Oh, I know. The workers who replaced my windows after they were broken said the same thing had happened about 7 or 8 years ago."

"And Mary had been on vacation then." Trudy nodded. "I remembered how upset Mary was when she returned home that time."

"We're still working on collecting evidence, but Mr. Martin seems quite willing for us to know how clever he is. He said he and Peter eventually decided it might cause more problems if Ethan's body was discovered later on since they'd gotten away with murder and no one suspected them. That is until Kyra insisted on staying in the house after Mary's death. They started worrying that she might want to fix up the basement before selling the house or just to eliminate the creepiness factor." He shook his head. "At that point, Ms. Martin, they wanted to terrify you into going home. He keeps insisting he'd like to talk to you, but we don't think that would be a good idea."

"No way!" Sam's face screwed up in anger. "But I'll volunteer to go meet him instead, officer."

"Um, I don't think that's a good idea, but thanks for your offer, Mr. Atkins."

Kyra rested her head on the back of the chair and tried not to think at all.

The detective moved toward the door and looked around the room. "Again, Ms. Martin, I'm sorry to be the bearer of bad news, especially after all the difficulties you've had in the past month. However, I can see that I'm leaving you with a caring group of people." He stopped at the doorway and added, "Unfortunately, I'll still need statements from you and Mr. Atkins, so I'll be in touch in a day or two. In the meantime, you're free to return to your house, if you wish."

Kyra saw his reluctance to leave and said, "We appreciate you taking time to personally give us the news, Detective. Thank you."

He nodded and walked away. Surprised at herself, she felt an emptiness when she realized she wouldn't have any reason to see him in the future. No arguments or sparring with words, or any reason to share warm muffins on a Saturday morning.

"Are you all right?" Lee asked. "You look like you've lost your best friend."

"What?" Kyra stared at Lee. Why would he say that? As if he'd completely understood what she didn't dare articulate to herself. She shrugged and said, "I just don't think I can take it all in. I'm exhausted and confused and need time to think." She studied Lee's face and realized that he looked as exhausted as she felt. "Oh, Lee, you look completely worn out." She stood and kissed his forehead. "We shouldn't have stayed this long." She held up her hand when she saw he was ready to argue. "I know you're worried about me, but I'm going to need you in the days and weeks ahead. So, please, get your rest and recuperate so you can come home quickly."

Lee smiled. "I like the sound of that word 'home.' Thank you, Kyra."

"Don't worry. We'll take care of her," Trudy said, wrapping an arm around Kyra's waist.

"I'm picking up Tex tonight." Sam shook hands with Lee. "We'll be camped out on the front porch all night. Your daughter is safe with us."

Kyra kissed Lee goodbye again, and his eyes were already drooping when she glanced back as they left his room. That night Trudy stayed with Kyra and they slept in Mary's room where Kyra took comfort in being surrounded by Mary's possessions. Earlier, Sam had cleaned out the hallway and Kyra's bedroom and promised to patch up the bullet holes and repaint the walls.

Trudy insisted on making breakfast the next morning for Kyra and Sam, and Kyra agreed when she realized Trudy wanted to take care of her.

"Great eggs," Sam said, scooping up another forkful of eggs scrambled with tomatoes and cheese. Tex lay by the door, his head resting on his front paws.

Kyra accepted the second cup of coffee from Trudy and then insisted she sit down and enjoy her own breakfast.

"I really appreciate everything you've both done for me, but I think it's time for you to go home for a while. I'll be fine now, and this afternoon I'll visit Lee in the hospital."

"If you want, I could drive you there or go with you," Sam offered.

"Thanks, Sam, but I'm all right."

Sam nodded as Trudy said, "I think she's hinting that she needs a little time alone."

"Oh, please. I didn't mean I wanted to get rid of you—" Kyra hurried to say, worried that they didn't know how much she valued their friendship.

"I understand," Sam said, smiling. "Just let me know when you want me to do the patching work upstairs."

Kyra hesitated and then asked, "Sam, that day I picked up the change of clothes at your house, I saw Mary's statues of the Tivoli fountain and

Romulus and Remus with their wolf-mother. It surprised me and I wondered . . ."

"You thought that maybe I took them from Mary?"

Kyra felt her face redden as she shook her head. "No, I couldn't believe that, but at the time, everything was so confusing, and I didn't know for sure who I could trust. I'm so sorry."

"I could understand that," Trudy said. "It's why I went to talk to Lee that afternoon you found me at his hotel room. I wanted to pick his brain."

Sam looked from Kyra to Trudy, frowning. "You ladies thought I was the bad guy?"

"No!" they both exclaimed and Kyra thought she was about to lose one of her dearest friends. Why had she even mentioned the statues?

"It's okay. Don't cry." Sam grinned. "You know how protective Tex is—he'd never let me hurt a hair on your head!" Before Kyra or Trudy could say another word, he added, "Mary gave those statues to me. I told her one day I'd never get to Rome, but I enjoyed the stories she told me about its history. The next day she brought them over and insisted I keep them to remind me of the time we spent together."

"Oh, Sam, I should have known." Kyra walked around the table and hugged him. "I'm glad you have them."

Trudy smiled, saying, "That sounds so much like Mary. She was a wonderful friend." She brushed her hand across her eyes and Kyra tried not to cry.

"Hey, none of that." Sam stood up. "I didn't tell that story to get you ladies all in a tither."

That made them all laugh.

Later that day, Kyra wandered around the house trying to decide what to do. Should she go back home to Pittsburgh or stay here in Stonecliff? She had happy memories of living in both houses, although she wasn't sure if that was really true of the last year she'd spent with Brad. In the early months of their marriage, Kyra had been contented and pleased to share her home with Brad. Then she'd slowly come to the realization that they actually had little in common, and he hated it when she suggested doing things together that she enjoyed. When she began writing her book, he openly ridiculed her efforts.

Thinking of her book, she walked into the den and turned on her laptop. She clicked on the file titled *The Cresthaven Mystery* and began to read.

When her cell phone suddenly trilled, she jumped and hurried to answer.

"Kyra, it's Dave Andrews."

Kyra frowned and then realized who it was. "Oh, Detective. How are you?"

"I'm fine. I know everything is finally settling down for you, but I need to ask you something."

"Um, okay."

"Is there any way you'd agree to speak to Mr. Martin if I stayed in the room with you? He insists he'll only explain himself to you."

Kyra hesitated, not sure she ever wanted to see Brad again.

"I'll understand if you say no." The tenderness in his voice almost undid her, so she responded quickly.

"Yes, I'll do it. Maybe it will resolve some issues for me, too, and I can finally put this all behind me."

"All right. If I pick you up in about thirty minutes, can you be ready?"

Kyra agreed and clicked off before she could change her mind. She hoped she wasn't making a mistake. Her stomach already felt queasy and she stared back at her pale face in the mirror. Drawing a deep breath, she hurried upstairs to change her shirt and freshen up in the bathroom.

The doorbell rang on her way back down, and Kyra rushed to the door.

"Oh, hi," she said, surprised to see Mr. Berchtold.

"May I come in?" he asked, although he didn't wait for her answer but stepped right past her.

"Um, sure." Kyra looked up and down the road and then closed the door. She followed Mr. Berchtold into the living room and indicated the sofa directly across from the chair she sat in. "Is there something I can do for you?"

Mr. Berchtold avoided her gaze, crossed and uncrossed his legs, and finally murmured, "I came here hoping to see if we could agree not to discuss Peter's involvement in your husband's crimes. After thinking it over, I'm sure Peter was forced into helping Mr. Martin, and I'd prefer not to drag Berchtold and Berchtold through the mud, causing bad press."

"Mr. Berchtold, I'm so sorry about all this, but I don't think I have any say in what the police do. I'd rather it was all swept under the rug, too, but your nephew and two other men have died." Kyra studied Mr. Berchtold. His body seemed to have shrunken in the last few weeks. His normally pristine pin-striped suit was rumpled and the shirt collar wilted around his neck, as if he'd worn it for several days in a row.

"I know Peter and Brad were friends in college, but I had no idea that your husband was the grandson of Jasper Owens. I would never have allowed that friendship to continue had I known."

"You're not the only one who's been hurt," Kyra managed to say. "I just found out my whole marriage was a sham." Then she narrowed her eyes. "Wait a minute! Who told you that Brad was Jasper Owens' grandson?"

"What?" Mr. Berchtold's gaze turned inward. "Oh, that was . . . oh, I remember. Brad confessed to that, too, when he wanted me for his lawyer."

"Funny, but I didn't hear about it until after you left Lee's room and the detective gave us that information."

"Well, then, I heard it later from the detective, too. It doesn't matter, my dear, because the important thing is that Peter was obviously led astray by Brad and had nothing to do with the murders of Ethan Owens or that other man."

"But the police have Peter's fingerprints on the knife that killed Max Keller . . ."

Suddenly, Mr. Berchtold's eyes blazed with anger and he shouted, "You mean that Detective Andrews, don't you? I know you have a thing going with that detective. I'm sure if you asked, he'd do anything for you!"

Shifting back in her chair, Kyra stared at him in surprise and a little bit of fear. "I think you've allowed your worry and sadness to cloud your judgment. I'll forget about your comments, but I'd like you to go now."

Before she could stand up, he jumped off the sofa and leaned over her, his face red with anger. Spittle shot from the corners of his mouth as he leaned toward her. "I was a good lawyer for you and Mary. The least you can do is help me in this one little request. If not, I might discover a more recent will of Mary's that proves she wanted her worldly goods given to charity."

"Please, Mr. Berchtold, please step back," she began just as the doorbell rang again. Relief flooded through her until the lawyer pressed his hand against her mouth.

"Not a word," he whispered. "We'll wait until they go away."

Fear coursed through her, but the detective would expect her to be home. She felt the lawyer's arms tremble, and she gathered her strength and shoved both hands against his shoulders. He staggered back onto the sofa and she ran for the front door. In moments she had it open and fell into the detective's arms. She saw his surprised face before his arms closed around her.

"This is nice," he murmured before pushing her back slightly and looking at her face. "You're trembling. What's wrong?" Kyra heard a noise behind her and then the detective's voice hardened. "Mr. Berchtold! What's going on here?"

"We . . . we were just having a little conversation," he said as Kyra turned to stare at him. His hands nervously tried to straighten his tie and he avoided her eyes. "I'll just be leaving now. Remember what I said, Ms. Martin."

She stiffened and Detective Andrews said, "Perhaps you'd like to tell me what she's supposed to remember."

Kyra waited a few moments, but when Mr. Berchtold stood silent, she said, "He wants me to make sure we cover up Peter's involvement in the crimes. He'd rather Peter be seen as another victim of Brad's evil schemes."

"And what about the truth?" Detective Andrews moved toward the lawyer, who backed into the hallway. "Perhaps you'd like to join us in a ride down to headquarters?"

Mr. Berchtold raised his hands in a placating manner and said, "All right. I was out of order. I shouldn't have approached Ms. Martin today."

"Damn right you shouldn't have. What kind of lawyer are you, anyway?"

"Sorry, it was a mistake. I've just been so upset that my mind hasn't been working clearly since Peter's death." He shifted his feet and tried to back up more but the wall was behind him. "Then the more I thought about it, the less likely it seemed that he was in cahoots with Brad Martin. After all, he was a victim in this fiasco, too."

"Maybe, at the end, but we have pretty conclusive proof that he was the person that murdered Max Keller."

Mr. Berchtold's face paled as he mumbled, "Then my law practice is finished. No one will trust my advice again." Suddenly, he seemed to gather strength again. "Or maybe not." He looked up and down at the detective in front of him, smiling slightly when he saw his protective stance in front of Kyra. "After all, I could point out that the fact Ms. Martin is your lover rather clouds the whole case." His eyebrows lifted and his eyes took on a crafty gleam. Kyra laughed at the absurdity of his statement and she saw Mr. Berchtold bristle at her reaction.

"Really, sir, you're grasping at straws now," Detective Andrews said as his shoulders stiffened. "You'll be the laughingstock of your profession if you try to prove such a claim."

The lawyer studied their faces and must have realized the truth because he closed his eyes and sighed, before saying, "All right. I just thought that maybe my pronouncement would catch you by surprise, and we could make a deal. I must be slipping."

"I'm sure Mary never understood what kind of lawyer you were, or she wouldn't have placed her confidence in you," Kyra said. "I'll be looking for another lawyer as soon as I can."

Mr. Berchtold nodded and turned to the detective. "Am I free to leave now?"

"I haven't heard an apology yet," Detective Andrews said, his voice steely.

"Fine. I was out of line and I apologize." As the detective moved out of the way, Mr. Berchtold walked quickly to the door. He stopped there and looked back over his shoulder. "If you're not lovers, then you're bigger fools than I thought." With a nasty laugh, he hurried away.

Kyra tried to shrug it off, but she caught the detective's gaze and couldn't look away. For several moments, neither one of them said anything, and then she murmured, "No, I can't do this right now," as he almost shouted, "You know we can't do this." Still, Kyra felt herself stepping closer as his arms reached toward her. The detective's cell phone rang.

CHAPTER 31

◆ ◆ ◆

They both froze and then the detective pulled his phone out of his pocket.

"Yes?" he barked, and Kyra hoped the person on the other end of the line couldn't hear his frustration. "What?" Suddenly, his voice held a mix of surprise, anger, and disbelief. "How did that happen? Who? You're kidding me. I'm at Ms. Martin's house and he just left. Okay, I'll be right there. Get out an APB on him. He drives a dark green Mercury Grand Marquis."

He slipped his phone back in his pocket and rubbed his hand across his face. Finally, he looked at her and Kyra knew something was drastically wrong.

"What?" she whispered, her heart contracting. "Is it Lee? What happened?"

"No, no," he said. "It's not Lee." He sucked in his breath. "It's Brad. I'm sorry."

"Brad?" Confused, Kyra shook her head. "But I thought his injuries weren't life-threatening. There must be a mistake."

The detective touched her arm, saying, "I'm afraid he managed to grab a gun from one of the officers assigned to keep an eye on him. They fought and the gun went off."

"Why would he do that? I thought he wanted to talk to me." Kyra's brain couldn't put the facts together and make any sense. "He was determined to stay married to me so he'd be around when I inherited Lee's money. What made him do something stupid like that?"

"Kyra, he obviously realized everything was falling apart. Look, right now we have to get in the car. I can't leave you alone."

He pulled lightly on her sleeve, but she resisted for a moment while she studied his eyes. When she saw his worried frown, she relented and allowed him to place an arm around her shoulders and hustle her out to the passenger side of his car. He darted looks left and right, which made Kyra even more frightened.

"Maybe I could stay with Sam," she said, but he shook his head.

"I'd rather you were where I was sure you'd be safe."

He backed up and drove through the neighborhood, constantly checking his surroundings. Kyra sat rigidly in the front seat, afraid to say anything else and distract his attention. Finally, he glanced at her and said, "Mr. Berchtold spoke to Mr. Martin shortly before the incident. My officer allowed him because he identified himself as Brad's lawyer. Then he heard Berchtold say something about you having a detective lover and taunting Brad that he'd end up in jail for the rest of his life. Officer Bergman interrupted them and sent the lawyer on his way with instructions not to come back again."

"Mr. Berchtold?" Kyra stared out the window. "I'm confused. I know the man was desperate to prove his nephew wasn't guilty, but why would he approach Brad that way? It sounds like he spurred Brad into trying something stupid."

The detective slowed to turn into the hospital parking lot and said quietly, "I believe he was trying to get rid of anyone who could testify about his involvement in this whole scheme."

"No, I can't believe that!" Kyra thought of Mary's trust in her lawyer. How she'd been happy to do business with him and all his kind words over the years. "What would have made him do that?" she asked.

"When the lawyer Mary used for many years retired, he recommended Mr. Berchtold."

"Are you sure?" he asked, pulling up to the emergency exit and putting on his flashers. "Maybe he approached her."

Before she could say another word, he got out of the car and came over to open her door.

"Stay right beside me, and once we get inside, I'll have an officer come and stay with you."

"No," she said after they were safely inside. "Let me see Brad." She tried to sound resolute, but her voice wobbled.

"I'm sorry," he said softly, "but I can't do that. It's considered a crime scene now."

Without warning, she found herself crying, and the more she tried to control it, the harder the tears fell. Whether she was crying for Brad or the loss of something she'd never really had, she didn't know. The detective wrapped an arm around her and walked with her to the side of the emergency room desk.

"Kyra, don't, please. I promise I'll do everything I can to help you get through this fiasco." When she looked up, his face was taut with sadness and his eyes held some deeper emotion. She leaned into his chest and his arms tightened around her before he gently held her away from him. "The problem is that right now I have to do my job. Later we'll have time to sort out our relationship. I'm going to take you upstairs to stay in Lee's room and Officer Jensen will meet us there."

She nodded automatically as his words kept spinning around in her head. *Our relationship!* Did they have a relationship? Is that what she wanted? As Detective Andrews led her away toward the elevator, she tried to wipe away the last few tears and sniffed hard. Without a word, he handed her a wad of tissues he fished out of his pocket.

"Like the proverbial Boy Scout I was, a policeman must always be prepared," he said.

She felt a smile tug at the corners of her mouth despite the sad events that had brought them here. The policeman was waiting when the elevator doors opened, and Kyra stepped out to join him. Before walking away, she turned back once to see the detective nod as the doors slid closed. When she reached Lee's room, she was surprised to see Lee sitting up in the chair, dressed in his street clothes with his left arm in a sling and a small bandage on his forehead.

"Kyra, perfect timing," he said, smiling broadly. "As soon as I see the doctor again, they're letting me go home. I've convinced them that I'm almost fully recovered."

She hugged him and then frowned. "I think you're bamboozling them to a certain degree, but I'm glad you'll be coming home with me today."

When Lee noticed the policeman standing in the doorway, he glanced at Kyra in surprise.

"Officer Jensen, this is my father Leonardo Napoli."

"Pleased to meet you, sir." He nodded to Lee and then turned away to stand guard.

Kyra shook her head at Lee's questioning look and said, "There have been developments." She sat on the chair beside Lee and holding his hand, she filled him in on all the details. Her voice wobbled when she spoke of Brad's death and Lee hugged her tightly.

At first Kyra didn't notice the commotion in the hallway, and then she saw the officer stiffen. He spoke quietly into his shoulder radio, but Kyra knew he was calling for backup.

"Sir, sir, you can't go down that hallway," a woman shouted and Kyra heard several people rushing toward Lee's room.

"Stay here!" Officer Jensen said as he stepped into the hallway and unclipped his gun.

"Don't come any closer, mister!"

"I'm visiting a client!" Kyra instantly recognized Mr. Berchtold's voice. "You have no right to stop a lawyer from his legal business. What is wrong with you people?"

"Stop!" shouted Detective Andrews. Moments later, they heard a scuffle and Mr. Berchtold cursing. "Officer Jensen, please escort this man to headquarters and place him in a holding cell. I'll be there shortly."

Kyra finally released her stranglehold on Lee's hand just as the detective walked into the room. She stood and they shared a look of relief, mingled with sadness about the whole situation.

"It's over now," he said, his voice hoarse. "We've learned enough about Mr. Berchtold's background to know that it looks like he was the mastermind behind the whole plot. He used his nephew, who was willing to go along with any scheme as long as he didn't have to work too hard, and your husband, Ms. Martin, to get back at Mary for choosing to stay friends with you, Mr. Napoli, after her husband died. Mr. Berchtold thought Mary would fall into his arms after Jasper died, but she turned down his offer of marriage."

"I can't believe he carried a grudge all these years," Lee said. "I knew Simon liked Mary many years ago, but she never gave him any encouragement. He seemed intent on finding a career and making lots of money, and I never suspected he had enough emotion in him to love anyone strongly. That's why I thought he became a lawyer and ended up marrying Thomas Cartwright's daughter. He thought he'd get some of the Cartwright money."

"I still can't believe I loved Brad in the beginning," Kyra murmured. "He must have been faking it all along. He always liked working at insurance agencies and managed to make good money. Although . . ." she hesitated and sighed. "Although I should have suspected something when he always bragged about how he could schmooze people into buying all kinds of insurance, even when they didn't need it."

"Now, Kyra, that could just mean he's a good salesman." Lee patted her arm as the doctor bustled into the room, a look of concern on his face.

"Is everyone okay in here? I guess there was a little problem in the hall, but the police have taken care of it."

"We're all right now," Lee replied quickly, and Kyra knew he didn't want to go into any details.

The doctor nodded. "Good. Well, Mr. Napoli, I hear you're ready to go home today." He shook Lee's hand and then turned to Kyra. "I'm Doctor Wilson. Are you the daughter he'll be staying with?"

"Yes, I am." Kyra's heart swelled with happiness knowing she was able to provide Lee a place to stay.

"Good. I wouldn't let him go home if he was alone." The doctor turned to the detective and asked, "You're her husband?"

"No, I'm . . ." he hesitated before saying, "a friend." He checked his watch before saying to Kyra, "I need to leave now, but I'll have a patrol car waiting for you downstairs. They'll be glad to take you home. I'll be in touch, Kyra."

The doctor looked at him in surprise, but just shook his head. "Sorry for my mistake." He smiled at Lee. "It looks like you'll be in good hands, so I'll send the nurse in so she can go over your discharge instructions and then you'll be on your way."

An hour later, Kyra and Lee were settled in the living room with coffee and some oatmeal raisin cookies Kyra had dug out of the freezer. They heard barking outside, followed by a knock on the door.

"It must be Sam," Kyra said. "He's probably dying to know why we came home in a police car." She laughed when she opened the door to have Tex greet her with a gentle woof as he walked down the hall, followed by Sam and Trudy. "I see the gang's all here."

Trudy and Sam took turns hugging her, and then she waved them into the living room before heading back to the kitchen to pour two more cups of coffee and defrost more cookies.

"I can't believe it's over," Trudy said when Kyra and Lee finished recounting all the events of the day. "I'm sorry about Brad's death, Kyra, but he wasn't the man you thought he was."

"It's better for her this way," Sam rumbled. "Now she don't have to feel bad and she can move on with her life."

"Sam! It's not that easy!" Trudy darted a worried look at Kyra.

"The police still have to wrap up their whole investigation so there could be more questions," Lee added. "But I kind of agree with Sam."

Kyra sat in the corner of the couch and listened to her friends' reactions to Brad's death. She felt tired and uncertain and still shook up by his death and Mr. Berchtold's treachery. When they all turned toward her, she scrambled to think of what to say. Instead she just shook her head and sighed.

"I feel like I should cry, but no more tears will come. Part of me is sighing with relief, and the other part wants it all to be a dream so I don't ever have to think about it again. But all these events are in my brain and it will take awhile to move them into past memories." When Lee shifted closer to comfort her, she waved him back. "Just a minute, Lee. I wanted to say that I will move on soon because I have Mary's example to guide me. She lived through a terrible time and kept on living and loving. And I have all of you here to support me along the way."

Much later that night when Lee was settled in Kyra's bed, Kyra sat at Mary's desk. From now on she had decided this would be her bedroom. She needed to write in her notebook some of her thoughts of the past few weeks because that helped her to ease some of the pain, confusion, and sadness.

She fell into a deep sleep that night but awoke in the early morning remembering how she used to crawl into bed beside Mary that first summer after her mother's death. Mary's love and understanding had allowed her to move on with her life and become the person she was today. Her father loved her, but he simply didn't know how to deal with his daughter when his own loss was so devastating. Slowly, she and her father worked out how to adjust to their new normal, but much of the credit belonged to Mary. If only Kyra had known that Mary was her biological mother sooner.

Kyra drifted off to sleep again and when she woke up, she could smell coffee and bacon and hurried to dress and join Lee downstairs. She found him whistling in the kitchen as he cracked a couple eggs into a frying pan.

"I heard you moving about so breakfast is almost ready." He grinned at her as he motioned to the coffee maker. "Pour us each a cup to get our engines going."

"Lee, you shouldn't be doing the cooking. I'm supposed to be taking care of you. And where is your sling?"

"I'm fine," he said. "My shoulder feels pretty good." Seeing her frown, he added, "Okay, I'll put it back on in a minute. In the meantime, let's just share this beautiful morning together," he pointed to the window at the blue sky and trees swaying in a light breeze, "and pass the time away talking about inconsequential things."

Kyra nodded. "Okay, I can do that. Thanks."

After they finished breakfast, Kyra picked up their coffees so they could move onto the patio. Lee had sighed, but obediently replaced the sling on his arm before they stepped outside.

"I hope you don't mind, but I took a quick peek at your laptop this morning," he said. "Thought I might check my email, but then I saw a file called *The Cresthaven Mystery*. Being a mystery writer, I couldn't bear the suspense, so I opened it."

"Lee!" Kyra wasn't ready to share her writing with anyone yet, especially her father. He was a famous mystery writer, and now he'd have to find a way to let her down easy so she didn't keep pursuing a dream that was only a dream.

"Come on, Kyra, you can't blame me for being curious. I wanted to know if I was passing down any writing talent to my only child." He smiled at her. "Your writing's pretty good, you know, and I liked the plot about a young man thinking Jennie is seeing his father when she's actually trying to get them to reconcile. It's got some rough edges, but I'd be glad to help with editing."

Kyra shook her head. "I don't want you to say nice things, just because you're my father. If it's bad, say so."

Lee said, "Don't worry. If it was bad, I *would* say so. I just gave you an honest opinion. I teach classes occasionally at the local college, and you can ask any student there if I give them honest opinions. No use babying writers or they never become better writers." Kyra studied his face for truthfulness as he took a sip of coffee. "Besides," he added, "you haven't seen the hatchet job I can do when I edit. You may not think I'm being so nice then."

"All right. I'll accept your offer. But . . ." She frowned at him. "But you have to promise not to peek at my book again until I'm finished and have done my own revising first."

"Agreed."

Kyra finished her coffee and stood up. "You made breakfast so I'm going in to clean up. You stay here and enjoy the sunshine, and that's an order. Pretend you're in Italy."

Just as she reached the kitchen the front doorbell rang. Thinking it was Sam, Kyra hurried down the hall and flung open door. Instead it was Detective Andrews holding a bouquet of red and white carnations.

CHAPTER 32

SIX WEEKS LATER

Kyra finished typing the last word of her novel and sat back in satisfaction. She knew it wasn't completely done; that weeks or months of revisions lay ahead of her, but she was mostly happy with the characters and plot. The windows of the den were open to the late summer breeze that helped to lift her spirits. She'd finally made the agonizing decision about staying in Stonecliff or moving back to Pittsburgh after several events fell into place. The nightmare of Brad's funeral followed by Simon Berchtold's confession to the police about the plot to acquire Lee's money was over. When Mrs. Perry, the librarian, had offered her a job as a front desk clerk and library aide, she decided it was a sign she was meant to stay.

Just then Lee tapped lightly on the door frame and asked, "Is now a good time?"

She smiled at him and nodded. "It's a perfect time. I just finished."

"Congratulations!" He came in and sat on the wingback chair in the corner. "I won't burst your bubble by saying that now the real work begins."

She groaned before saying, "Allow me a day or two of satisfaction first. A couple weeks ago I didn't even know if I'd ever get back to writing."

His expression turned serious. "It's hard to believe that Simon Berchtold started planning to gain access to my money so many years ago. All that time he continued to treat Mary as a friend, he never got over his anger about her relationship with me. He used his nephew to recruit Brad after he found out about Brad's desire for revenge against Mary for his grandfather's death. What a manipulative man!"

Kyra stared out the window at the perennial garden she had helped Mary plant in the summers. "I still don't understand how anyone could hate Mary when she was so loving. Mr. Berchtold had to be blind not to see her goodness."

"You must remember that we all saw the Simon we thought he was: a good man and a good lawyer. He figured if he was tricking people for years, other people were doing the same to him."

They sat in silence for a while until Kyra reached into the far right pigeonhole of the desk and pulled out the homemade card with the dried wildflowers on the top. She handed it to Lee. He took it from her, glancing at her face. "Open it," she murmured.

He sucked in his breath as he recognized Mary's writing. Kyra watched as he read and then reread the note. After closing his eyes for a moment, he smiled at Kyra. "Thank you for sharing this."

"So many secrets were revealed this summer that I'm not sure how I feel about keeping them. I've seen how a secret can bring pain or joy, but I sometimes think that maybe I should have been told as a child that Mary was my mother. What if I had been too upset or angry when I discovered I hadn't been told the truth all these years? What if it made me hate Mary?"

Lee frowned. "I think that maybe Mary kept that letter all these years just in case she missed the opportunity to tell you. And maybe she watched you grow and saw your inner strength over the years and knew you'd be fine whether she told you or not."

Kyra bit her lip as she contemplated his words. "Okay, maybe you're right. I know Mary and I had a wonderful relationship, so I guess it didn't matter if she was my aunt or my mother."

Lee heaved a great sigh. "Good. Then that's settled. And you're right that the relationship between Mr. Berchtold, Peter, and Brad brought terrible consequences for everyone they touched, but thankfully we all survived. Sadly, Simon is the only one left to pay for his crimes and three young men are dead."

"All in a horrible type of domino effect. Peter was responsible for Max Keller's death, and Brad for Peter's death, and then Simon instigated Brad's death. But it could have been even worse." Kyra trembled at the memory of Brad's attack on her and Sam.

Lee stood up. "Enough, Kyra. We've discussed this before and we decided we need to focus on the future. It will take time, my dear, but today we have plans. Remember?" He reached for her hands and she let him pull her up into a hug.

Brushing away the tears, she said, "What time did we decide to meet at Christo's Diner?"

"Six o'clock, so you'd better scurry upstairs and find something nice to wear for that detective friend of yours. He's picking you up in half an hour."

"I thought we were meeting Dave there. He doesn't have to—"

"I agreed when he asked, so don't worry about it. I told him Sam and I will probably visit Trudy afterwards, so he might have to run you home."

"What?" Kyra stepped back and studied his face. "So when were you talking to him?"

Lee looked at his watch again. "Time's flying, Kyra. Now you only have twenty-seven minutes to get ready."

"All right. Fine." She turned and tried not to give Lee the satisfaction of hearing her rush up the stairs.

Several hours later, after an evening of talk and laughter, Dave Andrews stopped his car in the driveway. As usual, he hurried around to open her door.

"You know, you don't have to do that," she said as she got out. "I'm perfectly capable of doing it myself."

"I know," he replied. "I thought I'd start out on the right foot. Besides, I was going to ask if I could come in for a cup of coffee."

She hesitated and then started for the door. "Um, okay, but I'm ready for a glass of wine. I'm all coffee'd out from dinner."

"Better yet."

Kyra heard the lilt in his voice and wondered if they should have stuck to coffee. She knew he'd been watching her quietly during the evening when he thought she was absorbed in the talk around her. He might be the detective, but she wasn't without her own observation skills.

"White or red wine?" she asked when they reached the kitchen.

"I'll have whatever you're having." He took off his jacket and hung it over the back of the kitchen chair.

"Okay, two glasses of sauvignon blanc coming up." When she joined him at the kitchen table, she decided he looked rather serious.

"What is it?" she asked. "Did something new come up in the case against Mr. Berchtold?"

"No, nothing like that." He sipped the wine and studied her eyes. "It's about me."

"Oh." Trying to keep it light-hearted, she said, "I already know you're a detective, you spend long hours at work, you like things to run smoothly, and you don't like other people trying to play detective."

Kyra saw a brief smile flit across his face before his expression grew earnest. "That's all true, and that's basically what I wanted to address." He shoved his hand through his hair before continuing in a rush, "I was married years ago, but it didn't work out. Jamie hated my job; she always wanted me to change and work somewhere from 9 to 5. We've been divorced for eight years and we never got around to kids. Just thought it was fair that you knew my background."

Kyra swirled her wine around her glass and then set it back down. "You already know my background, but I want to remind you that I'm a writer. I just finished my novel, and I already have an idea for the next one. Can I pick your brain for details about how the police work?"

"Sure," he agreed. "As long as we can do it over dinner and you don't mind the occasional interruption when I get urgent calls from work."

"Okay, and exactly why are we carrying on this discussion?"

He reached for her hands resting on the table and said, "Because, dammit, I think we're about to have a serious relationship and I didn't want any secrets between us!"

Kyra sucked in her breath and tightened her grip on his hands. When she looked up into his eyes, she whispered, "I think you're right, Dave, but I need a little more time. So much has changed in my life in such a short time, the good and the bad." She hoped he would understand as she continued, "I need a breather. I'll be going to Italy next week with Lee. We decided that it would be the best time for me to visit his villa before I settled into my life here in Stonecliff."

"Sounds like a good idea," Dave said. "Just don't let the Italian atmosphere seduce you into staying there. Lee seems to have made it his home for many years."

"Don't worry, this is my home. As long as you can wait for me."

He nodded and then slowly smiled. "If you can seal the agreement with a kiss?"

Still holding hands, they stood up and Kyra walked into his arms. Thinking of Brad, she hesitated a moment but Dave gently touched her closed eyes with his lips and murmured, "Trust me." When she relaxed, he kissed her lightly before his touch became firmer, and she found herself kissing him back.

ABOUT THE AUTHOR

Alicia Stankay is a fiction writer and photographer. She has written short fiction for many years, and eventually she published two books of short stories. Inspired by one of those stories, she wrote her first novel, *Beyond the Bridge*, a story of young love lost, a crime, and how the repercussions touched many lives for nineteen years. "Cabin adventures" at state parks allow Alicia to enjoy hiking, taking nature photos, and using those surroundings as settings in some of her stories. Several of her nature photos have been chosen for the Merrick Art Gallery's local artist shows, and in 2017 she was invited to present her own photo exhibition. Her photography also graces the covers of her books, including her recent teen novel, *Cathi and Katrina: Adventure in Old Economy Village*, which showcases the living history museum in her hometown of Ambridge, Pa. This book, *Summer of Secrets: A Stonecliff Mystery*, is her third novel, and she hopes the reader enjoys the many secrets as they unravel in the story. She may be reached at aliciastankay@gmail.com.

Made in the USA
Middletown, DE
28 July 2017